New York Tim...
bestsel...
CINDY GERARD
and the scorching hunks of BLACK OPS, INC.
are on fire!

"I'm hooked on Gerard's tough-talkin', straight-shootin' characters. Her story is exciting, taut, sexy, and just plain fun to read."

—*New York Times* bestseller
Sandra Brown on *Dying to Score*

"Gerard's deadly series kicks romantic adventure into high gear."

—Allison Brennan, *New York Times* bestselling author

"A great writer . . . head and shoulders above most."

—Robert Browne, author of *The Paradise Prophecy*

"Gerard artfully reveals the secret previously known only to wives, girlfriends, and lovers of our military special-operations warriors: these men are as wildly passionate and loving as they are watchful and stealthy. Her stories are richly colored and textured, drawing you in from page one, and not simply behind the scenes of warrior life, but into its very heart and soul."

—William Dean A. Garner, former U.S. Army
Airborne Ranger and Corporate Mercenary and *New York Times* bestselling ghostwriter and editor

With each new book in the series
"Gerard just keeps getting better and better"
—*Romance Junkies*

WHISPER NO LIES

"An incredible love story . . . hot, sexy, tender, it will steal your breath."

—*Her Voice Magazine* (Winter Haven, FL)

"Excellent stuff!"

— *RT Book Reviews*

"Heart-stopping, electrifying."

—Fresh Fiction

TAKE NO PRISONERS

"A fast-paced tale of romance amid flying bullets."

—*Publishers Weekly*

"Keeps the danger quotient high and the revenge motivations boiling . . . This author has truly found her niche!"

—*RT Book Reviews*

"A spicy, stirring romance . . . I found myself racing through the pages, nearly as captivated by the action-packed story as I was by the sizzling romance."

—*Library Journal*

SHOW NO MERCY

"Clever. . . . Action-packed from beginning to end!"

—*RT Book Reviews*

"Fast-paced, dangerous, and sexy."

—Fresh Fiction

"Cindy Gerard's roller-coaster ride of action and passion grabs you from page one."

—Karen Rose, *New York Times* bestselling author

These titles are also available as eBooks

Also by Cindy Gerard

Show No Mercy

Take No Prisoners

Whisper No Lies

Feel the Heat

Risk No Secrets

With No Remorse

GERARD

LAST MAN
STANDING

Pocket **Star** Books
New York   London   Toronto   Sydney   New Delhi

Pocket Star Books
A Division of Simon & Schuster, Inc.
1230 Avenue of the Americas
New York, NY 10020

Copyright © 2012 by Cindy Gerard

First Pocket Star Books paperback edition February 2012

POCKET STAR BOOKS and colophon are registered trademarks of Simon & Schuster, Inc.

For information about special discounts for bulk purchases, please contact Simon & Schuster Special Sales at 1-866-506-1949 or business@simonandschuster.com.

The Simon & Schuster Speakers Bureau can bring authors to your live event. For more information or to book an event contact the Simon & Schuster Speakers Bureau at 1-866-248-3049 or visit our website at www.simonspeakers.com.

Manufactured in the United States of America

10 9 8 7 6 5 4 3 2 1

ISBN 978-1-4516-0682-9
ISBN 978-1-4516-0686-7 (ebook)

The characters in my novels are fictitious; however, each and every one has been inspired by my admiration, pride, and gratitude for the men and women who serve in the United States military. This book, in particular, is dedicated to the fallen and those left behind.

"Life is eternal, and love is immortal,
    and death is only a horizon;
and a horizon is nothing save the limit of our sight."
—Rossiter Worthington Raymond

Acknowledgments

I have so many people to thank at Pocket Books for supporting and publishing this series so enthusiastically. My brilliant publisher, Louise Burke; my insightful editor, Micki Nuding; the amazing publicity department headed by Jean Ann Rose and assisted by Ayelet Gruenspecht; and the creative genius of the art department, specifically Lisa Litwack. Thank you and everyone else behind-the-scenes for working so hard on my behalf.

If a man does his best, what else is there?
—George S. Patton

Prologue

Joe Green was as good as dead. He'd known it the moment he'd started digging for answers to questions no one wanted asked.

What he hadn't known was the havoc his hunt would create.

What he hadn't wanted was for the priest to die.

"No, man. Oh no, man. You—"

"Quiet," Joe snapped when Suah's whisper echoed through the cavernous nave of the Sacred Heart Cathedral.

The teenage boy at his side was frozen in shock. On the cold stone floor blood pooled beneath the holy man's head, crept around the base of the chancel rail, then spilled down the step to the altar.

Joe dropped to a knee and pressed his fingers to the cleric's neck. No pulse. And no life in the eyes that stared blankly at the stained glass windows.

He swallowed heavily.

"Is he—?"

"Yeah. He's dead."

Regret, self-disgust, and defeat pounded through his veins, a reminder that what he had started would come to no good end.

No good end? Jesus. The priest was dead. Ends didn't come much worse than this.

He glanced up, beyond gold candlesticks on the high altar, above yards of maroon velvet cascading from an alcove that hosted a life-size statue of a benevolent Christ. Pale candlelight flickered eerily through the church, casting his and Suah's shadows in tall, wavy relief along the far wall, like ghosts already here to claim the priest's soul.

He lowered his head into his hand. *God help him . . . what had he done?*

The thick wooden doors at the front of the cathedral swung open with a heavy, echoing thud. Joe whipped his head around to see several police officers storm into the nave; Freetown's bastion of corrupt law enforcement had arrived in force. No hope of a quick search of the cleric's body now.

"Hide before they spot you," he whispered urgently to Suah, who stood, petrified in shock. "Hurry! Duck under the high altar."

He shot to his feet and gave the boy a shove as the gunmen raced down the center aisle between the worn wooden pews. Satisfied that the kid was well hidden beneath the draping cloth, he made sure the men got a glimpse of him, then sprinted for the sacristy, leading them away from Suah.

He got as far as the epistle door and swung it open. The rattle of rifles being shouldered and the *snick-click* of a dozen safeties switching to off position greeted him. The beams of as many flashlights blinded him.

He was surrounded.

"Hands in the air," a voice shouted from behind him.

Slowly, he did as he was told. Slower still, he turned around and stared into the dark, angry faces of the men who had passed the priest's body to get to him.

Without warning, the butt end of an assault rifle swung around hard and slammed into his temple.

He fell to all fours, fighting the screaming pain and the hard pull of unconsciousness. Yeah, he thought again, just before darkness sucked him under, he was as good as dead.

1

The last thing Stephanie Tompkins needed was for him to show up again. Joe knew that. Yet here he was, drawn like a storm-battered ship to the welcoming waters of a calm home port.

Jesus, it was so not fair to her. But he didn't have it in him to leave without seeing her one last time. Possibly the very last time, if this solo mission ended the way he suspected it would.

He walked slowly along the dimly lit hallway, then stopped in front of her apartment door. All of his life, he'd stood for right. Stood against wrong. Yet the choice he'd made to see this thing through blurred the lines so badly, it was hard to say where one ended and the other began.

For the first time in his life, he was scared. Not of the fight; he was scared that Stephanie was right. That he was losing himself in his need to settle a score. And he was scared spitless of losing her.

Lot of losing going on, he thought grimly. No matter how he sliced it.

It wasn't like he had any real options.

Swallowing the rock of guilt lodged in his throat, he stared down at his boots, trying to screw up some courage. The melting snow that clung to his soles had left slushy tracks on the tiled third-floor hallway. Like he was going to leave tracks all over her heart.

He checked his watch, stalling. It was going on midnight. She'd be asleep. And he was going to wake her up to tell her something that was going to kill her. Hell, just thinking about it was killing him. But he couldn't check out on her without saying good-bye. And lie through his teeth while he did it.

His hand was cold when he finally lifted it and, after a heart-thumping hesitation, gave the door a soft rap. Maybe she wasn't home. Maybe she'd gone to her parents' in Virginia for the weekend, and would escape dealing with the shitstorm he was about to dump on her. Maybe he should turn the hell around and be gone.

Too late. He heard the soft whisper of footsteps inside the apartment, then the tentative turn of the doorknob before she slowly opened up as far as the safety chain allowed, and peered into the hall.

"Hi," he said with a clipped nod when he met the surprise in her soft brown eyes.

Everything about Steph was soft. Her lush, curvy

body. Her generous smile. Her gentle nature that made a hard man like him want to play white knight and save her from the dragons that could hurt her.

But tonight he was going to be the dragon. A fire-breathing, breath-stealing, soul-defeating dragon. And he was going to hurt her bad.

If Bryan was alive, he'd damn sure kick Joe's sorry ass from here to the next zip code. Her brother wouldn't let him within shouting distance of his kid sister.

But Bry wasn't here. A lump welled up in his throat. Even fifteen years later, Bry's death was the reason Joe didn't sleep most nights. It was also the reason he had to let Stephanie go.

"Joe." Equal measures of relief, happiness, and concern colored her tone. "Hold on."

She shut the door, unhooked the chain, then swung it open again.

Her long sable hair was bed-mussed and tumbling around her shoulders. She'd hastily wrapped up in a short robe. Folds of the pale blue silk gaped open, exposing warm, sleep-flushed skin and the generous curve of a breast. She was gorgeous, sexy, spell-binding. Yet as beautiful as she was, it was her eyes that always got to him. Those soulful, deep brown eyes were like windows to her heart.

So many emotions. So little guile. And no defense at all against the onslaught of pain he was about to level.

"Come in." She stood back, opening the door wider so he could step inside. "It's freezing out there."

Another woman would have laid into him. Another woman would have slapped him hard, demanded to know where the hell he'd been for the past four weeks, then called him every name in the book before slamming the door in his face.

But she wasn't another woman. She was Steph. Giving. Forgiving. Vulnerable.

"You've *got* to be freezing." She turned on bare feet and headed for the kitchen. "I'll make coffee."

"Don't," he said with a stiffness in his voice that stopped her cold.

She didn't turn around. He knew that despite the brave front she was putting up, she was suddenly on the verge of losing it.

Why not? A man who loved a woman didn't treat her the way he'd treated Steph the past month—he didn't clam up, didn't not call, didn't refuse to explain himself. And he didn't show up unannounced in the middle of the fucking night and expect coffee before he sliced open a vein.

She just stood there, her silence and the rigid set of her shoulders giving away how uncertain she was, and he almost lost it himself.

"You don't have to make coffee for me," he said inanely.

Her shoulders sagged; her chin dropped to her chest.

Aw, hell.

In two steps, he came up behind her and pulled her back against him, wrapped one arm around her waist and another around her chest. With his forearm sandwiched between her breasts, he caressed her throat and tipped her head back beneath his jaw.

"I'm sorry," he whispered, lowering his lips to her hair. "Steph . . . I'm . . ." Hell.

She turned, lifted her arms around his neck, and with a desperation as sharp as the hurt in her eyes, drew his head down to hers.

"Don't talk," she murmured against his mouth. "I've missed you. I've been so scared."

He tasted the salt of her tears on her lips, and it was all over for him. He had no defense against this. No resistance.

The instant the heat of her body moved into his he reacted, like he always did when surrounded by the feel and taste of her. She was the woman he'd been waiting for his entire life, and it had been too damn long since he'd held her.

His mouth covered hers and he took what he'd been missing, but had no right to claim anymore.

"Joe," she whispered. No censure. Only giving. Only love, as he scooped her up and carried her into her bedroom, where soft lamplight cast the room in a pale glow.

Consumed in the moment, he kissed her deeply, then laid her on the bed that still held her lingering scent and warmth. Then he swiftly began shucking his clothes.

Her gaze followed every move and sent his pulse slamming as he tossed his jacket on the floor, then whipped his black sweater over his head and reached for the snap on his jeans.

Hunger flamed in her eyes as he stripped off his

boots and pants and finally, naked, sank a knee onto the mattress beside her hip.

"I've missed you," she whispered again, her fingers skimming slowly up his thigh, then circling over his hip before trailing across the tightly clenched muscles of his belly.

"Missed you," she repeated on a throaty breath, and finally brushed her fingertips along the throbbing length of his erection.

His breath caught on a groan. "Steph . . ."

"Shh . . . let me."

He tunneled his fingers through her hair, urging her closer.

Her gaze locked on his, she sat up. Her robe slid off one shoulder to reveal the creamy round of a bare breast as she slowly, and with great attention, pressed her mouth to all the places her fingers had been, trailing fire in her wake.

He was one live electric nerve, one raging sexual urge, when she finally caressed the most sensitive part of him with a slow stroke of her tongue . . . and damn near blinded him with her passion.

He sucked in a harsh breath, let his head fall back, and knotted his hands tighter in her hair losing himself in the sweet, wet suction of her mouth.

It was always this way with her. She drove him out of his mind with the selflessness of her giving. Humbled and thrilled him with the passion of her sighs and urgency of her touch, until mindless pleasure gradually transitioned to the dawning realization that her fervor had changed to desperation. That her desire had become a plea.

Don't leave me. Please, don't leave me.

It was clear that she knew he'd come to say good-bye. With every kiss, every wild and reckless touch, she told him she knew, and she was begging him not to go, bargaining with him to stay.

"Steph," he whispered, stilling her. He couldn't let her do this. "Steph, don't."

He tilted her head back and saw the tears trailing down her face, her beautiful eyes so full of pain.

And he hated himself then; hated that he'd made her beg. He was so far from worth it.

"I'm sorry." He gently laid her down, then settled her with a brush of his fingers across her cheek.

"Don't." She caught his face in her hands, dragged his mouth down to hers. "Don't talk. Just love me. Please . . . just love me now."

A better man would have resisted. A better man would have done the right thing.

But he'd stopped being a better man when he'd chosen the course that was going to take him away from her and could destroy everything he'd ever stood for.

Helpless to fight her, he lowered his body over hers and captured her mouth. And when she wrapped her ankles around his hips and opened herself for him, he drove deep. And kept on driving urgently inside her, indulging one last time in the one good thing he'd ever had going for him.

2

Stephanie lay back on the bed, focused on the man who stood naked and brooding across the room. His back was to her; his palms were braced above his head on the window frame as he stared silently into the wintery night.

Snow drifted past her third floor window in pristine, fluffy flakes. If she'd been in a daydreaming mood, she might have dwelled on the memory of a cherished snow globe she'd loved as a child. But tonight wasn't about woolgathering. Tonight . . . frankly, she wasn't sure she wanted to know what tonight was about. For the moment, she was just relieved that Joe was here.

Seeing him so troubled was haunting. Like the tattoo running down the length of his bare back was haunting. The intricate serpentine design, set against his large, muscular frame, never failed to move her, as did the sheer size and brute strength of him that so contrasted with his innate gentleness.

She studied the ink work that was as complex as the man. It began at the nape of his neck and trailed down his spine, ending a few inches below the point where it would have disappeared beneath the waistband of his jeans.

Cobalt blue and scarlet red, powder white and rusty gold, it twisted like an unfurling ribbon down the ridge of his backbone, forming an abstract banner of red, white, and blue, braided with a gold cord imprinted with the names of his fallen brothers-in-arms and the dates they had died.

Her brother's name was among them.

She knew that Joe still mourned her brother's death as gravely as he had the day Bryan had fallen in combat. Was Bry's death working on him again tonight? Or was it more than that? A man didn't do what he did for a living and not live with a host of ghosts haunting him.

"Joe?" She needed him close to her. And he needed her.

He turned slowly to face her. The hard cut of his jaw was cast in dark shadows, his high cheekbones and brow thrown into stark relief. He wanted to resist her—that was apparent in the tight clench of his jaw and the thin line of his lips.

She wasn't having any of it. There was too much pain, too much conflict in his eyes. It broke her heart.

She patted the sheets beside her. "Come back to bed." Where she could hold him. Where she could feel the hard, warm strength of him and fool herself into believing that if she tried hard enough, if she loved deeply enough, he would find some peace in her arms.

"Please," she whispered, feeling a small measure of

relief when he finally walked across the room and lay back down beside her.

"Your feet are cold," she murmured as she snuggled up naked beside him, never more aware of the softness of her body than when aligned with the steely strength of his. She was totally at a loss for what to say to ease the tension strung so tightly between them.

"You should be asleep," he said gruffly.

She laid her head on his shoulder and after a moment of hesitation, he folded her against his side. This was the man she loved; the man she missed. Caring, loving, tender.

"Mean" Joe Green. She smiled every time she thought about the nickname his teammates at Black Ops, Inc. had given him. On a mission, in combat, she had no doubt he was a fierce and ruthless warrior.

But when she was in his arms, a more gentle man did not exist.

He was a quiet man, and she had grown comfortable with it. But tonight, his silence was far from easy.

She hadn't wanted to talk before; she'd been too desperate with wanting him. But now she had to take that plunge. She had to know what was going on. Even before he'd disappeared four weeks ago, he'd grown emotionally distant.

She'd like to think he'd come back because he couldn't stay away. But the vibe she was getting—the edginess, the restlessness, the way he looked away rather than at her—told another story. One that terrified her.

She raised up on an elbow. His soft hazel green eyes

were more of a smoky gray in the dim light. "Please tell me what's working on you."

She felt that emotional distance between them grow to a chasm when he lifted his arm from around her and crossed his hands behind his head.

He stared at the ceiling. She stared at his face. His captivating and intriguing face. The strong, prominent nose. The clean-shaven jaw. The deeply set, mysterious eyes.

She loved looking at him. She loved everything about him, right down to the sandy brown hair that he kept cut military short, and his quiet confidence that always made her feel comfortable and safe. She'd told him so in one of their very first conservations.

"You're very comfortable to be around, Joe Green."

He shot her a doubtful look.

"Okay, maybe comfortable *isn't quite the word. I feel safe around you."*

He gave her a rare smile. "That's funny. Usually I make people nervous."

"Ah. The Mean Joe Green persona."

"That would be it."

"And you perpetuate it."

He lifted a shoulder. "I don't have to. This face doesn't exactly say 'nice puppy dog.'"

She smiled. "No, I don't think puppy dog. Should I?"

"Rottweiler, maybe." He smiled again and she'd been thoroughly charmed.

"Is that what you want people to see?"

"Most of the time, I guess I do. And most people don't bother to look further."

"*Well, I'm not most people.*"

The whine of a distant siren jarred her back to the present.

It seemed like a lifetime ago that she'd first met him. That she'd gotten to know him as well as he'd let her. A lifetime since she'd discovered that she loved him — though it hadn't even been two years.

She watched the pulse beat in a strong, steady rhythm along his throat.

Could she have been wrong? Was the love only on her side?

No. He loved her. She hadn't doubted it since the first night they'd spent together. But something was gravely wrong.

It was his last mission, she was certain. Something had happened on the operation that had unexpectedly taken the Black Ops, Inc. team back to Sierra Leone last month.

Sierra Leone — the words had become synonymous with pain. Bryan had died there in an ambush by a squad of Revolutionary United Front soldiers, whose reign of terror had decimated the people of Sierra Leone for almost a decade.

Like Bry's death had decimated her family.

She understood that Joe felt responsible. All of the guys felt some responsibility, but Joe seemed to carry the load even more heavily than the others.

Back then they'd all been U.S. military, pulled off their Special Ops teams to form a multi-branch unit. Bry, Gabe Jones, and Sam Lang had come from their

Army Delta squads, Rafe Mendoza from his Ranger battalion. Luke Colter had been imported from his Navy SEAL team, Johnny Reed from his Force Recon Marine unit, and Wyatt Savage and Joe from their CIA posts. Together they'd become Task Force Mercy, an elite, top-secret, handpicked unit of fighting men under the direct command of the president and the Joint Chiefs. Their mission had been to carry out covert operations in third world hot spots under the leadership of Captain Nathan Black, U.S. Marine Corps.

Bry had been so proud to be part of the unit, and he'd written about the others in his letters home. She hadn't met them but discovered why they were so special when they'd gathered in Virginia to pay their respects to her and her parents at Bry's memorial service.

They'd been more than teammates then. And they were now more than Black Ops, Inc., a private and highly covert paramilitary organization based out of Buenos Aires, Argentina, once again under Nate Black's leadership.

They were brothers. Like Bry had been their brother.

She sighed heavily and laid her hand on Joe's chest. *"Please* talk to me."

He'd only opened up to her once before, giving her a glimpse of the horrors that lived in his memories. Everything in her told her that Bryan's death was still at the root of his struggle, but he had to be the one to expose that wound, not her. "Tell me what's wrong, Joe."

He remained silent for another moment.

"This isn't working for me anymore," he said without looking at her.

For several heartbeats, she just stared. She couldn't have heard him right. But his silence said she had. And her brain finally accepted.

Her fingers felt numb. Her head felt like a balloon—light, unstable, and floaty.

"Wh-what isn't working?" She wasn't certain how she managed to form the words, let alone string them together into a coherent question.

The muscles in his jaw clenched. "This. You. Me. Us," he said with a weary finality that sent the blood rushing from her head and stole her remaining powers of speech.

"I thought I could make it work," he continued, still avoiding her eyes. "I care about you, Steph, but I just can't do this commitment thing."

"Is there someone else?" she finally managed around the knot of shock lodged in her throat.

"No," he said quickly. "Jesus, no. I'd never do that to you."

"Then what?" She felt physically ill. "What does that mean, you can't do the commitment thing? And when have I ever asked you to commit?"

She understood that in his line of work, it was difficult to plan a future since *tomorrow* was always an iffy proposition. She knew that they had miles to go before he gave her access to all the life experiences that had shaped him, that still haunted him, that had made him the man he was today. But she'd been willing to wait, certain they were on the same wavelength. Certain that the natural progression of their relationship would involve a commitment to each other someday.

It was hard to think above the rush of blood pounding in her ears. "I've never pressured you, Joe. Never."

She heard the desperation in her voice. Hated herself for it, but he was ripping her heart out.

"But it's what you want, right? A commitment? You think I don't know it's what you deserve?" He scrubbed a hand over his face, looking as miserable as she felt. "That's not going to happen with me. I'm not cut out for long term. I thought I could do it. I wanted to. But I can't."

He rose swiftly from the bed, then bent down and snagged his clothes from the floor.

"Look. I shouldn't have come here. I'm sorry." He stepped into his pants, jerked his sweater over his head, then shoved his feet into his boots. "I never meant to hurt you."

He grabbed his jacket and headed for the door.

"Wait!" She grabbed the sheet and covered her breasts. "You drop a bomb like that, and then just leave? Can't we at least talk about it?"

He didn't turn around. "There's nothing to talk about."

Blind rage rolled over the hurt and confusion and burst out of her like gunfire. "So why *did* you come here? Jesus, Joe, you could have phoned that in."

He stopped with his hand on the doorknob. "I'm sorry," he repeated, offering no defense.

She scrambled off the bed, ripping the sheet free and wrestling it around her body as she stormed across the room. "Sorry. I'm getting real tired of hearing that word."

He still didn't say anything.

"So what was this? A drive by? One last chance to get lucky?"

The guilt that flashed across his face devastated her.

"Oh, God. It was." She pressed the heel of her hand against her forehead in disbelief. "Wow. That worked out well for you. You drop by for a late-night confession, and cash in on a booty call before you leave."

"Christ, no," he said, sounding wretched.

Something in his eyes—more than regret, more than guilt—gave her a kernel of hope.

"You know what?" She touched his arm. "I don't believe you. I don't believe any of this. Tell me what's *really* going on—you owe me that. Look me in the eye and tell me what's going on with you."

He finally met her eyes. "What's going on," he said without an ounce of emotion in his voice, "is that I don't love you."

She gasped.

"Not enough," he added apologetically. He shoved his hands into his hip pockets, tipped his head back, and stared at the ceiling. "I thought I did. I thought I could. But I don't. I'm so—"

"Don't!" She held up a hand. Her heart felt too big for her chest; it physically hurt to hold it inside. "Don't you *dare* say that word again." She blinked back the tears that threatened to destroy what little pride she had left.

She'd wanted an answer? Well, she'd gotten it.

She turned away from him and stared at the rumpled bed, knowing it was still warm from their entwined bodies, knowing she'd never feel his warmth in her bed or her heart again.

I don't love you. Not enough.

"Go, then. Just . . . go."

Several long moments passed. She was certain he would tell her it was all a mistake, that he hadn't meant what he'd said, that he loved her and would never leave her again.

But then the door opened behind her. An icy draft from the hallway skittered across her bare feet and wrapped around her heart.

Then the latch closed quietly behind him and he walked out of her life.

3

"Steph, I think you should take a look at this."

Stephanie looked up as Rhonda Burns squeezed into her cubicle. Like Stephanie, Rhonda was a cryptologist in NSA's Signals Intelligence Division. Unlike Stephanie, who dressed in dark pantsuits, crisp white blouses, and sensible two-inch pumps, Rhonda pushed the limits of acceptable professional attire. Today, her anti-establishment statement consisted of a very short red skirt, very high black heels, and a *very* tight, low-cut white sweater.

Despite her flamboyant style and the untold pleasure she took in her ability to turn heads with her blatant sexuality, Rhonda was a damn good cryptologist. Stephanie also considered her a good friend. And in many ways, Rhonda was her "she-ro."

The pretty blonde added color and life to the division. Most days, she was the only bright spot on the open floor buzzing with worker drones. Rhonda was a shining beacon within the industrial gray walls and hundreds of small, sterile cubicles marching in rows beneath fluorescent lights suspended below dingy white ceiling tile.

Join NSA. Be a spy.

Be a drone, Stephanie thought sourly. It was exactly how she felt these days. And it was exactly what Rhonda fought against becoming.

"Take a look at what?" she asked without much enthusiasm.

Rhonda parked her curvy hips on the edge of Stephanie's workstation and handed her a file folder.

"Don't tell me." Stephanie tossed the folder onto her desk without bothering to open it. Since it was Friday morning and almost the end of the workweek, she figured she knew what was inside. "Randolph has a project that can't wait until Monday."

Randolph Browne was their supervisor, who periodically took delight in messing with her life.

Of course, since Joe had left her five weeks ago, she didn't have a life outside work anyway. Her choice. And right now, it suited her fine.

She supposed she should be angry, and should probably hate him. At the very least, she should feel vindictive. But she wasn't made that way. Mostly, she just felt sad. And foolish.

"Steph?"

She shook herself away from thoughts of Joe and glanced at Rhonda. Her soft blue eyes were pinched with concern; Rhonda knew exactly where her mind had wandered. Not much got by her.

"It's not a project." Rhonda laid a hand on her arm.

"It's something that came across the wire a while back. I didn't connect it. Kind of forgot about it until I was cleaning up loose ends this morning."

"Connect what?"

Rhonda notched her chin toward the folder. "Just check it out, okay?"

Stephanie watched Rhonda walk away, then frowned at the folder. Her disenchantment with life overrode what little curiosity Rhonda had managed to pique.

Would it always be this way? she wondered, glancing at the clock sharing a shelf with a photo of her parents. It was only nine a.m. and it felt like she'd been here all day. Another day without Joe.

Would she always measure time in terms of before Joe and after Joe? God, she hoped not, because after Joe sucked.

I don't love you. Not enough.

Okay, he wanted out of her life. Fine. But no one at BOI had heard from him, either. And that, she did not understand. The guys at Black Ops, Inc. were his brothers. Why would he walk out on them?

"Not your problem," she muttered under her breath.

If a black ops warrior decided he wanted to disappear, he disappeared. And if that warrior was Joe Green, there wasn't an army on earth—or an NSA spy—who could find him.

She had just enough pride left that she hadn't tried.

She was thankful that her career demanded her undivided attention. Day after day, her time was filled sifting through encrypted cyber chatter, searching for certain patterns, phrases, repeated terminology, anything out of the norm or simply out of place. She finessed the software, compiled her reports, and stayed focused and vigilant in her search for some tidbit of information that could reveal a threat to national security.

It was all about the bigger picture. The little picture—her life—had faded to dismal shades of gray.

God, she was pathetic.

She glanced toward her lucky talisman, on the corner of her desk. She rarely took out the ring Bry had given her one Christmas. The "magic decoder" ring had represented such promise for a nine year old who'd dreamed of an exciting and dangerous future as a spy.

Well, she was a spy. A spy who sat at a desk, before a computer screen, performing complex, time-intensive work, trying not to bemoan the fact that she wasn't the James Bond–style spy of her childhood fantasies.

Just like she tried not to mourn the fact that Joe Green had charged into her life two years ago, taken her away from her mundane existence, and made her a believer in white knights, spy thrillers, and happily-ever-afters.

Would you just get over it?

Finally, more out of duty than curiosity, she picked up Rhonda's mysterious folder.

When she pulled out the photograph paper-clipped to the inside flap, her heart stopped. So did her breath.

The low drone of chatter from neighboring cubicles, the hum of hundreds of CPUs, and even time and place faded as her entire world shrank to the size of an 8 x 11 inch sheet of paper.

A photograph of Joe.

A wave of dizziness hit her. She gripped the edge of her desk to steady herself, then stared hard at the picture.

The photo was black and white, and grainy, and of horrible quality, but she had no doubt that it was Joe— head down, his arms cuffed behind his back, blood trailing down his temple.

She squinted harder, horrified. He was surrounded by armed guards carrying assault rifles who appeared to be leading him into a government building. An angry mob had closed in around him.

The photograph was from a newspaper article dated . . . oh, my God . . . almost a month ago. The print was so small she couldn't read it clearly. Without tearing her gaze away from the picture, she felt around inside her top desk drawer for her magnifying loupe.

When she finally found the loupe, her hand shook so hard she had to force herself to breathe deep for calm as she positioned the glass over the newsprint text.

When she managed to make out the caption, the magnifying glass fell from her suddenly numb hand.

Freetown, Sierra Leone . . . unidentified man arrested in the brutal slaying of revered Sacred Heart priest . . .

"It's some horrible mistake," Stephanie told Raphael Mendoza when she reached him at Black Ops, Inc. headquarters in Buenos Aires. She'd pleaded sick, clocked out of work, and headed for her apartment as soon as she'd seen the picture. She'd had to talk to Rafe, and she wanted to be as far away from prying eyes and ears as possible. "Joe couldn't have killed that priest."

"Of course he didn't kill him," Raphael replied after she'd filled him in on the little that she knew. "You're certain it's him in the photo?"

"It's him. You'll see for yourself. I scanned the article and e-mailed it. It should pop up in your in-box any second."

She paced back and forth across her living room, holding her cell to her ear and staring at the photograph. She kept telling herself that she shouldn't care what happened to Joe. But she did. She cared too damn much.

As she'd raced across town to get home, searching her memory for something to make sense of this, she'd snagged on one haunting midnight conversation.

She'd awakened in bed one cold, rainy night several months ago. Joe had been lying in the dark, staring at the ceiling. He was wet with sweat and she immediately knew he'd had another nightmare.

She'd touched a hand to his face and felt the track of a tear trailing down his cheek.

Devastated by his pain, she'd wrapped him in her arms and begged him to tell her what was haunting him.

She hadn't expected him to answer her. But instead of telling her it was nothing like all the other times, he'd started talking. And what he'd said still chilled her.

"Some never see it coming." His tone lacked emotion,

but the heart that beat heavily beneath her hand told her he was anything but detached. "Some look me right in the eye and I can tell. They know I'm the last thing they're ever going to see. Not their wife. Not their mother. Not their kid. Me.

"Now I see them. In the dark. In the night . . ."

"Hold on," Rafe said, bringing her back to the moment. She heard a keyboard clicking in the background. "I think it just arrived."

She sank down on the sofa and waited for Rafe to open the message with the attached photo. She could picture Rafe's darkly handsome face pinched with concern when he cursed softly.

And when he gravely muttered, "Jesus. What the hell has he gotten himself into?" Stephanie knew that he was just as frightened for Joe as she was.

"When can the team get over there?" she asked, hearing the panic in her own voice.

The heavy silence on his end sent a wave of apprehension through her.

"I don't know, Steph," Rafe said, in a tone that foretold of bad news. "Right now, we can't do a damn thing."

It took her a moment to find her voice. "Because he left the team?"

"Hell, no. And he didn't leave the team. He . . . damn. I don't know what's been eating him, but he needed a time-out. So Nate told him to take it; get whatever was working at him out of his system."

So she wasn't the only one who had sensed a change in him.

"Did you know he was going to Sierra Leone?"

"No." The single word relayed Rafe's confusion and concern. "And it doesn't make any sense that he'd go back there. Unless . . ."

"Unless this has something to do with Bryan," she concluded. "Someone needs to help him, Rafe."

"And we would if we could. But the guys are deployed. Even Nate is in on this op. B.J. and I are the only ones manning the fort."

"Then contact them." Fueled by nervous energy, she paced to the window. Taking care of each other always came first. "Let them know Joe's in trouble."

"Not that simple. They're total blackout status, *cara*."

"Blackout?"

"They're so deep undercover even I don't know where they are. They've been off the grid for seven days now. Could be another seven, maybe more before they surface."

"But you can still contact them, right? You *always* have a way to contact them." She knew she was starting to sound frantic.

"Not this time. This op is strictly 'no commo,'" he said wearily, and her heart dropped. "Fact is, I have no way of reaching them. Even if I did, I wouldn't. The wrong person monitors a satellite up-link, gets a lock on their position, and the guys are as good as dead."

She stared blindly outside. "Just like Joe is as good as dead if someone doesn't help him."

"Steph, I'd be there yesterday if I could." The frustration in his voice matched hers. "You know I would."

Yes, she knew. Rafe was recovering from a severe bout of malaria that had hospitalized him for almost two weeks. He'd just been released yesterday. Stephanie knew this because she'd talked to his wife and BOI teammate, B.J. Chase-Mendoza, in what had become a series of weekly phone calls that B.J. had initiated shortly after Joe disappeared. The usually hard-boiled B.J., whose baby was due any day now, had surprised Stephanie with her empathy and support.

"What about Ann? Can your mother intervene? Pull some strings?" Rafe asked, searching for another solution. "Maybe put a little pressure on the U.S. embassy to get someone over there to check on him?"

"The U.S. embassy isn't an option. The article doesn't refer to him by name or claim that he's a U.S. citizen. They called him an 'unnamed' assassin. It's pretty clear that they don't want to link him to the United States and unleash a media storm.

"Besides," she went on, her feeling of helplessness growing, "I can't ask Mom or Dad for help. Not until I know all the facts."

She'd been tempted to call her mother but until she could figure out exactly what was going on, she didn't dare involve either of her parents. Both were high-profile figures in Washington, her mother in particular. Ann Tompkins held a power position with the Department of Justice.

"I doubt I can reach them anyway," she added. "They left yesterday on vacation, somewhere in northern Minnesota. According to Dad, it's so remote up there that cell service is spotty at best."

Her dad had been as excited as a kid. Her mom hadn't been quite as pumped about getting away from it all in the wilderness, their first vacation in years.

"The cabin is something out of Log Home Digest," her dad had said, showing her a picture of the isolated, beautiful cabin nestled on the shore of Lake Kabetogama, Minnesota, a place her father had fallen in love with as a child.

"It's a winter wonderland, Steph," he'd gone on, his excitement clear. "We're going to snowmobile, cross-country ski, sit by the fire, and get romantic." He'd winked at her mother, who had rolled her eyes but looked exceedingly happy.

So, no, for many reasons, her parents couldn't help. Which left, what? What were Joe's options?

There were none, she realized, feeling heartsick.

"Okay, look," Rafe said, interrupting her grim thoughts. "We wait it out, okay? Joe's resourceful. He's tough. He can take care of himself for a while."

"Rafe, it's already been a month."

"In a week, maybe ten days tops," he continued, attempting to instill calm confidence, "the guys will be back. And if they're not, then screw doctor's orders. I'll go after him."

"No, you won't," she said on a heavy sigh. He was still too ill. And there were B.J. and the baby to consider.

He must have heard something in her voice—something that even she hadn't realized she was contemplating. "Stephanie. What are you thinking?"

She didn't answer.

"Listen to me. Do not do anything foolish, okay? I repeat, Joe knows how to take care of himself. Let him do it. Just wait for the team."

"I guess I don't have much choice, do I?" She walked over to her desk, where she opened up her laptop and logged on to Expedia.

"Steph, you still with me?"

Heart beating wildly, she typed in a request for flight information to Freetown.

This was crazy. She was insane for even thinking about flying over there.

"Stephanie?"

"Yeah, I'm here," she said, distractedly.

"Please tell me you're not thinking about doing anything stupid."

"I'm not a commando, Rafe. I know my limits."

Major limits. She had no business flying to Africa. The hard fact was, she had no business in Joe's life. Not anymore.

"Let me know when the team gets back, okay?" she said. "Or if you come up with anything."

"You know I will. In the meantime, we'll start working contacts on this end. If there's anyone in place over there who might be able to help, B.J. and I will find them. Just hang tight."

"Right. Okay, look, I've gotta go," she said abruptly and disconnected before he could give her another warning.

She sat down and stared at the details on flights bound for Freetown, Sierra Leone, via the Lungi International Airport. There were several seats left on a flight that left Dulles at eight p.m. that night. Her passport was up to date. Her shots weren't. And she didn't have a visa. Maybe she could get one there. Or maybe . . .

She glanced at the picture lying on her desk beside the laptop.

Arrested in Sierra Leone.

So many ghosts there. Bryan's ghost, specifically. She kept coming back to that as her finger hovered over the escape key.

A rush of adrenaline shot through her blood as she contemplated the unthinkable. Then she drew a deep breath and felt a decisive calm and sense of resignation wash over her.

And she booked the flight, because in the end she really had no choice.

4

Joe leaned against the only wall of his cell that was not constructed of iron bars. The crumbling cinder block was damp with sweat and mold. Once it may have been painted gray, but the only thing that covered it now was the stench of filth and misery.

His cell was one of a dozen 8 x 8 foot boxes in the cell block. Six cells lined each side of the central incarceration area. Only one had a window: Number three was the farthest away from his on the opposite side of the aisle.

He could see the window and a slice of blue sky if he stood in just the right spot with his face pressed against the bars. The window was the only outside light source, the only source of fresh air. And the poor schmuck who occupied it was subject to whatever weather Mother Nature chose to dump through the opening. Mostly she dumped in heat, the stink of rot, and the noise of the city that rattled by outside, with no regard to the miserable wretches locked inside without the benefit of jurisprudence or basic human rights.

There was no running water here. His bathroom was a bucket. He slept on the bare dirt floor along with the rats, cockroaches, the occasional lizard, and a host of other creepy crawlies. Twice, he'd had the pleasure of sharing his "bed" with a viper. Both times, he'd had to kill it or be killed by it. Both of the dead snakes had been turned over to his jailers, who promptly cooked them and served them to the "crazy" American whom they both feared and held in awe for his ability to survive the vipers' deadly attacks.

The snakes were the only protein he'd had in the thirty days since he'd been arrested and charged with murdering the priest. He had not yet had a trial, but hadn't missed a daily beating. He expected more sessions with the nunchakus long before he got a session with a judge.

As he did several times each day, he willed himself to count the bars of the cage holding him prisoner. Counting kept him level. Counting kept him from locking himself into his own mind, where the utter loneliness of his isolation and the helplessness of his situation played games with his sanity. Counting the bars helped him to keep hold of reality. Mathematics did not lie. Occasionally, his mind did.

Approximately eight feet above him, an 8 x 8 foot grillwork of sixty-four, inch-thick iron bars made his ceiling. The walls to his left and right were composed of thirty-six bars each, with four crossbars dissecting the inch-thick cylinders on both walls. There were another forty-eight bars in the wall facing the aisle—ten

of them making up the door that hung on four sol-
dered hinges and was secured with double locks both
top and bottom.

One hundred eighty-four bars. His life had come
down to counting, devising an escape plan, and, of
course, the nunchakus. His only respite from the un-
relenting reality of his imprisonment came in the early
hours of the morning, just before he came fully awake.

For a precious few moments, Steph would be there
with him. And God, it was heaven to lie beside her. To
watch her breathe as she slept. To feel her heat snuggled up against him.

Then a key would rattle in the outer room, a prisoner
would groan, or a muscle cramp or hunger pains would
wake him up to the truth that ripped him back to reality.

Stephanie was back home in Maryland, safe, which
is exactly where he wanted her to be.

Those keys rattled in the distance now. Two guards
held separate sets that they carried on rings attached
to the woven belts on their green uniforms. When
they came, they entered the cell block through a set of
locked doors, each one opened by a different guard with
a different set of keys.

All in all, tidy security for a medieval-esque facility. It
was almost overkill given that they pretty much starved
the prisoners into total submission.

The same two guards patrolled the cell block three
times a day. Once with meager portions of stagnant
water. Once with a bucket of gruel that passed for a
meal. Once to allow the prisoners to dump their waste.

Five-star digs all the way.

Joe dragged a hand over his bearded jaw, felt the loss of muscle tone in his arm. He figured he'd dropped close to twenty pounds since the beginning of his stay in Hotel Hell. Still, he'd been lucky. The open wound on his temple from the blow with the assault rifle had pretty much healed. And though he was fairly certain he'd had a concussion, the nausea and double vision had subsided within a week. The daily beatings were mostly body blows. He knew how to deflect the worst of them and still look like he'd taken enough of a pounding to make them back off.

He figured his unshaven beard, shaggy hair, bare feet, and filthy, ragged clothes gave him a distinct Robinson Crusoe look. But other than being dehydrated and malnourished, he was okay. Banged up a bit, but okay. The same couldn't be said for some of the men who'd been arrested since his arrival.

At least three prisoners—one of them not much more than a boy—had been carried out dead. Based on the fact that the moaning had stopped in cell number three a few hours ago, he suspected another body would soon be added to the death toll.

Such was life on the wrong side of Sierra Leone law.

He closed his eyes in frustration and leaned his head back against the bars. Waiting was all he could do now. Wait for an opportunity. Wait for a mistake. Wait to die in this shithole. Alone.

He never would have ended up like this if he hadn't turned his back on the team. "No man left behind" wasn't just a trumped-up sound bite for the benefit of the media. For the men and women who fought for their country and each other, it was a code they lived by. No man *was* left behind. Ever. Not when he was part of a team.

If this had been a sanctioned military or a Black Ops, Inc. team mission, he wouldn't be feeling this desolation because he would know without a doubt that an unstoppable determination would compel his team to get him out of here.

No matter what had to be done, no matter how many had to be killed, no matter how many of them died in the process, his team would have come for him. He still might die, but it wouldn't be alone.

But he was alone now, because no one knew he was here. Which was exactly the way it had to be.

He'd known when he'd started his hunt that if he ended up being right about who was responsible for Bryan's death, the fallout from exposing the traitor/murderer would be tantamount to aligning the Pope with Satan. And because of the power that traitor wielded, Joe knew that if he made his allegations public, he would become a target for assassination and the truth would never be revealed.

He grunted and took in his surroundings. Sometimes it was hell being right. He'd barely scratched the surface of the lies and deceit, and he was going to end up dead before he had a chance to expose the traitor.

Shoving back the despair that constantly fought to break him, he forced himself to his feet. Gathering every ounce of strength from his waning reserve, he threw his hands above his head and jumped. He barely made it high enough to grasp the crossbars overhead.

Fire screamed through his weakened muscles as he pulled himself up, let himself down. He repeated the grueling process twenty-five agonizing times before the burn ripping through his muscles and joints forced him to let go and drop, exhausted, to the floor. Sweat oozed from every pore as he lay there gasping for breath, feeling himself grow weaker with each passing hour.

Jesus. At his peak, he could do eighty pull-ups without breaking a sweat. Could push it close to a hundred if there was a bet on the line. Well, his life was on the line now, and twenty-five was the best he could muster.

Fuck.

He had to get out of here soon. He just hoped to hell that it wouldn't be in a body bag.

He closed his eyes. Thought of Stephanie. The pain in her eyes when he'd said good-bye. The lies on his tongue when he'd told her he didn't love her.

This was why he'd lied. This was why he'd separated himself from her, from his family, and from Bry's parents and from his team at BOI. He'd known that he could end up in deep shit, and it was better for everyone that they didn't know why.

Stephanie worked for the NSA, for Christsake. Her mother had worked her way up—and worked damn hard—into a power position in the Department of Justice; her father had been an advisor to former president Billings and was now in private law practice. None of them could afford to be associated with him if things went FUBAR.

He didn't want the fallout from his actions to reflect on them as individuals, as professionals, or as a family. Ann and Robert were as important to him as his own parents. He couldn't drag any of them into the quagmire of lies and treachery he'd known he would uncover, because the odds were slim to none that he could ever prove what he thought he knew, or exonerate himself from the charges stemming from the crimes he would commit in the name of justice.

He'd made Stephanie cry.

He could never get that picture out of his mind. Never forgive himself for getting involved with her in the first place. She hadn't needed him to fuck with her life. Hadn't needed the baggage he'd brought with him to the party. And she sure as hell hadn't needed the pain he'd inflicted when he'd left her behind.

He rolled onto his back. Listened as the guards rattled their keys. Time for dinner. His stomach knotted at the thought of the swill they would bring him.

He'd made her cry.

It was for the best. Much better for her that she didn't know he had come after the man responsible for Bryan's death . . . and was most likely going to end up dead because of it.

Eight hours after she'd talked with Rafe, Stephanie sat at the gate at Dulles, waiting impatiently for her flight to be called and fighting a sense of impending doom.

She'd added a healthy debt on her credit card with the airfare from D.C. to West Africa, and had put a substantial dent in her savings account for the hastily forged U.S. embassy identification papers, visa, and vaccination records tucked in her wallet. Two grand in cash for a fake ID that might get her in to see Joe, or might get her arrested. Five grand for the ticket, and it was still going to take her nearly twenty-four hours to get there. It was plenty of time for second thoughts to set in, and she'd already had many.

She was alone in this, with no clue about what she was going to do once she arrived. At least she knew why she was risking her life, her career, and possibly her sanity going after Joe.

Two years ago, Joe had literally saved her life. If not for him, the man who had been sent to kill her would be alive, she'd be dead, and her parents would be mourning the loss of both of their children.

B.J. had foiled the hired assassin's initial attempt to kill Steph, but it was Joe who had taken out the second wave of killers, then kept her safe for a wild several days on the run, while the rest of the BOI team ferreted out and dealt with the mastermind behind not only the contract on her life, but a plot to attack the U.S. and bring an already wavering economy into total collapse.

She absently massaged her right wrist, remembering the violence in which it had been broken. The break had healed long ago, but her wrist still swelled up on occasion, reminding her of the ordeal she'd been through, and of how gentle Joe had been with her. How he had taken care of not only her safety, but of needs she'd never known she had—until she'd met him.

Before Joe, she'd just gone through the motions of living. With him, she'd lived *in* life instead of orbiting aimlessly around the outside of it. He'd given her a taste of passion. A sweet, small taste that had shown her there was more to life than work, and hopefully, that someday there would be more to life than the pain of losing him.

No one dies of a broken heart. She would recover. She would move on, but she would never be able to free herself from his memory if she let him die over there.

"It's your story. You can tell it any way you want to," Rhonda had said with a worried scowl when she'd dropped Stephanie off at the airport, after they'd picked up the fake credentials from Rhonda's shady "acquaintance." "But we both know the real reason you're risking your life, not to mention your career. You're still in love with him."

It never paid to crack a bottle of red with Rhonda. One long, slightly buzzed evening, she'd spilled her guts and her heart.

She stared blankly ahead of her now, not seeing the bustling foot traffic rushing from gate to gate. Yes. She still loved him.

He still loved her, too, damn it. She didn't care what he'd told her. She was sure this whole disappearing act was because he was trying to protect her from something he was certain would hurt her. Something that could land him in prison and drag her into an international incident. Something, she still suspected, that had to do with Bryan.

He should have confided in her. He should have trusted her. Instead, what he'd done was leave. If she somehow managed to help him get out of this mess, and they were both in one piece when it was over, she had no illusions about where they went from here.

If he couldn't see her as an equal, as a full partner in his life; if he would always close her out when it came to what ate at him; if he always needed to play protector and see her as a responsibility; then they were doomed anyway.

Don't think about that now. She fought to keep the depth of the damage to her heart from crippling her with indecision. *Stay focused.*

She needed to spend her energy coming up with a plan to get him out of that prison. She was a methodical, organized thinker. Yet for the life of her, except for getting the forged U.S. embassy ID that she hoped would get her into the jail to see Joe, she was coming up blank.

Well, I have twenty-four long hours of travel to come up with something, she thought with grim determination. To keep her mind off what she didn't know, she turned her attention to one of the TV monitors suspended above the rows of chairs.

The evening news was running footage of the president's press secretary, Karen Cramer, as she'd conducted a briefing earlier today to confirm the rumor that the current secretary of state intended to step down from his post at the end of the month.

Cramer went on to read a short list of candidates in the running to replace the retiring secretary of state. Most of the names barely registered. Stephanie had all but tuned out the TV when she heard Greer Dalmage's name, and the reporter pointed out that Dalmage, a retired U.S. Army one-star general and one-term state representative from Arizona, was the current liaison between the United West African Nations and the United States.

Her heart picked up a beat. The UWAN included Sierra Leone.

She sat up straighter, riveted on the TV. Dalmage was a constant figure in the news, and she combed her memory banks for what else she knew about him. He was sixty-something, known for his military bearing, close-cropped salt-and-pepper hair, and expensive suits.

Then the report cut away to footage of Dalmage. Several reporters had caught him on the Capitol steps earlier in the day and, fueled by speculation, had thrust their microphones in his face.

"Will you accept the post of secretary of state if it's offered to you, sir?"

"My life's work has been serving my country," Dalmage said with sincere patriotism. "If I'm asked, of course I'll accept."

"On a more pressing note, sir." A reporter from the *Catholic Press* stepped forward. "Could you please comment on a story that's recently surfaced out of Sierra Leone, indicating an American citizen has been imprisoned for almost a month for the murder of a priest?"

Stephanie's heart nearly stopped. This was the first she'd heard that Joe had been identified as an American, and it could only be good news. It meant that the embassy there, or perhaps even Dalmage, could intervene and help him. Maybe she wasn't alone after all.

Buoyed by the prospect, she rose quickly from her seat and rushed closer to the monitor so she could hear every word Dalmage had to say.

He had sobered abruptly—whether in shock or simply because of the gravity of the situation, she couldn't tell.

"I am aware of that unfortunate situation. However, neither I nor any of my staff have received corroboration that the man being held for the murder is, in fact, an American. The last I knew, his identity hadn't even been determined. Best check your sources before making such a serious assumption," he added with a critical look and turned to leave.

"So you're saying, sir, that the accused is *not* an American?" the reporter pressed.

Stephanie waited with her breath trapped in her chest.

Dalmage's shoulders stiffened beneath his tailored black suit jacket and he turned again to face the reporter, the winter wind painting his cheeks bright red. He did not look pleased. "That is not what I said. I said there is no confirmation that the man is an American. If in fact he is, we will offer any and all assistance at our disposal. Now if you'll excuse me, I have pressing matters that need my attention."

The footage ended but the TV anchor continued with the story. "Our sources have since confirmed that the pressing matters Liaison Dalmage referred to involved a flight to Freetown, Sierra Leone, where it is assumed Dalmage will look into the citizenship of the suspect now being held in maximum security in a Freetown, Sierra Leone, jail while awaiting a court date. In other news . . ."

Oh, my God, Stephanie thought, as the first boarding call for her flight was announced. Dalmage had flown to Freetown. But when? She got in line with the other passengers waiting for their boarding zone to be called.

Maybe Dalmage would be there when she arrived, which meant she could have an ally on the ground when she got there. Now Joe might actually have a fighting chance of surviving this.

For the first time since she'd seen that horrifying photograph, she felt stirrings of hope.

5

Suah Korama was fifteen years old and did not recall ever having a permanent home. To his knowledge, he had no living family. He'd been eight when the old man who ran the food pantry at the Kissy mission, in a crime-ridden slum on the east edge of the city, had told him that he had known Suah's mother. Suah had acknowledged the information with a blank stare; the concept of a mother's love was already as foreign to him as a full belly.

He had lived on the streets of Freetown and fended for himself as long as he could remember. Three years ago, when he'd been big enough and strong enough to handle a rifle, he'd been grabbed in broad daylight and dragged into a military transport truck at gunpoint. No one had dared defy the rebel soldiers who had taken him. Even before he'd been driven to a remote encampment outside the city, he'd known what his fate would be. He was to become one of hundreds of boy soldiers that Augustine Sesay had recruited for his resurrected Revolutionary United Front army. He'd been twelve years old.

Starting that day, his life had consisted of military drills, regular beatings, and one meal a day. Even though he would carry the scars from Sesay's whip on his back for the rest of his life, his existence had still been a step up from life on the streets. He had been certain he would die there either by Sesay's hands or in battle, a virtual prisoner of the RUF. But fate had had different plans for him. In the end, he had out-lived Sesay because of one man. The American, Joe Green.

Green was the reason Suah had held vigil outside the city jail for twenty-nine days in a row.

Leaning a shoulder against the side of a build-ing facing the jail across the busy intersection, he watched again today and struggled with the idea of going inside. To do what, he didn't know. He only knew that Joe Green was inside that jail and that once again, he owed the American his life. If not for Green, he would be imprisoned in that jail, too. Or dead by now.

He squinted against the sunlight beating down and the heat radiating from the broken concrete sidewalk be-neath his bare feet. He did not like being in debt to any-one. Neither did he like the unwelcome sensation that filled his chest when he thought of the big, hard-faced warrior who had first spared his life, then later saved it. Trust was not an idea he could easily embrace. He knew he should be as distrustful of the American's help as he was of the concept of trust—and yet he did trust him. Friendship, also, was a privilege he withheld from everyone but a chosen few. So he did not choose to befriend the American, even though he found himself wanting to—another reason to question his own judgment.

Though physically he was still a boy, Suah considered himself a man of honor. A man with a debt to repay. So here he stood, watching the jail and waiting. For what, he didn't know . . . until a dusty city cab pulled up in front of the high security building and a fair-skinned, dark-haired woman stepped out into the street.

He stood at attention and watched her stare uncertainly at the jail. Finally she drew a deep breath, smoothed a hand over the long, loose braid at the back of her neck, and then walked slowly up the steps and through the door.

She was American. Suah was as certain of that as he was that he hadn't eaten since last night. And he was certain that there was only one reason an American woman would walk into a jail in Freetown, Sierra Leone, of her own free will.

She was here to see Joe Green. This was the moment he had been waiting for.

"What you ask is not possible."

The stern-eyed, round-bellied officer regarded Stephanie with an inflated air of authority and a firm determination to keep her from seeing his prisoner.

"Look, we can do this the easy way, Lieutenant, or we can make it difficult—more for you than for me."

She held her ground even though her knees had turned to rubber. "Either allow me access to the American prisoner, or I'll be forced to call Liaison Dalmage to intervene, right after I contact my friends at CNN."

She prayed to God that her tough as nails, "I don't take no crap from no underling" attitude wasn't as transparent as the scratched glass covering his battered desktop.

The police lieutenant stared back at her through unblinking eyes set deep in his dark, fat face. How did a man in a country of hungry people manage to glut himself to the point of obesity?

He was probably on the take, his hand deep in some politician's back pocket. Money and corruption talked in any language.

If he didn't buy her bluff, she was sunk, and so was Joe. She didn't know Dalmage; hadn't had time to track him down in the two hours since her plane had hit the tarmac, she'd cleared customs, had managed to hail a cab, had finally caught a ferry and ridden it across the bay from Lungi to Freetown. She'd experienced a frustrating flight delay with her connection in London . . . lengthening her trip by almost ten grueling hours and increasing her sense of urgency that insisted she get to Joe as quickly as possible. She'd headed straight for the jail after she'd cleared customs.

Now that she was inside the antiquated facility and had watched, in horror, the treatment of a man who had just been arrested, urgency had turned to a deep, primal fear.

Joe was inside a cell in this building. She was desperately afraid for his life.

She made a show of impatience by glancing at her watch. The lieutenant—Saidu Bangura, said the placard on his desk—cut his implacable gaze from her face to the forged documents she had handed him upon introducing herself.

She had to pray that dropping Dalmage's name got results, since the credentials identifying her as a vice-consulate with the U.S. embassy in Freetown hadn't done the trick.

Bangura continued to study the fake ID in silence, all the while flicking the tip of his thumb back and forth over the corner of the paper.

"Officer Bangura," she said impatiently. "I have both Mr. Dalmage and Lou Dobbs from CNN on speed dial."

For a long, agonizing moment, she thought he was going to call her bluff.

"You have five minutes with the prisoner," he said, sounding displeased but resigned to avoid any potential political attention that might cast him in a bad light.

He stood and handed the fake papers back to her. She was thankful to see he was looking toward another officer to assist him. Her hand was shaking as though she was about to jump out of a plane without a parachute, which was exactly how she felt.

"This way, please, miss," the younger man said.

"Five minutes," Bangura repeated as the door closed behind her.

She followed the officer out of Bangura's office, down a hall, and waited as he unlocked a door that led to yet another hallway. They weren't even halfway to the end of the hall when the overpowering stench of human waste, filth, misery, and despair almost sent her to her knees. Her eyes burned. She fought back the roiling nausea. For a horrible moment, she thought she would lose the meal she'd been served on the plane several hours ago.

She cupped her palm over her nose, took several breaths through her mouth, and focused on the reason she was here.

Joe had lived in this horror for a month. She could handle it for five minutes.

She steeled herself as the smell intensified when they neared a heavily fortified door. A barred window approximately eighteen inches square had been cut into the center of the door at eye level. The officer stopped, knocked, and a few moments later, a man's face appeared through the bars. The jailer nodded to the officer and after the rattle of keys in the lock, the door swung open.

Reeling from the appalling conditions, Stephanie waited while the two men exchanged words. The jailer slowly looked her over as he pulled a set of keys on a retractable chain away from his belt.

Without comment, he unlocked a second door made entirely of iron bars and swung it open.

"Number six," he said as Stephanie stepped into the cell block.

She flinched involuntarily when the door slammed shut behind her with a heavy thud of metal against metal.

"Stay away from the bars. We may not be able to arrive in time if one of them grabs you," he added from the other side of the barred door. His tone made it clear that no one would hurry to help her.

Still fighting queasiness, she turned back toward the cell block, trying to shut out the moans of misery from the shadowed recesses of the cage-like cells on either side of the aisle. Her heart pounded like thunder as she pushed past the fear and walked haltingly toward the cell with a worn number 6 imprinted in the stained concrete floor in front of the door.

Her senses were so saturated with revulsion over the conditions, and the light was so dim, that at first she didn't see the figure hunched low in the corner of the cage.

When she spotted him, her breath caught. His head was down, resting heavily on the knees he'd pulled up to his chest and encircled with his arms. His feet were bare; he was shirtless and filthy. She actually found herself praying that it wasn't him.

"Joe?" she said tentatively from the center of the aisle, heeding the guard's warning.

No response.

"Joe Green?" she repeated more firmly.

Her breath stalled as she waited. Again, there was no response. But then, very slowly, the man's head came up. His eyes opened and met hers . . . and her wildly racing heart kicked up to warp speed.

Oh, God.

It was him. Or what was left of him.

Jesus, oh, Jesus, *what had they done to him?*

Her eyes had adjusted enough to the dim light to see signs of the horror he'd been through. Through the dirt and grime coating his body, she could see a multitude of dark bruises coloring his chest, arms, and the legs showing beneath the tattered remains of his pants. An angry wound slashed across his forehead.

But the full measure of what he'd endured showed in the cold, vacant stare of the eyes that met hers first with denial, then with confused recognition, then with an unvarnished panic that broke her heart into a million pieces.

She'd seen his eyes when he had his warrior face on. Seen them tender in the aftermath of passion; haunted after living through a nightmare.

But she'd never seen them like this. Tortured, caged, even a little crazed.

She touched trembling fingers to her lips, feeling sick and afraid and . . . But she had to keep it together.

"Joe," she whispered around the knot in her throat. "Joe. It's Stephanie."

Dropping all pretense of being an uninvolved embassy employee, she rushed forward, pressing close to the cage.

"Joe?"

"What the fuck are you doing here?" he snarled in a harsh whisper.

She'd expected shock, and knew his outrage was a manifestation of that.

"How badly are you hurt?" She clutched a rusted iron bar in each hand as hot tears trickled down her cheeks. "Can you stand? Can you walk?"

"Get back," he growled hoarsely and with difficulty, rose to his feet. He cut a wild glance past her shoulder toward the locked door, as if he expected the guard to arrive at any moment. "You can't be here."

His hostility is because he's frightened for me. And because he's wounded and trapped like an animal.

"I'm going to get you out of here."

A wildness filled his eyes. "No. They'll lock you up, too," he warned in a voice made harsh by pain.

"They wouldn't dare imprison a U.S. embassy official," she said, wishing she believed it.

Bewilderment flashed over his face before it dawned on him that she'd gotten in with a fake ID.

"You have no idea what they would do," he hissed under his breath. "Now get the hell out of here before they catch on that you know me."

"Joe . . . listen to me. The guys can't come. They're on a blackout mission. We don't know when they'll be back. So I'm it—*I'm* the cavalry. Tell me what to do to help you, before they make me leave," she pressed, undeterred by his warnings.

"You don't get it," he gritted out between clenched teeth as he half lurched, half stumbled to the cell door. His hands were shaking, his knuckles bleeding from fresh wounds as he gripped the bars on either side of her hands. "There's nothing you can do. Just get out of here. Now."

Her heart was breaking. Up close, the signs of the beatings he'd taken were even clearer. He was skin and bones; clearly, he was fed starvation rations. His hair was over an inch long, his beard was matted and shaggy, his bare feet stained with only God knew what.

He was in a living hell.

She had to get him out of here before they killed him. She covered his hands with hers. "Help me help you. *Please* tell me what to do. Who can I contact? Surely someone can be bought off to get you released."

For an instant, the Joe she knew came back to life in his eyes. She thought he was coming around. Then he jerked his hands out from under hers and slammed them against the bars above her head.

"Guard! Guard! Get her out of here!" he roared in a hoarse, angry yell, his eyes going from cold, flinty gray to hot, smoky ash.

His rage was so unexpected, so violent, that she jumped backward before she caught herself and realized what he was doing. Protecting her. Again.

"Don't," she pleaded in a strained whisper. She glanced desperately behind her. "Don't do this."

"Guard!" he yelled again, slamming both hands against the bars with a brute strength she hadn't thought he could possibly possess.

"Step back, miss."

She jerked her head around to see the jailor entering the cell block.

She met Joe's eyes, and her heart fell as she saw his total and unbending determination to get rid of her.

"Get her the fuck out of here!" Joe demanded as he shifted his gaze to the guard. "I don't want any counsel from the U.S. goddamn embassy. And I don't want this woman let in here again."

He turned his back to her, and she had no choice but to walk away.

Her head was fuzzy with shock and disappointment and fear for Joe's life when they reached the locked door to the cell block.

"What will happen to him?"

"I do not know, miss. As of tomorrow, he will no longer be my problem."

She stopped abruptly, touched a hand to the guard's arm as he fit a key in the lock. "What happens tomorrow?"

"Tomorrow he will be moved to a maximum security prison to await his trial date."

Her knees threatened to give out again. "Maximum security? Where?"

The guard swung the barred door open and lifted a hand, gesturing for her to walk through it ahead of him.

He'd already tuned her out. She wasn't getting any more information out of him.

She'd failed, she realized as she was led down the hallway, let out into the outer office, then escorted to the front door and shown outside into the blistering morning heat.

She stood on the top step of the jail, feeling ineffective and disgusted with herself for her inability to function in Joe's world. She'd come to help, and she'd proven that she could help with exactly nothing.

But she couldn't give up. A renewed sense of urgency filled her. She had to get in contact with Dalmage. He was the man with the teeth around here. Somehow, someway, she would convince him to help her, and she would go to extreme measures to make certain that he did.

6

Fueled by new determination, Stephanie rushed down the jail's steps to the sidewalk and scanned the busy block. Her cell phone was useless here—she hadn't had time to get an international SIM card—but if she could locate an Internet café or a Wi-Fi connection to access her Skype account, she could call Rhonda to find out if she'd gotten a lead on where to find Dalmage.

She'd taken several steps down the sidewalk when she felt the hair on the back of her neck stand at attention. Stopping abruptly, she looked behind her, a gut feeling telling her that she was being followed.

The foot traffic was as heavy as the street traffic, which rushed by with a reckless disregard for anything that resembled a speed limit. Everyone seemed to be in a very big hurry as horns honked, dust swirled, and bicyclists wove in and out of the melee at their own peril.

No one seemed to be paying any attention to her. She moved on, trying to shake the persistent sense that she was being watched. But the sensation kept after her

like a cobweb, and she stopped again, whirled around—
and saw a teenage boy watching her intently from about
three yards away.

Great. She was going to get mugged.

She started walking away from him as fast as she
could.

"Miss? You are American?"

Okay. Muggers didn't announce themselves. Maybe
he was a beggar. She walked faster, ignoring him in the
hope that he'd leave her in search of another mark.

"Miss, please. Are you here to see Joe Green?"

That stopped her like a bucket of ice water. She
turned around.

The boy—he couldn't have been more than thirteen
or fourteen—stood in bare feet, wearing a ragged white
T-shirt that hadn't seen detergent in a very long time
and baggy, sand-colored shorts.

"You are a friend of Joe's?" he asked, sounding
hopeful.

She glanced around to see if anyone was watching
them. Satisfied that no one was, she looked back at the
boy and studied his face. "You know Joe?"

He nodded and repeated his question. "You are a
friend?"

"Yes," she said as her heart fluttered with an irratio-
nal anticipation. "I'm Joe's friend."

He assessed her through eyes that were old beyond
his years.

"And you? Are you also a friend of Joe's?" She met
his probing stare with one of her own.

He hesitated, then finally nodded. "I am," he said reluctantly.

A friend who didn't want to be a friend. That was clear. *And only a boy*, she thought again. Yet she could see in his bearing that he had endured more trials than most men three times his age.

"He is in very bad trouble," the boy said.

Yes, he was. "What's your name?"

"Suah," he said and drew his shoulders back. A very proud boy.

"How do you know Joe?"

He ignored her question. "I can help."

"Help do what?"

"Get him out." He hitched his chin toward the jail.

She shook her head. "I couldn't help him. How can you help? Why would you help?" What could this boy possibly do?

"I will help," he repeated with a solemn determination that made her want to believe him.

"Look. Joe is fortunate to have you as a friend. But you can't help him now. I'm sorry. I have to go talk to someone who can," she said apologetically. She had to get hold of Rhonda and Rafe.

"Talking will take time. And do no good." The warning in his voice chilled her blood despite the oppressive heat. "I know what happens to men who are arrested in Freetown. They die. You must come with me," he insisted. "I have a plan."

She stared at him. Common sense told her to walk away, because he was a child. Because she didn't know him from Adam. Because the logical thing would be to get a lead on Dalmage.

But this boy had a plan. Something she didn't.

She'd been running on gut instinct from the moment she'd seen the photograph of Joe being marched into the jail. She'd broken the law, obtaining forged identification on instinct. She'd flown here on instinct. Gone to the jail on instinct.

"We must hurry, miss," he insisted.

When he turned and motioned for her to follow him, she went with her instincts again and trailed after him down the street, praying to God that she was doing the right thing.

"Madre de Dios! Stephanie, what the hell were you thinking?"

She'd known before she'd called BOI HQ that Rafe wouldn't be happy when he found out she was in Sierra Leone, and she was glad for the thousands of miles that separated them.

She glanced at Suah, who stood sentinel behind the street phone booth where she'd used an international calling card she'd just bought.

"Look, Rafe, we don't have time for this. Can you transfer the money into my account today or not?"

"Of course I'll transfer the money—that's not the issue!"

"I know what the issue is."

"Jesus, Steph. How do you know you can trust this kid to deliver?"

She'd known Suah Korama all of two hours, and she was betting Joe's life on that trust and asking Rafe to do the same.

"I *don't* know," she admitted. "But I'm not looking at many options here. Joe's close to the edge." The memory of his bruised, starved body made her choke up. The look in his eyes had terrified her, making her wonder if she was already too late.

"If I don't do something fast, he's going to die before he ever gets to trial. And even if he makes it that far, they're still going to kill him."

"I'll say this again. Please try the embassy," Rafe persisted.

"You're not listening," she snapped, then settled herself down. Rafe was worried. He cared. He wanted her to go the safe route, even though he would do anything but play it safe if he was in a position to help Joe himself.

"The embassy hasn't received official confirmation that he's an American citizen. Because the police haven't released his name to the public, the embassy can't even initiate action that might help. The only reason I got in to see him was because I threw them off guard by knowing who he was and threatening to call my 'contacts' at CNN."

She paused and drew a frustrated breath. "I need that money in two hours, or I'm not going to be able to make this work. Can you deliver?"

"You'll get the money," he promised, sounding weary. "Just tell me what you and this kid are planning."

There was no way she was going to do that. Rafe would blow up again, and neither one of them needed the drama. She had enough to deal with.

"I'm out of time on the phone card," she lied. "I've gotta go."

"Stephanie," he snarled on a warning note.

"Do you need me to repeat my bank account number and the routing information?" she cut in.

"No, I've got it. But—"

"I've got to go," she repeated.

He surrendered with a frustrated breath. "Keep me posted, do you hear me?"

"I will. And Rafe, thanks."

She hung up, then stared at the receiver.

"We must hurry," Suah said quietly.

She turned around and searched the boy's face. A tsunami of indecision swamped her. This was it? This was the best thing she had going for her and for Joe?

How *did* she know she could trust him? No matter how hard she'd tried, she hadn't been able to get him to open up about his involvement with Joe. He'd told her only that he owed Joe and was obligated to repay his debt. She was pinning Joe's life on the shoulders of a wild, homeless boy who openly regarded her with disdain.

In the end, she had no choice. While she'd been able to get hold of Rhonda, who was now working on finding out how to get in touch with Dalmage, there was no guarantee that Stephanie could find him in time to convince him to intervene on Joe's behalf.

Maneuvering through the maze of international politics was like walking blindfolded through a minefield. Dalmage was bound to have reservations. And even if he did agree to help, by the time he got on board, it might be too late to save Joe.

She couldn't afford to hesitate any longer. She followed Suah as he ducked into an alley. They had a date with a local gang leader who just happened to dabble in illegal arms sales as a sideline.

Oh, God.

The bastards were getting better with the nunchakus. Either that, or he was wearing down. Every muscle screamed with pain. Every rib throbbed in agony when he drew a deep breath.

Biting back a groan, he carefully curled a little tighter into himself as he lay on his side in a corner of his cell. He didn't know if he should be thankful that they were done with him for today, or pissed that they'd saved enough of him for a repeat session tomorrow.

He tried to burrow into that place in his mind where now didn't exist, where both his body and his psyche were pain free. But the rattle of the key in the lock jarred him back to the filth and the stench and the reality that he was a dead man, time and date yet to be determined by these assholes.

"Get up."

A bucket of warm water slapped him hard in the face. He covered his head with his hands, gagging on the foul, brackish water and the taste of his blood from the split lip they'd given him.

"Get up." A booted foot kicked him hard in the ribs and searing pain shot through him like lightning.

"Fuckers," he gasped, struggling for breath.

Clutching his battered ribs, he pushed himself to his knees, then grabbed blindly at a bar. He managed to get a grip and, gritting out the pain, pulled until he was standing. Not straight, but at least standing.

"Hands behind your back."

He knew the consequences of stalling and did as he was told as fast as his aching body would let him. Not fast enough, apparently, because the jailor shoved him into the cell wall, then jerked both arms behind his back and slapped on metal handcuffs.

"Outside."

"Two dates in one day?" He shuffled painfully out of the cell. "I'm going to start to think you guys . . . are getting sweet on me."

He got another shove for his disrespect and crashed against the wall. He shook off the head-ringing blow and saw the large, utilitarian clock above the door in the outer hallway. His vision was fuzzy, but even a blind man could see those numbers: 11:07. Still morning.

Jesus. What now? It had been less than two hours since they'd finished with him. The bastards were bloodthirsty today.

And yesterday seemed like a lifetime away. Yesterday, when Stephanie had come to see him.

He still couldn't wrap his head around that. Sometimes he thought he'd imagined it. But then, with a clarity that sucked the breath from his lungs, he'd see her face—the pain, the fear, the hopeless determination. And he'd panic all over again when he thought about the danger she'd put herself in.

No, it had not been his imagination. Stephanie had been very, very real. She'd smelled like sunshine and fresh air and everything good that was missing from the cesspool that had become his world.

He trudged along the hallway. He'd wanted . . . hell. Didn't matter what he'd wanted. He'd had to get her out of there because goddamnit, he could *not* let her get sucked into this quagmire with him. So he'd made damn sure that she was good and gone.

But Christ, oh, Christ, he hadn't wanted her to leave him. He'd wanted to fall into her arms. Wanted to lose himself in her clean, pure softness, like a sleeping child lost in dreams of white clouds and a sweet breast and fields of dancing flowers.

Yeah, he was that fucking weak.

The guard shoved him from behind when he didn't walk fast enough to suit him. He'd rather die than to take one more beating.

And how pathetic was that? *Mean* Joe Green, worn down after a lousy thirty-one days in Hotel Hell. That ugly truth was as crippling as the thought of the beating he was about to take.

So, that's it? That's all you got, Green?

He had to dig deeper. Could not let these twisted fucks get the best of him with their nunchakus and their promises.

"*Confess to killing the priest and the beatings will stop.*"

Yeah. That was not going to happen.

He stumbled again and almost went down as the guard prodded him through the hallway. He knew the way to the interrogation room by heart; when the hallway T-boned, he turned right.

The guard grabbed his arm and shoved him down the opposite hall, which could only be bad news. He'd known they weren't going to be content with merely beating him much longer. Not when there were so many other fun options. Water. Electricity. Pliers. Acid.

His gut clenched in anticipation of what they had lined up for him next.

Then a door opened to blinding light, blasting heat, and a smell so foreign that it took him a moment to realize it was fresh air. He breathed deep, ignoring the pain from his battered ribs, and soaked up the first direct sunlight he'd felt on his face since they'd arrested him.

"Inside." A rifle barrel poked him in the spine, and nudged him toward the yawning black hole in the back of a transport truck.

7

Joe shuffled stiffly toward the rear of the truck, squinting into the dark opening. Iron hoops in five-foot-high arcs had been welded to the framework of the truck box. A heavy canvas tarp stretched over the hoops, Conestoga wagon style.

Finally, he could make out the stooped figures of several men sitting opposite each other inside. Other prisoners, none he'd ever seen before. They were all in as bad or worse shape than he was. All were handcuffed and chained.

He tripped up the cinder blocks they'd used to build temporary steps and ducked inside. The guard jumped in behind him and unlocked his cuffs while another kept the business end of an AK-47 locked on his chest.

"Hands in front," the guard ordered, then snapped the cuffs on him again before reaching up and snagging a heavy chain suspended from one of the hoops. After threading the chain through the link between the handcuffs, the guard padlocked it in place and drew Joe's hands above his head.

He felt like a piece of meat suspended from a hook, with only enough give in the chain to let him sit down on the bench along the wall.

He assessed his surroundings and his escape options. The truck was a small transport vehicle, possibly military, not much bigger than a pickup. The bench he was sitting on was a slab of thick, rough wood. And then there were the chains. It all led him to conclude that he wasn't going anywhere but for a ride.

He stared at the faces of the five other men chained up with him. None of them white. All in bad shape. All resigned to whatever the guards had planned for them.

"Where are they taking us?"

Silence.

"Does anyone know where they're taking us?" he asked again.

"Pademba," a man across from him finally said in a voice void of emotion.

Despite the oppressive heat, a chill washed through his body. So this was it. Joe had heard of the Pademba Road facility. The maximum security prison was set smack in the middle of the city. Prisoners were sent there to die. He remembered reading about an American citizen who died there several years ago, after being leveled with fabricated conspiracy charges. Joe remembered because after the man's death, he was exonerated.

Justice—when there was any—was slow in Sierra Leone.

And human life was highly disposable.

The guard lifted the tailgate, secured it, and slapped

his hand on the back of the truck, signaling the driver to pull out. The gears grinded, the engine groaned, and they rolled forward.

The ride across town was rough and hot as the truck jostled along the dusty, pocked pavement. The tailgate didn't meet the canvas roof, leaving a u-shaped gap three feet high and three feet wide. Joe stared out of the opening at the run-down buildings scrolling by like news footage from a documentary on poverty and urban decay.

Then he attempted to mentally prepare himself for the inevitable end that would come with phase two of his captivity. But all he could think about was Stephanie.

How he'd let her down.

How horrified she'd looked when he'd sent her away.

How he wished he had lived a life that she would have been safe being a part of.

They hit a deep rut that knocked him out of his thoughts and briefly sent him airborne. He hadn't recovered his balance when the truck made a hard, left turn. Planting his feet to keep from sliding off the bench, he used the chains binding him to the hoops for leverage, but damn near slid off anyway as they skidded to a grinding stop.

Swearing at the pain, he gripped the chain to keep the cuffs from cutting deeper into his wrists, then glanced past his raised arms to look out the back again as the truck went into reverse and started jockeying around, changing direction.

A multi-vehicle pileup of broken-down cars, trucks, and vans created a logjam in the middle of the intersection. And the street they'd just veered off was blocked. In the middle of the day, in light traffic.

Which made no sense. Something was wrong with this picture.

The situational awareness he'd honed to a sharp edge during years of combat and covert operations hummed to life. The most opportune time to stage an escape attempt was during transport.

A fleeting hope shot him full of adrenaline. This was exactly the kind of escape attempt the BOIs would launch.

But the guys were half a world away. And he was still on his own.

Gaze sharp, he glanced at the faces of the other men, wondering which of them might have a friend on the outside determined to set him free. They all looked as surprised as he felt.

When the truck started rolling forward again and nothing else happened, he knew that wishful thinking was as close as he was going to come to making a break.

The adrenaline rush dropped like a stone, and his abused body gave in to exhaustion. He let his head hang between his upraised arms and closed his eyes, resigned to his fate. And his failure.

He'd botched things up at every turn. He'd managed to get a priest killed *and* put Stephanie at risk, which was the one thing he'd been determined to avoid.

God, he still couldn't believe she'd come here. He was still half out of his mind with guilt and worry that she would try to get to him again.

At least there was good news in the transport. She'd have to find him first, and he had a real strong feeling that no one back at the city jail was going to offer any information about his relocation anytime soon.

The truck skidded to an abrupt stop again. This time Joe landed on his knees on the floor, the chains jerking his arms painfully above his head.

He scrambled to get himself upright, catching a glimpse of the street as he did. A huge pile of tires had been set on fire in the center of the intersection. Black smoke boiled up out of the flames, scorching the air, obstructing the view.

Tick, tick, tick. His mind whirled with possible explanations. One blocked intersection might be a coincidence. Two? No way in hell. Something was definitely going down.

His pulse revved up again in anticipation. Someone out there wanted someone in this truck out of the mix. And he was hanging here like a rack of beef, and couldn't do a damn thing to capitalize on the situation.

For the second time, the truck maneuvered away from an intersection, then started forward again with a jerky takeoff before Joe managed to get back on the bench. He fell back again, cursing along with the other prisoners, who were caroming around like tetherballs at the end of a short rope.

The truck's gears ground and complained as the driver shifted and picked up speed. Joe estimated they were doing around thirty or thirty-five miles per hour, too damn fast for inner-city driving, when the driver stood on the brakes again.

The truck fishtailed, heaved to the left, and then everything went to hell.

Out of control, the vehicle tipped further and further to the side as the driver attempted to stop the inevitable.

But inertia had taken over. The truck toppled onto its side, then skidded for several yards as steel scraped against pavement. The prisoners erupted in curses and pained cries as they swung and bounced around, victims of gravity and velocity.

Joe felt a glancing blow to his back—someone's foot—but somehow managed not to dislocate his shoulders as he muscled himself to his knees. He leaned into the pull of the chain as the truck finally jerked to a stop, the men quit yelling, and the engine heaved its last breath.

Then the first shot was fired.

Oh, shit.

The *chuck chuck chuck* of automatic rifles clattered into the sounds of the ticking engine, creaking chassis, and men's shouts. Bullets pinged off the upended truck's belly, ricocheted off the streets, and danced through the canvas that had been ripped halfway off the iron hoops.

The thought had barely crossed Joe's mind that he'd survived the crash but was going to buy the farm from an AK-47 round when the shooting stopped as abruptly as it started.

The smell of hot tires, motor oil, and gunpowder clogged his lungs as, very gingerly, he peered through the ragged canvas. A dozen masked gunmen descended on the downed vehicle, rifles shouldered, beads drawn on the driver and the two guards riding shotgun.

The three lawmen held their hands in the air and were quickly cuffed and chained to the truck's front fender.

As quick as monkeys, six of the gunmen converged on the truck, made fast work of the chains with bolt cutters, and set the prisoners free. Men scattered in every direction. Joe got slammed against the wheel well in the process, saw stars, and swallowed back churning nausea.

He had to . . . had to get out of here. Couldn't hang around to express his gratitude.

Head spinning, he pushed to his feet. A wave of vertigo washed over him and he fell flat on his face, tasted dirt and blood, and knew he'd split his lip open again. With his last reserve of strength he pushed to all fours, fighting the pain screaming through his body and the sucking weakness of his muscles. He actually made it to his feet, started off at an off-balance, hobbling run, only to be grabbed from behind and shoved through the side door of a beat-up panel van.

Before he could peel his face off the ratty carpet, the

van shot down the street like the hounds of hell were after it.

Fuck. This could *not* be happening. He could not survive that prison and the crash and the storm of firepower just to end up a captive again.

He battled to stay conscious. Struggled to sit up . . . and slammed into another wall of dizziness that had him crashing back down.

"Be still."

The voice that delivered those two words stopped him cold.

Stephanie.

Stephanie paced the small room on the second floor of the safe house Suah had arranged for them. Rain beat down in torrents, and the energy of the downpour made her restless and edgy. She made herself let the doctor do his thing, even though she had a hundred questions. Joe looked bad. Really bad. The doctor looked young. Really young. And really inexperienced. She felt helpless as he examined Joe, wondering if he knew what he was doing.

Suah sat in one of two wooden chairs in the corner of the little room, the butt of an AK-47 balanced on his thigh, trying to look impassive. She could tell that he was concerned, too, even though he had assured her that the young Dr. Bala Sankoh was a miracle worker, and that he could be trusted to keep their existence and their location secret.

It had been two hours since they had staged the escape and Joe still hadn't regained consciousness. When he moaned and shuffled his legs restlessly on the single mattress that lay on the floor, she couldn't keep her silence any longer.

"Why hasn't he come to yet?" she asked urgently. "Does he have a concussion? Is he in pain?"

Dr. Sankoh, a slight young black man with an easy, comforting manner, smiled up at her, revealing a wide gap between his immaculate white teeth. "There is no apparent concussion, miss. I do not believe he has any head injuries severe enough to cause one. Head injuries bleed a lot, so they look much worse than they generally are. And he sleeps because I have given him sedation and because his body needs an opportunity to recover. I will give you instructions for dosages over the next few days. As for pain, at least two of his ribs are either cracked or badly bruised. So I am certain, yes, that they are causing him pain. The sedation will help with that also."

"He's so thin," she said, more to herself than to the doctor.

"Malnourished, no doubt. That will be easily remedied. Dehydration is his major issue now. Again, the IV fluids will turn that around quickly. I'm also administering antibiotics to deal with any infections he may have contracted while imprisoned. I'll leave additional instructions for you.

"He's a strong man," he said, offering her a kind smile. "A fine physical specimen. That is all in his favor. In a few days, he'll be much improved. Give him a month and he'll be back to normal."

Looking at him now, his face gaunt, his skin pale and pasty where it wasn't covered with bruises or wounds, she couldn't imagine that happening.

"You will see." The doctor started gathering up his medical kit. "Even tomorrow, he will show more signs of life. I suspect the sedation will be necessary to keep him down, to give those ribs a chance to heal."

She panicked when he headed for the door. "You're leaving?"

"I must," he said with an apologetic smile.

"But you'll be back to check on him?"

He shook his head. "I'm sorry. I cannot. I have done what I can for him. Time will do the rest. And I have many patients much more in need of my attention. He will be fine," he assured her again, then went over his instructions on the administration of the fluids, the antibiotics, and sedation.

"Thank you so much." She handed him several bills. "This seems inadequate, given all you've risked."

He counted the money. "You are very generous. This will go directly to the clinic. Many people will benefit, so the risk was well worth it."

Suah rose and opened the door, then, leading with the rifle, checked to make certain there was no one in the hallway who wasn't supposed to be there.

"We have not seen much of you at the mission, Suah." Dr. Sankoh paused by the door.

"I've been busy," Suah said evasively.

"You are missed." He laid a hand on the boy's bony shoulder. "Please do not be such a stranger."

Suah gave him a noncommittal nod. "I am in your debt."

"If you feel so, then come back to the mission. We miss your smiling face." The doctor chuckled when Suah schooled his face into a mask totally void of emotion that Stephanie was beginning to realize was typical Suah fashion.

Just once, she would like to see him smile. Would like to see him react to kindness, to show some sign that there was still a little boy inside that too-thin body. A boy with hopes and dreams and plans for a future.

But Suah seemed to already know what the country that had abandoned so many children knew. That every day of his life would be a fight for survival, and no matter how badly he might want to believe in people like the kind Dr. Sankoh, he could only depend on himself.

It hurt her heart to know that his pretense of detachment came from so many hard lessons. She felt helpless because there was nothing she could do to help him, either. If she managed to pull this off, she and Joe would be gone soon. Suah would still be here, still be an orphan, still be on his own. It would still be—always be—him against the world.

When Suah left the room with the doctor she turned back to Joe, someone she *could* help, and looked him over with a critical eye. He appeared to be resting comfortably. She chose to believe that the doctor could be right: that he'd soon be back to normal.

For the first time in ages, she drew a breath that didn't choke her with tension.

They'd actually done it. They'd gotten Joe out of that evil situation. None of Suah's boys had gotten hurt, thankfully, and no one, not even the guards, had died in the escape.

Joe was free. He would heal. They'd find a way out of Sierra Leone, and then . . . then what?

She knelt beside the mattress, pulled the bucket of rainwater Suah had collected earlier closer, and reached inside for the cloth Dr. Sankoh had used to clean Joe's wounds.

What happened next for her and Joe? The answer was simple: nothing.

No matter what his motives were—whether he really didn't love her, or whether it was some misdirected attempt to protect her—the bottom line was that he *had* left her. He'd been determined to write her out of his life, confirming a truth she'd been denying for a very long time. With Joe, there would always be something bigger than the two of them. He would always be committed to his job and his team and his code of honor that told him it wasn't fair to subject her to the risks. He'd always be haunted by ghosts from his past and not want to subject her to the fallout. And now he'd have new nightmares from his horrifying imprisonment to muddy the waters even more.

She stared at his bruised and battered face, sadness tightening her chest. Despite all that she knew about what couldn't be, all that she knew about his inability to stop playing protector long enough to engage in an equal partnership, she still loved him. Still loved a man who didn't have the ability to trust that what they could have together would outdistance any obstacles that got in their way.

Yeah, she thought with a newfound resolve to deal with a future without him. She still loved him. But when they got out of this place, she was going to let him go.

"Your loss, Joe Green," she whispered into the quiet room.

Hers, too.

With tender care and as dispassionately as possible, she started bathing him. He still reeked of the jail. She knew how much he would hate that and wasn't going to make him suffer it a moment longer.

As she gently administered to his body, she tried to look but not see or remember what it felt like to lie beneath him. Tried to touch but not feel. Tried to pretend that the tears suddenly trailing down her face were all about the cruel damage inflicted on this strong, resilient body. Tried, even, to convince herself that some of her tears were for Suah, who had never been allowed to be a child. That they were tears of relief, even, that the worst was over. That they had nothing to do with the fact that she had finally accepted the truth.

She would never touch this man again as a lover. Never give and take pleasure from this body ever again.

Never look in his eyes and know this was the man she hoped to spend the rest of her life with.

She wiped her eyes with the backs of her wrists, and rinsed out the cloth. Then she finished the job she'd started.

8

"Do I have to tell you again what will happen to you and to your family if the American is not found immediately?" Pain clutched at his chest as he leaned over Saidu Bangura's desk. *You should be afraid,* he thought darkly, gratified that the fat police lieutenant was nearly cowering.

"Are you . . . well?" Bangura asked cautiously. "You do not look well."

"I'm fucking fine," he ground out as what felt like a searing hot iron spread flames through his chest.

Sweat poured off his face as he reached blindly into his breast pocket. His hand was shaking with rage and weakness as he withdrew a prescription bottle, then fumbled to uncap it. He shook two nitro tablets into his palm and quickly tucked them under his tongue.

The relief was almost immediate. The pain lessened and the nausea subsided as the drug dilated his blood vessels and eased the pressure.

Fucking angina. Fucking inept bastard, whose

bumbling loss of the American could cost him everything.

"Perhaps you should sit down," Bangura prodded as he planted his palms on the desk and rode out the tail end of the attack.

"And perhaps you can explain to me why a lone American who'd been starved and beaten for a month managed to escape your transport vehicle."

"The men responsible for letting him escape have been punished."

"That doesn't answer my question."

"I do not know yet what happened. I know only that he had assistance from outside."

"Assistance?" Not from Green's employer or his teammates. He'd made sure that the Black Ops, Inc. team was otherwise occupied deep in the Amazon, chasing their own tails on the trail of a bogus intel report of an al-Qaeda splinter group setting up a base of operations. Once his eyes on the ground had informed him that there was an American in Freetown snooping around, then positively identified him as a former member of a U.S. special operations group that had made trouble for him at the onset of his operation here, he'd made certain the rest of the team had been kept very busy. Before that, he'd arranged to have them tagged to go to Colombia to deal with a bona fide U.S. security threat. When Green was arrested last month they'd been conveniently unavailable in Bogotá, where there was no chance of the news reaching them. The BOIs—Black's Obnoxious Idiots—were out of the picture. Green wasn't getting any help from them.

That was the degree of power he wielded. The power he had earned. He had the ear of the secretary of defense. The confidence of the joint chiefs. And had been noticed by the president.

None of it was by accident.

Every step of the way, he'd meticulously plotted and skillfully placed all of his chess pieces in play. It was all about finesse and intellect, about winning and reaping the rewards.

Most of all, it was about power. He'd been taught that from a very early age, and what he hadn't learned fast enough had been beaten into him. Defeat had never been an option. Not in little league baseball. Not in a school spelling bee. Not on the gridiron.

Weakness led to defeat. And he'd never been allowed to be weak. The angina was an unforgivable weakness, but it would not win. And he would not lose.

After several long years, he was one step away from checkmate. Only one man stood in his way: Joe Green.

In retrospect, he should have shut him up right away. Letting him live this long had been one of his few mistakes. But he'd wanted information before he had Green eliminated. A stay in Bangura's jail had seemed the perfect way to weaken his will and loosen his tongue. A transfer to Pademba Road prison, a final interrogation to determine what, if anything, Green knew about his Sierra Leone operation, and he'd quickly become a casualty of a prison system known for its high mortality rate among inmates.

"I assure you, we will find him." Bangura attempted to reassert himself in the silence he had taken as a threat, with good reason. "My entire force is searching as we speak. I have divided the city into grids and—"

"I don't give a fuck how you do it." Now that the attack had passed and he was capable of self-control, he reverted to the chillingly calm tone that he had always found a more effective terror tactic than shouting. "And I don't want your assurances. I want results."

Sweat beaded on the fat man's brow.

Message received: Bangura understood that his family wasn't safe until this was resolved.

"Hourly reports," he said over his shoulder as he walked out of the lieutenant's office.

Inside the building had been stifling. Outside, the sun was unbearable. He hated this fucking barbarian country. Despised the fact that he was even here. But here he would stay until Bangura delivered.

The crooked cop was a joke at his job, but he loved his fat, busty wife and their three heathen children. He'd made it a point to know everything about Bangura. Knew specifically that the man's interrogation tactics would be brutal. Bangura wouldn't hesitate to lop off a digit or even a limb to obtain the information he wanted. That unapologetic brutality was one of the reasons he'd recruited the former RUF officer in the first place.

If Green had help, Bangura would find those responsible. And then he would dispense with them all.

Joe woke up in the dark. In a bed, or maybe a pallet on a floor. Not mired in filth. The air didn't smell foul. No moans of misery and pain formed perpetual white noise in the background.

He had no clue where he was, only that he was not in prison. What he *did* know, with absolute certainty, was that he was not alone.

He lay still to determine if the other person in the room represented a threat or a promise. But his head felt so damn fuzzy. His thoughts were like sludge, sluggish and vague and disjointed. Only his body sent crystal-clear messages. If he so much as drew a deep breath, the pain was vicious and crippling.

The sweet oblivion of unconsciousness was a powerful lure, so he drifted again, floating in and out of sleep.

And then he caught a scent.

Warm. Fragrant. Clean.

Familiar.

Stephanie.

Another trick of his mind? Hadn't he made certain he'd sent her away?

A soft hand lay gently on his brow.

"Joe."

His heart kicked like recoil from a rifle shot. Disbelief came in a distant second to hope as he lifted a hand, curled his fingers around a slender wrist, and hung tight.

"Jesus," he whispered, part prayer, all sheer, selfish relief that rolled over the regret.

"It's okay," she murmured and with the gentlest of touches, settled his wildly beating heart. "You're safe now. All you need to do is rest."

It had been so long since he had rested. So long since he'd felt safe. She was offering both. And Jesus God, he wanted both. He'd *never* felt this weak. Physically. Mentally. It shamed him.

"It's okay," she murmured again, and with exquisite gentleness pried his fingers away from her wrist. "Just rest."

The hell with it. He didn't want to fight it.

So he believed.

You're safe now.

And he obeyed.

Just rest.

And he let the tension slide out of his body on a slow, shallow breath.

This time when the darkness took him under, he welcomed it with open arms.

"I was starting to think you were never going to come around."

Stephanie. Beside him. Sleep-soft and fragrant. She shared his bed on the floor. The only bed, he suspected.

Jesus. Joe still had trouble believing it, and coming to terms with what had happened.

He'd been awake for several minutes, silent. Assessing. Trying to clear the cobwebs and get a bead on the time of day. Based on the angle of the sunlight slanting in through an open window, he finally decided that it was late morning.

He was naked beneath a thin sheet and wasn't sure how he felt about that. He was clean. About that, he felt damn good, until he thought about Stephanie having to clean him up. He should remember something like that, but he was drawing a total blank.

The only thing he was certain of was where they were. Nowhere on earth smelled like this place: the faint but ever-present stench of rotting garbage, smoke from hundreds of charcoal grills, the salty scent of the sea, the bitter scent of cassava and rice. Add that to the intense heat and there was no mistaking that they were still in Freetown.

He had a million questions, but they could wait. He wanted to savor this moment a little while longer. Savor his freedom and the nearness of the soft, pliant woman nestled up against him.

Real. Not a dream.

And not right.

A staggering wave of panic shattered his temporary feeling of contentment. She was not safe here.

"I thought I sent you away." His throat felt raw and dry.

She pushed up on an elbow. "You tried to." Her smile was full of concern, speculation, and discomfort. Yet it was so heart-wrenchingly beautiful, it humbled him.

She had every reason to hate him, yet she was here. He couldn't even begin to assemble the questions on that front.

"Last thing I remember . . . I was chained in a truck. And then I wasn't. You did that? You got me out of there?"

"*We* got you out."

"We?"

She sat up stiffly, folded her legs beneath her hips, and stretched her arms above her head. Sunlight from the east-facing window cascaded over the dark, tangled hair that fell over her shoulders and trailed down her back. A line creased her cheek where she'd been lying on her arm. A softness in her eyes revealed a heaviness in her heart that made his chest ache.

"Why don't we see how you're doing first, then we'll play twenty questions." She checked a tube that he only then realized was attached to an IV port in his arm.

"Fluid and antibiotics," she explained when he looked from the tube to her face.

Antibiotics were as hard to come by in Freetown as running water. He didn't want to think about how she had gotten them.

Someone had patched him up. A bandage covered the cut on his forehead, he realized after feeling it gingerly with his fingertips.

He lifted his head, felt the room spin, and let it fall back down. He was as weak as a damn baby. All he could do was lie there as she rose to her feet, stretched out more morning kinks, and walked across the small room on bare feet.

"How long have I been out?"

She returned with a bottle of water, knelt beside him again, and supported his head so he could drink. Compared to the brine at the Freetown jail, it tasted like ambrosia. He latched on to her wrist and guzzled, not caring that it ran out of the corners of his mouth and down his neck, or that the plastic rim bit into his cut lip.

"Easy, Joe. Your system can't handle that much water that fast. You're going to make yourself sick."

He reluctantly let her go, let his head fall back, and closed his eyes.

"How long have I been out?" he asked again as he willed down his stomach's attempt to reject the water.

"Almost forty-eight hours."

Christ. He'd lost two days. "How the hell did that happen?"

"Dehydration, malnutrition, your injuries—pick one."

"I shouldn't have been out of it for two days."

"The doctor said you needed the rest."

His eyes snapped open. "You've been sedating me?"

She looked surprised at the anger in his tone. "Per the doctor's orders, yes."

"Is it in this?" He glanced suspiciously at the IV port. He'd rip the sucker out of his arm if he was getting a steady drip of it.

"No. I dose you every six hours."

"No more," he said flatly.

"But if it will help you heal—"

"No more sedation," he restated in a hard tone, and immediately regretted the bruised look he'd put in her eyes. "It's okay; you did what you thought was best. But I can't be sedated, Stephanie." Not and get back on his game.

"Fine. No more," she said, looking wounded.

He looked away, overcome by emotions that ran the gamut from guilt to humility to gratitude to absolute astonishment, before ending with a frustrated sense of failure. *He* was the protector. *He* was the caretaker. Right now he couldn't take care of a paper clip.

"Joe. Look at me."

The softness in her eyes told him she'd read his mind. "You don't always get to be the hero. Some of us lesser beings need to get a shot at it every now and then, okay?"

No, it was not okay. And there was nothing about her that fell in the *lesser* category. "How did you pull this off?"

She looked relieved that he'd settled down, reminding him with a fresh wave of guilt that so far, he'd acted like a real asshole. "I had help. You can thank Suah."

"Suah?"

"A very resourceful young man."

There had never been any question about that. "Tell me."

"He rounded up some of his friends," she said with a shrug. "They planned it all. The place. The time. The diversions."

"The burning tires blocking the road." The image of billowing black smoke and red-hot flames came back to him.

"Among other things. The only thing we hadn't planned on was the transport truck tipping over. I thought we'd lost you then."

So had he. More images and sounds came back to him. "The boys had some heavy firepower."

She looked a little uncomfortable. "Yeah . . . we had to make a little deal with the locals."

Good God. Exposing herself to that criminal element could have gotten her killed.

Which was redundant as hell. Just *being* here could get her killed. And he was zoned out on drugs.

"Where are we? What part of the city?"

"North, in the hills. Suah arranged for the safe house. And for the doctor who treated you."

He gave her a measuring look. "All provided out of the goodness of their hearts?"

When she looked away, he knew she'd bankrolled not only the escape, but also the hideout and his medical treatment.

"If I had the strength, I'd yell at you."

"So let's work on that strength thing. Do you think you can handle some broth?"

"Yeah. Help me sit up."

He was breathing hard and wet with sweat by the

time they managed to get him upright and scooted back so he could lean against the wall.

A wave of dizziness hit him again and he had to hang on to her arm to keep from tipping over.

"Maybe this wasn't such a good idea." She looked troubled.

"I'm okay," he insisted.

He would be okay. He *had* to be okay. Because neither of them would get out of this alive if he wasn't.

9

Joe looked around, taking in his new digs. It wasn't much but it was one hundred steps up from his jail cell. The room was small and spartan, its peeling walls a faded blue. A single window—no glass, no screen, no blinds—faced the street. The level of the noise from outside told him they were not on the ground floor; second or third, probably. The only door faced him. On one side of the door were a couple of hooks hung with several items of clothing.

On the other side was a small apartment-size refrigerator, dented and scratched and rusted around the edges, its hum adding another layer of white noise to the street sounds. A card table sat in another corner with two beat-up wooden chairs, one facing the door. On top of the table were several boxes of ammo.

Whoever had set things up was playing heads-up ball. If someone who wasn't welcome came through that door, they weren't going to get far. An older model AK-47 leaned, barrel up, in the corner next to the table. Closer to him, another AK was propped within reach.

A well-used Glock 17, a full extra clip, and a KA-Bar lay on the floor by the bed.

He glanced back at Stephanie, hating it times ten that she was in neck deep, when the whole reason he'd walked away from her was to keep her out of the mix.

She handed him a toothbrush that she'd loaded with toothpaste. He'd never been so grateful for anything in his life, planning to brush until his gums bled. He didn't get far before the damn weakness made him quit.

"Where's Suah now?" he asked after rinsing his mouth.

"I don't know. He leaves sometimes." A hint of frustration in her voice told him Suah's absences were worrisome to her.

"But the boys are on lookout. We'll get plenty of notice if anyone suspicious gets too close."

His thoughts were still disjointed and fuzzy, but it finally occurred to him to ask "How did you two hook up, anyway?"

She brought a cup of cool broth from the minifridge, knelt beside him, and extended a spoonful. Another direct hit to his ego, but the simple act of brushing his teeth had worn him out, so he let her feed him. The broth was thin and a little salty and tasted slightly of beef. He had to will it to stay down.

"Suah found me, actually," she said. "The day I came to the jail, he was waiting outside. From what I've gathered he'd been holding vigil for the past month, trying to figure out a way to get you out of there."

He grunted, then wished he hadn't when fire shot through his ribs. He gingerly ran his fingers over them.

"The doctor says they're bruised. Possibly cracked, but not broken," she said, correctly interpreting the question in his eyes.

"Suah says he owes you. What's that about?" she backtracked after feeding him another spoonful. This one went down easier.

"Long story."

"Since you're not going anywhere anytime soon, I think we have time. Unless you don't feel up to talking."

"No, I'm good," he said, willing strength back into his body. "Last year, when we shut down the North Korean's arms deal?"

She nodded, well aware of the BOI op that had ferreted out an international gun smuggling network run by Jeong Ryang, and had also destroyed Augustine Sesay's hopes of resurrecting the brutal Revolutionary United Front movement in Sierra Leone.

"Sesay sent Suah and several other boy soldiers to pick up the gun shipment. We confiscated the weapons and captured Suah and the others. Kept the guns, but we let the boys go."

"Instead of turning them over to the authorities?"

"Instead of killing them."

Her face paled. "You would have killed children?"

"We would have killed soldiers," he said flatly, "armed with automatic weapons and the skills to use them.

"But no," he added, looking off into space as he remembered how close he'd come to pulling the trigger.

Where he'd been in his head and his heart that day, it wasn't a place he was proud of. "In the end, we could not have killed them."

Because that constituted the difference between the good guys and the bad guys. If he had pulled that trigger, he would have been no better than the Sesays and the Ryangs of this world.

"Suah apparently felt that he owed me for that."

She didn't say anything as she spooned up another mouthful of broth and held it out to him. He watched her face as he let her feed it to him like he was a child. But his body didn't react like a child's as his gaze strayed from her face and trailed slowly down the rest of her.

God, she was beautiful. Every soft, lush curve was accentuated beneath her slim khaki pants and tan tank top. Her sandals were brown and appeared to be local. She wore small gold hoops in her ears, a fine gold chain around her neck. Sometime between the water and the broth, she'd gathered her hair at her nape with a wide gold clip. Random curls had sprung free, framing her face, clinging to her neck in damp wisps caused by the heat. She was fresh faced, sweet smelling, and stunning. She was also the single sexiest woman he'd ever known, although everything from the way she dressed to the way she wore her hair was designed to undercut that sex appeal.

Only the red polish on her toes suggested that she ever indulged in a little bit of whimsy, or that she gave herself over completely to that sexy siren who lost her inhibitions when her clothes came off and she took him to her bed. The memory of her hands on him, of her mouth on his, shot another cloud of fog through his head.

It cleared as he zeroed in on the compact Glock 19 tucked into the waistband of her pants at the small of her back.

"You shouldn't be here," he said, his voice gruff with emotion.

She lowered her lashes, then looked directly at him. "I wouldn't be, if you hadn't walked away."

The words were softly spoken but the look in her eyes gave him a hint of the hurt and anger she was feeling. All justified.

"Why didn't you let me rot?" He didn't bother to ask how she'd found him—she had the resources of the NSA at her disposal. The bigger question was why she'd bothered.

A long silence told him that maybe she might be wondering the same thing.

"Because I was the only one available to make sure that didn't happen," she said finally.

And how was that for brutal honesty? What had he expected? That she'd tell him she came because she loved him? After what he'd done to her? Not a prayer.

"And because no matter what the news report said, I know you didn't kill that priest," she added, humbling him again with her trust.

"No. I didn't kill him. But he's still dead. And that's on me."

Her brows pinched together. "I don't understand."

"I was asking questions, Steph. Questions someone didn't want asked or answered."

Wariness filled her eyes. "What kind of questions?"

"You're not going to want to hear it."

"Oh, I think I *need* to hear it."

He tightened his mouth, then let out a long breath. "Questions about Bryan's death," he said and waited for the fallout.

She looked very tired suddenly. This was an old and sore subject. And despite the softness that was first, second, and third nature to her, the anger that had been simmering beneath the surface finally bubbled to the top.

"I'd *hoped* that you'd let that go. Bry died in combat, in an ambush. The investigation was conclusive. As far as I'm concerned, there are no more questions about his death."

"And you're wrong. There are too many questions, starting with why there was an ambush in the first place," he countered with more bite than he'd intended.

"What happened has never been in dispute." The frustration in her voice made it clear that she was trying to make some sense of where he was going with this. "Someone at Cent Com screwed up. Someone botched the satellite read. You walked into a trap. It was a bad call."

"It was more than a bad call. Someone wanted *all* of us dead that night. We weren't supposed to come out of

Sierra Leone alive. The RUF attack was just the vehicle to make it happen. Their mistake had been thinking they could kill us all."

"Joe," she said gently, "I know how difficult it was to lose him. It was difficult for all of us. But this is insane. For God's sake, you ended up in prison, could have ended up dead, because you're trying to turn Bry's death into . . . what? A calculated murder?"

"That's exactly what it was. And the man responsible also had the priest murdered and me framed."

"But why kill a priest? If he was after you, why not just kill you?"

"Because the priest could confirm what I'd finally figured out. And outright killing me would have raised more than a little suspicion, don't you think?"

She shook her head, still doubting. He got it. The possibility that Bryan's death hadn't been a mistake at all, that it was deliberate, was too much for her to process.

Tears filled her eyes. "Look," she said carefully, "let's . . . let's not talk about this right now, okay? Whether you think so or not, you still need recovery time. Your fever is down but you've still got a low-grade infection."

She sat back on her heels, her hands clasped tightly in her lap. "Give yourself a little more time, okay? We'll get you on your feet and you'll start thinking more clearly."

"There's nothing wrong with my thinking." But there *was* something wrong with him trying to force her to accept a truth she wasn't prepared to handle. "But fine, I'll drop it. For now."

Her shoulders sagged with relief.

Neither of them spoke as she fed him the rest of the broth. And when she encouraged him to lie down again, he didn't argue. He was a total disaster in the strength department.

But not for long. Just a little more rest, a lot more fluid and antibiotics, and some protein when his gut could handle it, and he'd be back on his feet.

Right now he was already drifting back toward LaLa Land.

Fucking weakness. Fucking jail.

Fucking bastard who was responsible for putting him here, for putting Steph in danger, and most of all for taking the life of a brother in arms who'd died way before his time.

"Stephanie." He grabbed her wrist just before he drifted off. "Thank you."

Stephanie hurried along the busy street, head down and covered with a long, mango-colored scarf. Bekah—one of the boys in Suah's little army—kept pace behind her as she wove through the crowd, her arms full of groceries. Had anyone been watching, they would have assumed she was alone, just a woman returning home from market. But Bekah was there for her protection. So was the boy walking point a couple yards ahead of her.

Both were Suah's boys. All of them *were* just boys.

Orphans. It made her heart hurt to know what they'd seen in their young lives, what they'd been forced to do. None of them had much to say, but it was clear that they shared a common bond. They'd all been stolen from the streets and forced to become soldiers in a madman's army. They were free now and on their own, literally living a dog-eat-dog existence. No stability. No support. No love.

They had no reason to help her, yet these boys stood for her and for Joe when she couldn't even get a meeting with the one American who might be able to help them.

It made her so angry. Before her last stop at the market she'd made contact with Rhonda, who had given her an address where Dalmage set up shop when he was in Freetown. Ironically, the government office the United States leased for Dalmage and any other dignitaries who needed quarters was only a few blocks from the safe house. She'd found the building an hour ago, only to be met by attitude from the self-important, fifty-something American receptionist who sat behind a polished mahogany desk and guarded Dalmage's inner sanctum door with the fierceness of a pit bull.

"Please, if you can't let me in to see him, *please*, just give this to Liaison Dalmage," she'd implored, extending the sealed envelope containing the note she'd written. "There are lives on the line," she'd insisted when the woman sat in pinch-lipped silence. "American lives."

"I will tell you again, miss, this is a matter for the

American embassy. Mr. Dalmage's duties do not extend—"

"The embassy can't help me," she snapped, weary of going over the same ground yet again. She'd already tried. There would be paperwork, and a lag time of a few days, possibly more before she would obtain a duplicate passport for an American citizen without identification. And even if they obtained the passport, he'd never get past security. They'd immediately haul him back to prison.

She needed someone who would bend and maybe even break some rules to help one of their own. Based on everything she'd heard about Dalmage, she was betting he was that man.

At the woman's continued scowl, Stephanie had taken a deep breath and settled herself down. "Look, Ms."—she glanced at the engraved desk plate—"Foster, I regret if I've been impudent. I understand that it's your job to protect Mr. Dalmage's time and position. But as I've told you, this is a critical issue. Please—just give him the envelope."

Ms. Foster glared for another long moment, then sighed heavily. "Give it to me," she said stiffly. "I'll see what I can do. Who shall I say it's from?"

"It's all in there," Stephanie had said, feeling a small measure of relief. "Thank you."

She'd left before the woman changed her mind—and before she could ask any more questions. There was no way she was going to reveal her identity or Joe's name. Not until she knew if her carefully worded note—which included the number for the disposable phone she'd just bought so Dalmage could call her— would net Dalmage's help. He could turn out to be a "by the books" diplomat and turn them in.

In the meantime, she was hedging her bets. She'd talked to Rafe again right after leaving Dalmage's office. He was working on transport to get them out of the country. A dicey proposition at best, but if Dalmage didn't come through . . . She couldn't think about that now.

Just like she couldn't think about the state of Joe's health—physical or mental—right now. It made her heartsick to hear him talk about Bryan's death as a murder.

Had the heavy weight of misplaced guilt finally broken him? All of his talk of murder, his leaving her, leaving the BOIs . . . were they all variations on the same theme? Was Joe searching for a way to deal with his demons?

She didn't know. But now she had some questions, too. Why *had* the priest been killed? Why had Joe been framed and thrown in jail? Could there actually be some truth to his conspiracy theory?

"Miss. We must hurry."

She hadn't even noticed that Bekah had walked up beside her.

"This is not a good time to be in this part of the city."

She'd been so lost in her thoughts, she hadn't been paying attention. She looked around and felt a shiver of unease. The hollow-eyed stares from a dozen different places reminded her that people died here every day for less than the cost of a loaf of bread, and that the sacks she was carrying were full of food.

She put her head down again and started walking faster, wishing the BOIs were here to help her get Joe home. And wondering if she had what it took to do it on her own, if Dalmage or Rafe didn't come through.

10

When Joe woke up again, Suah was sitting cross-legged in the corner of the room cleaning his rifle.

It was late afternoon, pushing toward dusk, if the heat on the sultry breeze drifting through the window was any indication. Joe had no way of knowing if it was the same day. He hoped he hadn't lost another one. When you were a hunted man, nothing good came from staying in one place too long.

He had to get moving so he could get himself and Stephanie away from here. And he wasn't going to get his strength back lying on this fucking mattress.

Besides the fact that he was now surely the top dog on Freetown's Most Wanted list, the man who had framed him for the priest's murder had no doubt launched a manhunt that would make the search that ferreted out Bin Laden look like a game of peek-a-boo.

Very carefully, he rolled a shoulder. It was sore but okay. Same for his neck. He painstakingly muscled his way to a sitting position, disgusted by the amount of effort it took and by the degree of pain that ripped through his ribs. Still, he felt a little stronger. His head was clearer, now that the night-night juice was out of his system. The IV antibiotics and fluids were doing their thing. And judging by the sudden growl of his stomach, his body was ready to take on a little protein.

"Where's Stephanie?" he asked Suah, who continued to clean his gun.

"She went for food," he said, buffing at a spot on the rifle barrel with an oiled rag.

Alarm bells went off like fireworks. "Alone?"

"Bekah is with her."

Joe recalled the tall, lean boy, his face marked with chicken pox scars, his belly gaunt with hunger. He was one of the boy soldiers they had set free last year along with Suah; a tough, war-worn kid accustomed to making it on his own.

His gut tightened with a new urgency. "Is that wise? To send her with him?" Christ, Bekah might decide to sell her to local slave traders rather than protect her. A Western woman built like Stephanie would bring a king's ransom in this depraved corner of the world.

Suah set the barrel aside and started cleaning the stock. "Bekah does what I say. He will keep her safe and he will bring her back. Plus, I sent Edward along to make sure."

It had become real clear, real fast, that Suah was the leader of his motley crew. And since they survived by relying on each other, respect for authority was a necessity.

He will bring her back.

A year ago, Joe wouldn't have trusted Suah as far as he could have tossed the transport truck taking him to Pademba Road prison. But that had all changed since he'd met up with the kid last month. Go figure, but he and Suah had inexplicably bonded—in a noncommittal and semi-hostile way. At the very least, they had an understanding. Suah pretended not to like Joe, and Joe respected the boundaries the kid set.

He understood. There was pride involved, and there was fear. Suah didn't dare let himself care about anyone. Experience had taught the kid that everything and everyone eventually left, no one could be trusted, and nothing in life came without a price. Joe suspected that the reason Suah never went without a shirt, like his buddies, was to hide the scars on his back. The kid didn't know that the thin white T-shirt couldn't conceal the ridges and raised welts left by some bastard's whip.

Yet as hard-core and hard-edged as he was, Joe also understood there was a part of Suah that wanted to open himself up to trust that Joe might be the exception to the rules he'd been taught by life and the RUF.

"You got a Plan B in case we need to haul ass out of here on short notice?" he asked.

"A better plan than you had when you let the police capture you."

He grinned at the kid's not-so-subtle dig, not just because Suah had a set of balls on him, but because he was right. Joe had been so focused on finally getting a solid lead that he'd walked right into a trap.

"So . . . you saved my bacon. Again. Why?" he prodded, even though he already knew the answer. It was important for Suah to clarify that it was honor and nothing more that had prompted his help.

"I repay my debts. If not for you, I would have been arrested in the cathedral. Now we are even. Again." In Suah's world, it was all about settling scores. Joe had just provided the opportunity for Suah to make that clear.

Joe was starting to wonder about the influence of fate. After he'd left Sierra Leone last year, he'd never expected to see Suah again. Hell, he hadn't even known the kid's name. So when he'd arrived in Freetown, asking questions and looking for leads to prove his theory, he'd been totally surprised, when, the night after he'd arrived, Suah had materialized out of a dark alley in Kissy.

"You're pushing your luck, kid," Joe said as they faced off. He fully expected the boy to challenge him in retaliation for their run-in last year over the arms deal, and he didn't need the aggravation. "I let you go once. This time I might not be so generous. You would be smart to get out of my face."

"You are looking for information," the boy said, standing up to Joe's threat. "I can help."

It didn't surprise Joe how fast word had gotten out on the street that there was an American asking questions. It did surprise him that this kid was offering to help.

"What's your name?" he asked as he weighed the odds that a whole gang of these little bastards might crawl out of the decay and jump him.

"Suah Korama."

"And why would you want to help me?"

"I do not want to help you. But I am a man of honor. I am in your debt. I must make the slate clean."

Joe considered this unexpected turn of events. Considered the boy who had grown a couple inches but still had a lean wiry frame, a baby face, and the skills to operate an assault rifle, RPGs, frag grenades, and any other tools of war tossed his way. The kid could probably set up an X-shaped ambush like a pro and kill anything that moved through it without qualms.

"How old are you?"

He pulled his shoulders back, stood taller. "Fifteen."

Fifteen, Joe thought reflectively now as he watched Suah work quietly on the rifle. He thought of his own childhood, of how he'd been raised with love and care on a farm in the deep south. He looked at this thin, rangy kid and wondered what his little brother, Bobby, would have looked like at fifteen. What kind of a man would he be now?

He pulled sharply away from those thoughts. No good ever came from walking that road. Or from remembering that at fifteen, he and ten-year-old Bobby had spent their summers lazing on a river bank fishing, and the only gun he'd owned was a shotgun for bird hunting, handed down from his granddad.

This kid tore down an AK-47 with the practiced precision of a pro. It was just plain wrong.

Suah had stood before him in that alley, knowing Joe could easily decide to finish the job he'd started last year—and that made him a man in Joe's book. He'd respected the guts it had taken for Suah to approach him. And he'd understood that it was a matter of pride for the kid.

In the end, he'd agreed to let Suah help. Suah had located the priest's parish the next day and arranged the meeting. And now they were back to square one in the debt repayment department, after Suah had helped Stephanie orchestrate Joe's escape.

Purely a business transaction—except for one little thing. The kid had grown on him. And though Suah would never admit it, the boy wasn't as detached as he wanted Joe to think he was.

"Must piss you off that you had to help me out again," he said, and couldn't help but grin when the boy snorted. "Or am I growing on you?"

"You are growing like a wart on my nose. I live only to be rid of you."

It felt good to smile. It had been a damn long time since he'd had anything to smile about.

He was thinking about trying to get another rise out of the boy when the door opened and Stephanie walked in, her arms full of groceries.

"You look a little better," Stephanie said after giving him a thorough once-over.

"I'm fine," he said around the huge lump in his throat.

He'd torn her heart to ribbons and she'd still come for him. What kind of a woman did that?

"*Fine* might be going a little too far," she said. She set

the groceries on the small wooden table in the corner of the room, then turned to Suah.

She nodded toward the door, an unspoken request for privacy. Carrying his gun, Suah got up and headed for the door.

"Wait." She dug into the sacks and pulled out a few items to keep, then extended the bags to Suah. "For you and the boys."

Suah shook his head. "We can take care of ourselves."

She gave him a look and shoved the bags into his chest. "I owe you. Don't deny me the chance to repay you. You, of all people, should understand."

Joe admired her intelligence and her compassion. She knew exactly how to play Suah. She was going to feed those boys no matter what, and the look on her face said she wasn't taking no for an answer.

His pride assuaged, Suah conceded with a nod and left the room with his arms full.

Stephanie stared at the door after it closed, then finally turned back to the table.

Her body language told him how anxious she was. Her shoulders were rigid. Her movements were jerky and precise as she filled a plate with rice and cassava and a slice of cassava bread, the two staples of the diet in Sierra Leone.

"Take it slow." She handed the plate to him along with a bottle of water. "If it stays down, we'll try some chicken."

She leaned back against the wall, crossed her arms beneath her breasts, and watched him eat, her face relaying her tension.

Because he was starving, and because she was apparently still working up to telling him what was on her mind, he quietly dug in.

It didn't take long to fill him up. His stomach had apparently shrunk to the size of a tennis ball.

And the knot in his chest had clamped into a fist. "I was a bastard earlier."

She looked surprised. "You were upset," she said, brushing it off.

"Doesn't make it right. I'm sorry."

"Apology accepted."

Her generous dismissal made him feel even more like an ass. But that was his cross to bear. Right now there were bigger fish to fry.

He handed her the half-empty plate. "We can't stay here much longer. They'll be canvassing door to door. Someone will have seen us. Someone will talk."

She set the plate aside. "The boys are on lookout. Their communication network is amazingly efficient. The first sign that the search is headed this way, we move. If we're not already gone."

It still stuck in his craw that he had to depend on her to get his ass out of a jam. *He* was supposed to be the one doing the saving.

"Can you handle that?" He glanced at her waist where he knew the piece was tucked into her pants, out of sight beneath her top.

"If I have to," she said.

That was the whole problem. She shouldn't have to.

Focus, he admonished himself. "Am I remember-ing right? The BOIs are running black? They're out of touch?"

She nodded.

"All of them?"

"Rafe and B.J. are holding down the fort, but they're both out of commission. She's due any day and Rafe had a bad malaria flare-up. He's out of the hospital but Nate has him on the D.L."

"We need to make contact with him. See what he can do about getting us some transpo out of here." Once he got her safely back to the States, he'd come back and finish what he'd started.

"He's working on it. I talked to him an hour ago."

"Tell me you didn't use a cell phone." Cell phones were always transmitting, looking to find the closest tower, so they could be located by triangulation of the towers.

She shook her head. "I didn't have time to procure an untraceable unit from NSA before I left."

By "procure," she meant "steal." Since it was easier to shove a watermelon through a keyhole than sneak something out of the NSA offices, he was glad she hadn't tried. She'd already risked too much.

"I'm using a calling card. Different pay phone each time."

He clenched his jaw. "Every time you go out, you're a target."

"Suah knows the city. Bekah and the boys do, too. They're not going to put me in jeopardy."

"Jesus, Steph—you're in jeopardy just being here!"

She was quiet for a long time. "Let's not go there now, okay?"

She was right. It was a waste of energy. And he still had fucking little to spare.

"I bought a razor," she said. "I was thinking you might be up for a shave."

If she had intended to distract him, she'd aced it. "A shave would be good. A shave would be *great*," he said. "The head, too."

Unless he was deep in an op, he never went a day without shaving and always wore his hair in a military buzz or totally shaved.

She walked to a small cabinet hung on the wall, removed a bowl and a small bar of soap. "This and room temp water will have to do."

"I'll make it work."

She rushed to his side when he tried to get up. "Let me help."

Like he had a choice. It took both of them to get him on his feet and get the IV line situated so he didn't pull it out. He held the thin sheet around his hips with one hand and slung his other arm over her shoulders. He managed two small steps when a wave of weakness slammed him.

"Give me a sec," he said, determined to support his own weight. When he finally felt steady, he walked the two steps more to the table and sank onto the wooden chair beside it.

Sweating like he'd run five miles carrying full gear,

he watched her walk to the far wall, then return with a pair of cammo cargo pants.

"Hope they fit. Suah rounded them up, along with a shirt and a pair of sandals."

His head had finally quit spinning. It felt good to be upright. "That boy is something else."

"He is," she agreed, sounding distracted.

When he looked up, he understood why. She was standing directly in front of him, her gaze on his bare chest. And he realized she was uneasy being so close to him.

The room was small, 10 x 10 feet max. And now that he was upright, the dynamic had changed. So had her comfort level. It was different when he'd been lying on the floor on the pallet. When he was down, she was up and he was dependent on her.

He was still dependent, more than she'd ever know. But even in his weakened state, he understood that his sheer size was intimidating.

Christ, she was so close he could smell her—a scent uniquely hers that, even in this heat, clung to her in sensual layers of floral and musk and citrus.

"Do you need help?" she asked tentatively.

The pants. And, yeah. He needed help. He couldn't bend over without a knife stabbing through his ribs.

Hating it, he nodded and handed them to her.

She knelt on the floor in front of him. He clutched the sheet around his hips and lifted his left foot so she could pull the pants up his leg.

And he did his damnedest not to think about the close proximity of her face to his lap.

The silence stretched and he lifted his other leg as she bent in so close, he could feel the warmth of her breath on his thigh. So close he could imagine her moving between his legs, taking him in her hands, in her mouth.

"I can take it from here," he said abruptly when he felt himself stiffen and swell beneath the sheet.

He grabbed the pants from her so quickly that she tipped backward, reflexively clutching his calf for balance—and inadvertently grabbing a handful of sheet and ripping it off his lap.

Fuck.

There was no hiding his reaction.

"Sorry," they both said, trampling all over each other's apologies and fighting to ignore the very obvious elephant's trunk in the room.

"It's okay." He felt like a jerk. They'd once been as intimate as a man and woman could be, but in the aftermath of his "I don't love you enough" pronouncement, his reaction was totally out of line.

"It's okay," she echoed, looking embarrassed.

She stood quickly and turned her back on him, more for her sake, he suspected, than for his modesty.

He pushed to his feet, pulled up the pants, and let the sheet fall to the floor. As soon as he'd tucked and zipped himself away, he sank back down on the chair, feeling ridiculous for dodging what had just happened.

"I really am sorry, Steph. I hadn't meant for that to happen."

"It's okay," she said again, a tentative smile tipping up one corner of her mouth. "Guess it's a good sign. You're getting your strength back, right?"

"Yeah," he said, his own smile involuntary and tight. "I guess it's a good sign." And they hadn't even started on that shave.

11

He could do this. Joe held the straight-edge razor up to his throat and glared into the small mottled and wavy mirror Stephanie held in front of him. He'd already chopped off most of the length with scissors, a task that had sapped the bulk of his strength.

So, yeah, he could do this—if his hand wasn't shaking, and he didn't mind nicking his carotid artery and bleeding to death in the process.

"Shit," he muttered and tossed the razor into the water bowl. "I guess this isn't happening today."

He grabbed a small hand towel that looked like it had been through a thousand wash cycles. Her hand on his wrist stopped him before he could wipe the soap off his face and neck.

"I can do it for you."

He grunted. "After the incident with the pants, you sure that's a good idea?"

"I can do it," she said again, more firmly this time. "Not a big deal. Let's just get it done."

She set the mirror on the table and fished the razor out of the bowl. Then she moved in close, touched a hand to the side of his face, and tilted his head back. "Hold still."

The edge of the blade scraped slowly up the left side of his throat to his jawline. Water sloshed when she rinsed off the stubble, then she repeated the motion with another slow draw of the razor over another section.

Sounds from the street faded to muffled background noise as the repetitive rasp of steel against stubble, and the sound of their breathing enhanced the unavoidable sense of intimacy. The tension resurrected a sensual memory of another time there'd been shaving involved.

She'd been naked in her tub, water lapping around her shoulders, bubbles playing peek-a-boo with her buoyant breasts. He'd been on his knees beside the tub, fully clothed, enjoying the hell out of the experience. He'd held her razor in one hand and her left calf in his other; soapy water trickled down her leg as he raised it and ran the blade in a slow, sensual glide along her silken, fragrant skin.

Soft sighs. Sexy smiles. The gentle splash of water against flesh.

He hadn't stayed dressed or dry for long.

Do not go there now. Not when she was this close. Not when her breasts were directly in front of his mouth, and the warmth radiating from her body rivaled the heat of the West African day.

"You doing okay?" she asked as she tended to his upper lip.

He grunted something that he hoped passed for a yes and closed his eyes. For all the good it did. He could still see her in his mind. Still knew that if he moved even a fraction of an inch, his mouth would be pressed against that warm woman flesh. His face would be nestled in the softest, most amazing place in the world.

Lust coiled in his groin, his abs clenched.

"Did I hurt you?"

Jesus. He must have groaned. He opened his eyes. Met hers. And saw that she'd figured out that he was having as much trouble with this as he'd had with the pants debacle.

He saw something else before she averted her gaze. She wasn't as immune as she'd like him to think. She was as affected as he was by the sexual undercurrents simmering between them. And she didn't like her reaction.

He could kiss her now. Even though she'd resist, he could grip her waist in his hands, guide her onto his lap, and kiss her. She wouldn't want to give in, but she would let him kiss her slow and deep, and mother of God, he wanted to.

But no matter how badly he wanted to, he would *not* take advantage. She was vulnerable now. She was conflicted and confused and in way over her head. He had no idea how she felt about him at this point, but as far as she was concerned, he didn't love her. He needed her to keep believing that, because until he nailed the bastard who'd killed Bryan and messed with him, this was far from over.

"Let's call it good," he said, fracturing the intimacy with his abrupt announcement. "Thanks. Appreciate it."

"What about your hair? We might as well take care of it while we have the chance."

He let out a heavy breath. "Fine. Just shave it all off."

So she did. He sat there, his hands clenched into fists on his thighs, his eyes closed, his mind occupied with multiplication tables, mental images of a street map of the city, a front and back run-through of how to assemble and disassemble the AK . . . anything to keep himself from thinking about her. About wanting her. About keeping himself from asking if he'd fucked things up between them forever.

"That should do it."

He snapped out of his self-induced trance, opened his eyes, and realized she'd finished. She handed him a towel, which he promptly dropped, then couldn't reach down and pick up because of his ribs and the IV line still attached to his arm.

"Damn, I'm tired of being an invalid," he muttered when she picked up the towel for him.

"The doctor said you'd need several days to start feeling human again."

He dragged the towel over his head. "Did he say the bad guys were going to wait for that to happen?" he snapped, and immediately regretted it.

"Damn. I'm sorry. I didn't mean that as a criticism. How you managed that escape, and this . . ." He lifted a hand to encompass the room. "I don't know how you did it. And I don't like you being here in the thick of this."

She lifted her chin. "Like I said, you don't always get to be the hero. And I know it's driving you insane that you weren't cast in the role this time."

"Yeah," he said apologetically. "It's driving me nuts. And making me stupid. I'm sorry. Again."

Things were going to change, starting now.

Conquer your mind and the body will follow. His axiom since day one of his service.

As Luke Colter always said of his SEAL experience, "The only easy day was yesterday."

When he looked up, she'd crossed her arms beneath her breasts and leaned back against the wall. "Maybe it's time for you to tell me everything."

He breathed a sigh of relief; the grim look on her face told him that she was ready to listen to him now. Her brown eyes were hyper-alert. Her nerves were clearly frayed. There was no way on God's earth to whitewash this, but he was determined to see it through.

"It's complex," he said.

She made a sound of derision and handed him a bottle of water. "Isn't it always? Just . . . just start from the beginning. The night Bryan died."

He tipped up the water bottle, winced when he bumped his split lip, then bit the bullet. "You know that it never rang true with me that the RUF just happened to be in the same area as our patrol. That it was dumb luck that they ran across us. Not when our intel—all filtered down from Command Central—hadn't placed any enemy combatants within ten miles of our position.

"After the official after-action report came down and they explained it as a monumental intel screwup, I still couldn't buy it."

"Even though the prevailing opinion was that it was the only plausible explanation?"

"Even though," he echoed flatly. "I get that everyone needed an outlet for the blame. It wasn't easy to accept that our own leadership fucked up, but at least it gave us an answer. Answers are important. Answers give closure. They help us move on."

"But you never did."

He focused on the plastic tubing still stuck in his arm that was attached to the IV drip. "It was just too pat. And it reeked of fabrication."

So he'd become obsessed. He was so screwed up over losing Bry that he'd done some fabricating of his own, looking for bad guys where none existed. That's what everyone had thought.

Sometimes he'd wondered himself why he just couldn't let it go. But day after day, year after year, it had consumed him. And, yeah, Bryan's death had gotten all muddied up with his confusion over his little brother's death. He should have been able to do something to save Bobby—just like he should have been able to save Bry.

"I tried to let it go, Steph. I swear to you," he said, meeting her eyes. "I'd finally stopped looking. I *had* moved on."

Because he'd met her. Because he'd fallen in love with her. Because he'd known that he needed to let the past go so he could have a future, and be with her the way she deserved.

"But then . . . last year something happened," she prompted. "When you came back here to Sierra Leone."

"It had to do with the mission, yes." He leaned back heavily in the chair, cursing his draining strength. "But it started before we even flew here. It started in D.C. with Marcus Chamberlin."

Her brows pinched together. "Chamberlin?"

She wasn't asking who he was, everyone knew the sensational story of senator Marcus Chamberlin's fall from grace. The senator had died last year in Sierra Leone during the same BOI operation that had taken out Sesay's camp.

"I was in D.C. watch-dogging Chamberlin for the team, while they were at HQ in Buenos Aires trying to put the puzzle pieces together."

He'd been tasked with extracting the truth from Chamberlin, who had been deeply embroiled in Ryang's illegal international gun-running operation. Ryang had been blackmailing Chamberlin into facilitating the arms shipments, using Chamberlin's ex-wife as a pawn and humanitarian aids shipments to Sierra Leone as a cover.

"We didn't even know that Sierra Leone was the end-game at that point. I was in Chamberlin's office, putting a little heat on him to give me something to help us tie things together, when I spotted this framed photograph on his wall. He told me it was a group shot of the volunteer team on the ground in Sierra Leone where the aid shipments were sent."

"The shipments that were a front?"

"Yes. I recognized one of the men in the photo. And every siren that I'd silenced in my head regarding Bry's death went off like an air raid drill. Right then I *knew* that I was looking at the man who had as good as fired the shot that killed Bryan."

She looked skeptical and confused. "You knew this because you saw a man in a group photo?"

"Not just any man. A colonel who had been on the ground in Sierra Leone when Task Force Mercy was running ops there. The same colonel who had sent us on our last mission."

That had her looking at him differently. Bry had died on TFM's last mission.

"When I saw him in that picture it was like a bomb went off, a bomb full of images and memories. Like how he'd sometimes show up in the field. And how he always seemed to feel like he was 'slumming' it with the grunts. I always got bad vibes from him. There was something about him . . . I don't know. I couldn't pinpoint it. But it didn't matter. In the military you followed orders, did as you were told, no matter who called the shots." He paused, the memories vivid even now.

"Joe?"

He hadn't realized that he'd fallen silent until her soft voice prompted him to pick up the conversation again.

"Something about an encounter I'd had with him hung around the edge of my mind but wouldn't gel. As I stared at the photograph, it finally came to me.

"One night, I was passing by the operations tent and overheard a heated discussion between the colonel and the general in charge of the entire offensive on the ground. At that point, we'd pulled mission after mission. All combat. All close quarters. Everyone on the team was running on empty. But this guy had insisted that we needed to infiltrate that particular area that night, arguing that even though it was dangerous, men died in battle all the time and the big picture needed to be considered."

He took a long pull of water.

"I kept staring at that picture on Chamberlin's wall and I kept hearing his words all those years ago, and . . . I knew something was off. I knew he had a hand in the gun shipments. And if he had his finger in one pie, most likely he had it in another. He had a hand in setting up the ambush. I just didn't know why he wanted us dead, or how to prove it."

She'd grown very quiet.

"So I did some digging into his service record. And I found out something interesting. Turns out he was the one who lobbied to get Task Force Mercy disbanded. That bit of info clinched it for me."

Now she looked confused. "I don't understand. What does disbanding TFM and Bryan's death have to do with each other?"

"Everything." He lifted a hand, imploring her to understand. "Like I told you earlier, he wanted us gone, Steph. One way or the other, he wanted TFM out of Sierra Leone. He didn't care who died to make it happen. He didn't kill us all, but he accomplished his mission anyway: We got pulled the next day. The team was disbanded shortly after that. All the work we'd done here just ended. The RUF took back all the ground we'd gained."

She processed that, sighed heavily, then opened up a bottle of water for herself. After a deep drink, she carefully measured her words. "You're working on an awful lot of speculation here. And a lot of gut feelings."

"I learned to trust my gut a long time ago. But you're right. At that point it was all speculation. I needed proof, so I decided to find it. And the only way to do that was to come back to Sierra Leone and start digging."

For the first time since they'd started talking, fire flared in her eyes. "You couldn't have told me that was your plan? You couldn't have leveled with me about what you planned to do? Or told the guys?"

"And have you tell me I was crazy? That I needed to let it go?"

Her silence was answer enough. That's exactly what she would have done.

"Steph, this guy is a big player in Washington now.

And he's ruthless. I had to play it close to the vest until I figured out what was so important to him here that he ordered that attack on our unit. If he got wind that I was after him, I was as good as dead before I'd have a chance to expose him.

"Case in point," he said, lifting a hand in a gesture that encompassed his body and his sad physical condition. "I was going to die in the prison. He was going to make certain of it. That's why I needed hard proof. Without it, my credibility is *nada*. It's my word against his, right? He's connected. He could easily convince the powers that be that the word of a former CIA operative is suspect. Hell, everyone knows that those guys are psychos, right? I'd be just another agent gone rogue."

He stopped to gauge her reaction. She remained silent, still listening. He decided to lay the rest of it out for her.

"And the fact is, going rogue wouldn't be far from the truth. If I couldn't pin anything on him, not only would I be cast as a loose cannon driven to delusions by the 'dark side' of my profession, but by association with me, BOI would take a hit. Their contracts would dry up. Nate would be out of business."

The furrow between her brows deepened.

"I know this is a lot to swallow, Steph. But I know how that game is played. Which is why I knew that if I went after him, I had to distance myself from everyone who meant anything to me. I didn't want anyone to get caught in the fallout."

"And what if you'd died in that prison? What did

any of this do but get you killed? No one would ever know why."

"Nate would know," he said soberly. "If I show up dead, my attorney has instructions to deliver a letter that spells every thing out."

Angry tears filled her eyes. "But it didn't have to come to this. We could have helped."

He shook his head. "No. You couldn't have. He's too smart. Here's the bottom line: Whether I can prove it or not, he's going to pay. And I will not take anyone—especially you—down with me."

She was quiet for a long moment. "So. The disappearing act. It was all about protection."

Aw, hell. He knew where she was going now before she even asked. He knew how much it cost her.

"And that night . . . did you lie about *everything* that night? About not loving me?" Her eyes were glassy with tears she was determined not to shed.

It was going to kill him to lie again, but until this was over—

A phone rang, breaking the thick tension.

"What the hell?" He glared at her. "I thought you said you weren't using your cell phone."

"I'm not. This isn't my phone. It's a burn phone." She reached into her pocket.

"Wait." He grabbed her wrist, stopping her from answering. "Who has this number?"

"Only one person," she said, looking as though a huge weight had been lifted from her shoulders. "The man who's going to get us out of here."

She quickly answered the call. "Mr. Dalmage," she said on a rush. "Oh, thank God. Thank you so much for calling."

"Jesus!" Joe sprang to his feet, grabbed the cell phone from her hand, and disconnected.

Stephanie's eyes widened, and even through his panic he felt her fear. "What are you doing? I've been trying to reach him since I got here!"

"Dalmage?"

"Yes. Greer Dalmage. He's the U.S. liaison to the UWAN."

"I know who he is."

"Well, he's here. In Freetown," she said, her voice rising with her confusion. "He can help get us out of here. Please, give me back the phone."

"Dalmage is *here*? Fuck. Dalmage doesn't want to help us—he wants to kill us."

He threw the phone on the floor, picked up the chair, and with a strength borne of a full-on adrenaline rush, slammed the chair leg repeatedly on the phone until it was broken in pieces and hopefully any tracking capability destroyed.

Breathing hard from the exertion, he looked up. Horror filled her eyes. "Do you not get it? *Dalmage* is responsible for Bryan's death."

He jerked the IV out of his arm as she stared, shell-shocked, at his face and the blood dripping onto the floor. She thought he'd lost his mind.

"Grab what you can't live without. We're leaving." He shouldered painfully past her and jerked open the door. "Suah!" he yelled, knowing that he would be standing guard in the hallway. "We've got a problem."

The boy rushed into the room, his eyes wide with questions.

"Time for Plan B." Joe reached for the T-shirt hanging on the wall hook. He wrenched it over his head, the adrenaline blocking some of the pain as he toed on the sandals. "Grab all the extra ammo you can carry."

Suah scrambled while Joe limped back to the mattress and retrieved the Glock and KA-Bar along with several ammo clips that he dropped into his pockets. Then he shouldered the rifle, grabbed Stephanie's arm, and headed back to the door.

She stood frozen, her eyes round with fear and confusion.

"Look," he said, rounding on her so fast the room tilted. "We don't have time for you to process this or decide if I'm psycho. We're leaving. Now. Before Dalmage can pin down our location from that cell call."

12

Sweat ran down between her shoulder blades, and stung her eyes. Her hair clung to her neck in heavy, wet curls. The insufferable heat, the exhaustion, the fear all combined to make her light-headed. But what weighed on her the most was the look she saw in Joe's eyes as she flattened herself beside him against a decaying two-story building.

He couldn't take much more of this running. He wasn't strong enough yet. The heat beat down like a battering ram; even in the shade it felt like they were standing at the mouth of a furnace.

"What's taking Suah so long?" she muttered. Joe might be upright, but he was barely conscious.

Suah had left them here several minutes ago while he and the boys went ahead, scouting the streets, making certain they didn't run into any city police patrols. Or, as they'd discovered the hard way several blocks ago when they'd almost burst recklessly around a corner, any military units. Apparently, the manhunt for the escaped American prisoner had expanded to a provincial if not national scale.

So here they waited, guns drawn, hearts pounding. She'd lost track of the number of back alleys, side streets, and buildings they'd snaked through. Lost count of the number of times Joe had stumbled, almost gone down, then miraculously dragged another fragment of strength from deep inside him to press on.

Dalmage. A murderer. A traitor. How could she possibly believe that? Yet, when she saw the raw conviction on Joe's face, how could she not?

She dragged the hem of her shirt over her face and wiped the perspiration away, then let her head fall back against the building, and caught her breath. She knew only one thing with certainty. If they didn't get Joe out of this heat and off his feet soon, he was going to need a hospital.

The gauze bandage she'd wrapped around the IV site on his arm was soaked with as much sweat as blood. She couldn't allow herself to worry about blood loss or infection or a hundred other things that could sideline him, so she concentrated on the positive. All things considered, his color was good. And up to a few moments ago, when he'd just sort of fused his back against the building, he'd been lucid.

She glanced sideways at him. His eyes were closed, his head lolled to the side.

"Are you still with me?" she whispered.

He grunted. "Unless I'm having an out-of-body experience, yeah, I'm here."

If his voice weren't so weak, she would have felt better. And if the situation weren't so dire, she would have pressed him to convince her they hadn't just shot their best chance of going home all to hell. But that bridge had been blown, so there was really no point.

Suah came scooting around the corner just then.

"Come." He motioned for them to follow him.

When Joe was slow to push himself away from the wall, she lifted his arm over her shoulder and banded her free arm around his waist. Then she shouldered his AK and started walking.

"There you go again," he said on a labored breath, "playing hero."

She grunted under his weight as they trudged after Suah. "That really doesn't set well with you, does it?"

He pushed out a sound that could have been a groan or a chuckle. "You have no idea."

"Don't worry," she said, relieved when Suah doubled back and moved in on Joe's other side, helping with some of his weight. "I have no intention of making this part of my daily routine. Now save your breath. No more talking."

Five minutes, one block, and one arduous climb up two flights of stairs later, they were once again tucked into an apartment—not nearly as tiny, but just as spartan and worn as the other one. And Joe was passed out cold.

Stephanie sat forward on a shabby rattan chair across from the small bed, her fingers linked together between her knees, her elbows propped on her thighs, and watched him sleep.

Just before he'd passed out, he'd grabbed her hand. "No drugs. No Dalmage. Promise me."

When she'd hesitated, he'd squeezed her fingers until they hurt. "Promise me. On Bryan's grave . . . *promise* me."

She'd finally nodded. "I promise. On Bryan's grave."

She'd trusted this man with her life once. Why was she having such difficulty now?

Because if she believed that Dalmage was a murderer, then she accepted Joe's wild story that Bry's death was the result of some sort of a conspiracy. And the idea that her brother had died because of a traitor's duplicity was just too difficult to stomach.

She was also having trust issues because she had believed in Joe completely at one time. Despite all of his secrets, and the fact that he withheld the parts of himself he'd decided she wasn't strong enough to handle, she had believed. He'd walked away from her anyway, and it was clear he hadn't planned on coming back.

She'd gotten her proof back at the other safe house. Just before the phone rang, she'd screwed up her courage and asked him point blank: *"Did you lie about everything that night? About not loving me?"*

She'd seen in his eyes that he had been about to say no, he hadn't lied. No, he didn't love her.

Exhausted, she slumped wearily back in the chair. And thought, with a slow and dawning realization: *Oh, he'd lied all right.*

That man loved her. He had *always* loved her.

She was certain of that.

Okay, why? Why was she so certain now?

The second revelation hit her. She was certain because she could always tell when Joe lied. Whether it was a flat-out lie, like, "I don't love you," or a lie of omission, like not letting her into those dark places in his soul that he thought would hurt her—she *knew* when he lied.

Because he was a terrible liar. It just wasn't in his DNA to be deceitful.

And that's when the third revelation hit. And oh, God, she'd been so stupid!

She shot up off the chair, fueled by a burst of restless energy. He was telling her the truth about Dalmage. It wasn't just true in his head, it was true in actuality. He hadn't gone over the edge. That had been her little bit of conjecture because she was so hurt and was having trouble dealing with his rejection—which really wasn't a rejection but his attempt to keep her out of the mix and out of danger.

Okay, fine. That wasn't news. She'd already figured that out. But she hadn't dug deep enough. Not nearly deep enough to realize that a man who loved a woman that much, only saddled that woman with as much as he thought she could handle. And Joe didn't think she could handle the heat.

Why would he? What had she ever done to make him believe she was strong enough to carry the weight of the issues he dealt with every day of his life?

She walked over to a window, shaking her head at her stupidity. And her cowardice.

You get what you give. You reap what you sow.

Well, all she'd ever given him was silent understanding. She'd never challenged, never bullied or badgered him to open up to her. Sure, she'd asked him to talk to her, but when he didn't, she'd accepted it. Never pushed. Never pried. Never prodded him to confide in her or to give her credit for being more than a woman who needed a man to take care of her.

Self-anger and humiliation added to the flush on her cheeks from the heat. Of *course* he'd lied to her. She'd invited lies every day with her misguided strategy of letting him pick his time, pick his place, to decide to trust her to handle his baggage.

Well, that all ended. Right now.

She'd had more than one self-discovery since she'd lifted off at Dulles four days ago and touched down at Lungi. First and foremost, she'd found out that she could handle herself. She'd lied to the police, manipulated the system with a fake ID, walked into the bowels of that hellhole of a jail, and brokered a weapons deal with a notorious street gang.

Not only that, she'd helped stage and execute a prison break. She'd harbored a felon. Kept him alive. Was still keeping him alive.

Talk about defining moments. Talk about revelations. Now that she had a moment to sit back and assess, she was seeing herself in a whole new light literally and figuratively, as she caught a glimpse of her reflection in the wavy, dust-streaked windowpane.

Her hand flew to her throat and she leaned in, looked deeper. It was her, all right, but a high-octane version. Her clothes were rumpled and damp. Her hair was a wild tumble of damp waves around her shoulders. And her face . . . even that seemed to have altered. Her soft, unremarkable features had transformed somehow. She looked . . . edgy. Decisive. Experienced and lean.

Kick-ass, she thought with a ridiculous little smile, and embraced the idea.

She looked not like a woman who needed a man like Joe Green to complete her life, but like a woman who could damn well complete his.

Then and there, she decided that she wasn't going to let him shut her out anymore. No more demure, retiring spy wannabe sitting quietly in the corner and letting life do unto her. She'd finally earned that decoder ring, and she was going to wear it proudly.

She looked at the sleeping man who had turned her life upside down. She was not going to let him get by with shutting her out and playing the protector anymore, and she was *not* letting him walk away.

They were getting out of this mess—she was going to make it happen. And when they did, Joe Green was going to find out that Stephanie Tompkins was a force to be reckoned with.

He didn't love her?

What a crock!

Fired up with resolve, she hurried across the room and opened the door.

"Suah," she called out, slipping out into the hallway. "Watch out for him. I've got to go out."

Even the boy seemed to sense her newfound sense of purpose, because he didn't warn her to be careful. "When will you be back?"

"When I'm back." She headed down the stairs at a fast trot.

Joe woke to lamplight and soft voices. Stephanie's. Suah's. He glanced around and bit back a curse. He was so fucking weary of waking up in rooms that he didn't recognize. If he was going to pass out and not remember how he'd gotten here, it only seemed fair that it be because he'd had a good time.

"Where are we?" He forced himself to sit up.

The effort wasn't as difficult as he'd anticipated. He was a little light-headed, but he was stronger. He could feel it.

"Kissy," Suah said without looking up from the table where he and Stephanie sat with their heads together, talking in soft tones.

The Kissy ghetto on the east edge of the city had sprung to life around ten years ago as a refugee camp during the bloody RUF-run government. Now it was a dangerous, crime-ridden, gang-infested no man's land. After thinking it over, he realized it was also a perfect place to hide out. Any police squads venturing into this part of the city did so at their own peril.

He rose carefully, waited for the slight dizziness to pass, and shuffled over to the window. It was dark but for the lone streetlight that hadn't yet been shot out. The murky shadows did little to soften the bleak landscape of littered streets and ramshackle buildings scrawled with graffiti and scarred with broken windows.

"So you're thinking this is the best route?"

Stephanie's words had him turning toward the table. Suah nodded. "Less congestion."

He walked over to see what they were doing. On a map of the city, Stephanie was tracing street routes with a pencil.

"What's this?" he asked.

"A map," Suah said with no attempt to hide his sarcasm.

Joe pulled out a wooden chair and sank down heavily. "I know it's a map, smart-ass. What are you charting?"

Stephanie sat back and finally met his eyes. "How are you feeling?"

"Like I had a head-on with a semi. What are you charting?" he repeated.

"A potential escape route."

"Yeah, about that." He leaned an elbow on the tabletop, dropped his head heavily into his hand, and closed his eyes. "I need to get to a phone. Talk to Rafe. Get something set up."

"I've already talked to Rafe," Stephanie said, "and I've got it covered. We're getting out of here tomorrow."

That snapped his eyes open and his head up.

"Do you want something to eat?" she asked suddenly.

"There's a cooler full of food over there. Or do you need me to get it for you?"

"No. I can get it," he said defensively, although he couldn't pinpoint exactly why he felt defensive. Or why he felt a little off-balance at the tone of her voice. Or the look on her face.

He studied her as she got back to business over the map. He'd always thought of Stephanie as soft. Sexy soft. Welcome-home soft.

She didn't look soft tonight. Didn't sound soft, either. She sounded all business. And . . . distracted, he realized. Maybe a little bothered.

Because she had to deal with him?

"Okay, let's back up," he said, suddenly feeling a need to assert himself into what should be his arena. "You have a plan? To get out of here tomorrow?"

She slumped back in the wooden chair, hooked an arm over the finial, and looked up at him. "Since the guys are still out of commo, Rafe reached out to Mike Brown. He's coming for us in the BOI corporate jet."

Mike "Primetime" Brown was a former Navy pilot. He'd been the TFM team's go-to pilot when they'd needed to infiltrate or extract. Brown was an independent now, ran an air cargo business out of somewhere in Argentina. Most important, he was damn good.

"Brown's hauled our asses out of more than one dicey landing zone."

"Which was why Nate tagged him for the Sierra Leone mission last year, right?"

Joe nodded. "Brown choppered us out of the hot zone after we blew up Sesay's camp."

"Well, let's hope we won't be drawing fire when we reach the airport tomorrow."

He stared at her. "Let's back up the truck here. Exactly how are we getting to the airport? It's a five-hour drive, and the bastards will have roadblocks set up at every exit road. We'll never get past them."

"That's why we're going by ferry. It'll cut the time by more than half."

"Ferry? Have you *been* to the docks?" He knew he sounded condescending.

"Yes, I took a ferry from Lungi to Freetown."

"Then you know that the piers are flanked by several square blocks of nothing. Wide-open territory. No trees, no buildings, no alleyways to hide in."

"We're not going to hide. We won't have to. The docks will be teeming with people."

"And you don't see a problem with us standing out like two pieces of white rice in a sea of black beans?"

She smiled tightly. "I've got it covered, okay?"

The assertiveness in her voice rattled him to the point that he had a brief "Who is this woman?" moment.

"You need to concentrate on getting your strength back, Joe. Leave the details to me, okay?"

There was that impatience again. A clear "I'm in charge here, so back off" tone that he'd never heard from her before. It wasn't that she was a doormat. She spoke her mind; she had intelligent opinions. And it wasn't that he didn't consider her an equal. It was just that . . . hell. He'd never seen her this assertive before.

As much as it rattled him, he kind of liked it. Not that she'd give a rat's ass what he liked at this point, but yeah, he liked it.

"There's a very small—and I mean *very* small—bathroom through that door," she added. "When I checked earlier, there was running water in the shower. No hot water, but still, it's running water."

That was a rare thing in this city, one of the wettest capital cities in the world. Even in the midst of heavy downpours, water taps often ran dry. The city fathers apparently hadn't had the foresight to plan ahead for the needs of the growing population.

"And I bought shampoo. You can have first dibs; then I'll change the dressings on your head and arm. There are clean clothes in the smaller suitcase at the foot of the bed."

He glanced toward the bed and for the first time noticed two expensive-looking leather roller board suitcases. He turned back to ask her when she'd gone shopping, but she'd already dismissed him. Honest to God, turned her back to him, huddled back over the map with Suah, and dismissed him.

Sonofabitch.

He opened his mouth to say something, but didn't have a clue what he wanted to say—so he shut it again.

Thoughtful, he turned toward the bed and silently rummaged around in the suitcase until he found a pair of men's tan walking shorts. No underwear. Good enough. Commando had never been his thing, but in this infernal heat and humidity, it worked fine.

He headed for the shower, unable to shake an unsettling and oddly satisfying feeling that he was leaving the grown-ups behind to do the heavy thinking.

13

Saidu Bangura sat alone in his darkened office. A small, rattling oscillating fan sat on the corner of his desk, doing little more than move hot, muggy air from one side of the room to the other. It was nearly ten p.m. on a day that had been painfully long and was getting longer.

With weary forbearance he held the phone to his ear and listened to Dalmage rant, realizing that he hated every American with whom he had ever come in contact. They postured, they demanded, they scorned his country's culture with words like *uncivilized* and *barbaric* and *backward* to bolster their sense of superiority and to denigrate time-honored Sierra Leone traditions.

They talked of justice and human rights. Then they sent a man like Greer Dalmage, who professed to educate and enlighten and initiate equality, while in secret, he pursued his personal agenda of exploiting Sierra Leone for his personal gain.

Dalmage was the true barbarian. Saidu had never

been more aware of that fact as Dalmage shouted into the phone, his tirade escalating to the point where Saidu thought the man might have another of those attacks that turned his face red, made him sweat like a pig, and brought him to the brink of passing out. It would not sadden him if that were to happen. No, he would not weep if the American were to shout himself into a heart attack, fall to the ground, and die.

But Dalmage's death would result in the loss of regular revenue, which would make Saidu's wife very unhappy. So he was bound by golden chains to do Dalmage's bidding. He had fallen in league with the devil, and his penance was Dalmage's wrath and a very spoiled woman. He had once taken pride in his ability to lavish her with luxuries most women in her position would never see. Now he regretted it. She would never be willing to return to a spartan existence. She liked her baubles, her nice clothes, the girl who came in every morning to cook and clean for her and see to the children—who were also spoiled beyond measure. And yes, it was true, Saidu had grown accustomed to the expensive and beautiful young women who took care of his own special needs.

He was in a situation of his own making, he thought with a heavy sigh, and endured Dalmage's rage until the sudden silence told him he was now expected to speak.

"They will not escape the city," he said again, and recounted all the reasons why. "The entire police force is on high alert. We have initiated foot patrols, vehicle patrols, and door-to-door canvassing. The Army has dispatched three fully armed companies that have been patrolling the streets in heavily armed Range Rovers since we found the apartment where they had been staying vacant."

They'd missed the Americans by minutes. Saidu cursed his bad luck, which had naturally been a failure in Dalmage's very vocal opinion. True, Dalmage had provided them with a pinpoint location based on a brief cell phone communication, but Saidu had had no officers within ten blocks of the address at the time. Truly—how was he to have caught them?

"They've gone to ground," he said, explaining why the American prisoner and the unidentified woman who had orchestrated his escape had not been captured. "Which means they are stationary for the time being. If we don't track them down before they move again, we will find them as soon as they appear in public."

Dalmage's rebuttal was short, clipped, and succinct. "Find them. Or find your family dead by morning." The line went dead.

Saidu's fingers clenched so tightly on the phone that they ached. When his head cleared and his heart rate settled, he did what he should have done this morning when this nightmare started.

"My love," he said when his wife answered the phone. "It appears I will be working all night. Please kiss the boys good night. Also give my regards to your auntie when she arrives in the morning."

The silence on the other end told him that she understood. A man did not straddle certain lines for as long as Saidu had without the expectation that his duplicity might catch up with him someday. And he took no chance that his conversation might be electronically monitored. Long ago, in preparation for the possibility of danger, they had agreed upon the prearranged message. "Give my regards to auntie" was code for *"Take the boys and leave the city immediately."*

"I will tell her you said hello," she said in a subdued and shaken voice before disconnecting.

Saidu breathed deep, his sense of relief undercut by the uncertainty of his future. He ran a sweating hand over his jaw, wondering if he would ever see his wife and sons again.

Joe felt almost human again after his shower. Despite their little race through the city, he felt stronger. It was about damn time. Just as it was time to tell Stephanie the rest of the story on Dalmage. Blind faith could only sustain her for so long.

Wearing only the shorts she'd bought him, he joined her at the table. "Where's your partner in crime?"

She looked up. She seemed surprised that he was there—and shirtless. She quickly redirected her gaze to his face.

"Suah slipped out to do some scouting. He'll be back in a few minutes. You look better, by the way."

"I'm fine. How about you? How you holding up?"

"You don't have to worry about me."

"This hasn't exactly been a stroll in the park."

"Strolling is overrated," she said. The vibes she was giving off said, "Let it go."

So he did, and got straight to his point. "You haven't asked me about Dalmage."

She fiddled with a corner of the map spread out on the table. "There hasn't exactly been an opportunity. But we don't have to go there now. You need to rest."

"So you believe me. Just like that."

"Obviously, not 'just like that.'" She leaned back in the chair and crossed her arms. "But yes, I believe you now."

"So what changed?"

She almost smiled. "There's not enough time left in this day to cover that territory."

He couldn't get a read on her mood. Maybe she was just weary. Maybe she was simply tired of fighting him on this issue. Frankly, he was tired of fighting it, too. "I want to finish this."

She clearly didn't like it, but said, "Fine. But please tell me you've got more than that picture and your gut instinct going for you."

"I've got plenty more. But the picture finally broke it wide open. My first night in Freetown, I started flashing around the photograph I'd taken from Chamberlin's office. I got a hit right away. A man who had once been forced to serve as a member of the RUF militia recognized Dalmage."

She shifted her shoulders, settled in. "From where?"

"From seeing him up close and personal in an RUF camp during the same period TFM was running ops there."

The look on her face told him he had her full attention.

"This guy was a personal attendant to the RUF general in charge, so he's as credible as it gets. According to him, Dalmage was a frequent visitor. Big buds with the general. He heard conversations that always involved an exchange of money."

Her eyebrows drew together. "Dalmage was on the take?"

He shook his head. "No. The general was. Dalmage was buying protection for a particular section of land that was always the main topic of their conversation."

She looked a little shaken, like she'd figured out exactly where he was headed. She asked anyway. "And this land . . . where exactly is it?"

"Within a mile of where the team was ambushed."

She closed her eyes as a sick look crossed her face. "So Dalmage was protecting the land. He ordered the RUF ambush to make certain that TFM didn't get anywhere near it."

"Yes. And then he arranged to have us shipped out of there the next day and made certain the unit was disbanded shortly after."

"So what was on the land that he didn't want you to see? Diamond mines? Was he was jockeying for position in the diamond trade?"

The brutal legacy of the Sierra Leone blood diamond trade was the logical assumption. But not the right one.

"No diamond mine within a hundred miles."

"Then what?"

"That's what I was tracking down the night I was arrested. The guy who ID'd Dalmage referred me to a woman who had lived in the region until just a few years ago. She wasn't much help, but told me she knew of a priest who had firsthand knowledge of some hinky land deal that had impacted his parish."

"The priest who was killed?"

"Yeah. Apparently he'd had a run-in with someone several years ago because he'd asked the wrong questions about the right people. They almost killed him. Had actually left him for dead, but one of his parishioners found him, patched him up enough that he could be transported, and helped him go into hiding. He assumed a new name, a new parish, and went on with his life."

"So how did you find him?"

"That's where Suah came in. That night, when he hunted me down and offered to help? I figured what the hell and told him what I knew, what I didn't know. Took him less than an hour to find the priest. He was right here in Freetown."

"That boy has sources that would make the NSA drool."

"Tell me about it. Anyway, the priest was skittish. Didn't want to talk to me at first, and I didn't blame him. For all he knew, I was there to kill him." He grunted. "How ironic is that?"

"You can't blame yourself for his death, Joe."

"Under what system of justice does it compute that I'm blameless?" The anger that burned every time he let himself think about that dead priest propelled him out of his chair.

It would always eat at his gut that an innocent man had gotten caught up in his vendetta. "I opened up that can of worms. I don't know how Dalmage found out, but he did. And he had that priest killed to keep him quiet."

"Exactly. Dalmage had him killed. Not you."

"Same result. And all for nothing."

"You never got to talk to him?"

"No. We were on our way to a meet that Suah had arranged. We were a block away when I heard the shots. Two men came out shooting when we reached the cathedral. I got off a couple of shots but they disappeared into the dark. When we went inside, the priest was already dead."

"That's when the police arrived?"

"Convenient, huh? And that brings us up to speed."

She was quiet for a long moment. "Dalmage is on the president's short list for secretary of state."

His gaze sharpened. "Say what?"

"I heard it on the news at Dulles just before I boarded my flight."

"Jesus. That can't happen."

"No. It can't. We need to find out what's on that

property," she said abruptly. "We need to find out what prompted Dalmage to risk losing everything he's worked for—his reputation, his status, even a potential presidential appointment."

Which was exactly what Joe had been thinking. But as he turned her words around in his head, it hit him. "Or maybe that's backward. Maybe what we need to know is what's on that property that will ensure he *gets* that appointment. Maybe that's been his goal all along."

"I don't follow."

"What if that property contains something that would give him leverage? Don't ask me what kind. I haven't gotten that far yet. But let's say it could place him in a major position of power.

"Hell," he said, warming to the idea, "third world countries don't have the corner on the market for egomaniacal despots who get off on the idea that they're destined to control the world. The history books are full of bloodthirsty tyrants who didn't give two figs about human life. Dalmage has proven he falls into that category."

He paced to the corner of the room, knowing in his gut that he was on to something. "We have to find out. That son of a bitch is not going to profit from another death."

And if they couldn't prove it, he was still determined to make Dalmage pay. Even now, he was running through scenarios to take him out and just be done with it.

"You know you can't kill him, right?"

He stopped mid-stride and turned back to her. Saw in her eyes just how well she knew him.

"Killing him is not enough, Joe," she said with a cold determination that chilled him. "I want him more than dead. I want him exposed for the traitor he is. I want him publicly humiliated. I want him to stand trial for killing my brother. For breaking my mother's heart and nearly breaking my father's spirit."

He wanted the same things. But first and foremost, he wanted Dalmage dead.

"We have to get out of Sierra Leone," she pressed, determined to convince him to do this her way. "We have to get back home and tap every resource at our disposal, then take a backhoe to his past until we dig out every business transaction, every donation, every acquaintance, every single detail of his life, and get to the bottom of this."

She pushed up from the table and walked over to him. "Killing him isn't going to solve anything, Joe. All it's going to accomplish is making him dead and making you a cold-blooded killer. Even if we're able to prove his complicity in Bry's death later, you would still be in prison and Dalmage would simply be dead. It's not enough."

She was right. He knew she was right. Yet the need for retribution burned like hot coals in his gut.

"No sleight of hand tomorrow," she said, more plea than command. "You fly out of here with me and we do this the right way. We make him pay with something even more important to him than his life: his pride. We expose him as a traitor and a murderer on a world stage, and he'll die of public humiliation a thousand times before his heart ever stops beating."

He looked into her eyes and knew there was only one answer he could give her. "Fine. We fly out of here tomorrow."

All the tension melted out of her body. He lifted a hand to her hair, his need to comfort the woman he loved as instinctive and necessary as drawing breath.

The instinct to kiss her overpowered him. He had no right at all. But when she leaned toward him, he knew that her need was just as immediate, just as strong as his.

Yearning filled her eyes as he cupped her head and tipped her face up to his. God, he'd missed the easy way she welcomed him. Missed this unapologetic surrender that made the victory hers.

He lowered his head until his mouth was a whisper away . . .

And Suah burst into the room.

She jumped back, flustered and embarrassed. "Is everything okay?"

Suah nodded, looking stoically—and a little proprietary—from her to Joe. "Is everything okay *here*?"

The little smart-ass knew exactly what he'd interrupted. And it hit Joe that Suah had a big crush on Stephanie. Interesting.

"Fine," they said in unison, pretending that nothing had just happened.

Thanks to Suah, Joe thought morosely, nothing had.

14

The boy was so thin. Stephanie had a hard time keeping her mothering instincts under wraps around him. She understood that she had to handle Suah carefully or his colossal independent streak would kick in and he'd refuse to eat, just to prove he didn't have to.

But the mothering worked tonight. She fed them both and avoided eye contact with Joe while Suah gave them a report of the situation on the streets. A sit rep, in Joe's vernacular.

The entire Freetown police force seemed to be involved in the manhunt for the escaped fugitive. The Sierra Leone military had been enlisted to help, upping the intimidation factor by patrolling the streets in swarms of Land Rovers with submachine guns mounted on their hoods.

"The rest of the boys? Are they okay?" They'd taken such huge risks for her and Joe.

"They know how to take care of themselves," Suah said.

Joe had remained silent through the entire report.

Now, he pushed away from the table and walked over to the bed. Without a word, he lay down and covered his eyes with a forearm.

She knew that silence. Guilt was eating at him again. And since there wasn't a single thing either of them could do or say to assuage it, she left him alone. She hoped he'd fall asleep; he still needed rest. He was going to need every ounce of strength to get through tomorrow.

So would she.

"You should stay tonight," she said when Suah rose from the table, pocketing a piece of bread. There was no reason to believe that Dalmage or the police had any knowledge of Suah helping them, but still, she worried.

"I have made other arrangements." He was already headed for the door. "Be ready at nine tomorrow morning."

"Suah." She stopped him before he could leave. "I don't know how to thank you."

His eyes gave away his embarrassment for a moment. He could maneuver these dangerous streets, handle himself with the dregs of this city, but he had no idea how to field the simplest thanks.

So he deflected with a disengaged look, as always, and turned to go.

She wasn't going to let him get by with it. She joined him at the door, placed both hands on his slim, bony shoulders, and turned him around to face her. "There may be no time for this tomorrow, so I want to say it now. You're a good man. A very good man."

Clearly uncomfortable with the praise and the affection in her voice, he nodded stiffly and made to leave. This time she stopped him by wrapping her arms around him and hugging him. She kept on hugging him, even though he stiffened like a thin tree trunk in her embrace.

When she pulled back and gently brushed her fingertips across his cheek, she saw that he was anything but rigid on the inside. For a brief, heartbreaking moment, those huge brown eyes spoke to her of longing and loss and a sorrow that cut straight to her soul.

"I will leave Bekah and several others on watch tonight," he said, pulling back his shoulders. "No one will approach without warning."

Then he was gone. And she was left staring at the closed door, wishing there was some way they could take him with them when they left.

It was a ridiculous idea; she knew that. There was no time, and they were in no position to try to arrange diplomatic approval to take him with them. Suah could never leave Sierra Leone—and even if by some miracle someone could make it happen, it would be highly unlikely that the horrors and abuses of his childhood would ever leave him. Or that he would want to go.

With a heavy heart, she locked the door and turned back to see that Joe was sleeping again. She thought about that almost-kiss earlier. Wise or not, she would have let him kiss her if Suah hadn't returned when he had.

She watched Joe sleep, feeling a sense of satisfaction

that although he was still banged up and far too thin, he was clean and bandaged. And for the first time since they'd dragged him into that van, he appeared to be comfortable and truly resting.

She quietly dug into the suitcase she'd brought back from her outing and pulled out a pretty blue cotton-gauze sundress that she'd bought at a street market when she'd picked up clothes for their great charade tomorrow. Then she headed for the shower, relishing the prospect of washing away several layers of dirt, sweat, and tension.

Clean and somewhat energized, even though she'd been functioning for days now on very little sleep, Stephanie walked out of the small bathroom wearing her new dress and drying her hair with a nearly thread-bare towel—another market find. Joe was still sleeping even though the dim lightbulb suspended from the ceiling was still on.

That they even had electricity was amazing. She'd figured out fast that the lights in Freetown generally failed at the first sign of a rain shower.

She walked to the window and inhaled the scent of the downpour that marginally cooled the air and cleansed it of the cloying city smells that were alternately an assault and an exotic feast to the senses.

She tipped her head to the side and worked the towel through her hair, thinking about home. She missed the crisp winter air of Maryland, even the snowy streets that sometimes made driving treacherous, and the frost-covered windshields that she grumbled about in the early morning when she needed to get to work.

She'd barely thought about work. Would she even have a job when she got back? She realized with only a small amount of surprise that she wouldn't care all that much if they decided to fire her. This "adventure" had changed her. Profoundly. She doubted that she'd ever be content with a desk job again. Rhonda might be miffed at her for leaving her to deal with the fallout, but she'd also be proud, Stephanie thought with a secret little smile as the rain peppered the building's tin roof.

She tossed the towel onto the back of a chair and started working a pick through her heavy, wet hair, taking pleasure in the normalcy of the methodical act. It was impossible to keep her mind from wandering to thoughts of the man on the bed—who, she realized when she heard the soft give of an ancient bedspring, was no longer asleep.

Not only was he awake, he was watching her. She sensed it in the sudden sensitivity of her skin, and in her hyperawareness of his altered breathing.

He was aroused, too. She knew it in the same way she had always known how to touch him, how to please him, how to entice him to take and give pleasure on levels she'd never known existed before.

It was wrong, she supposed, to take advantage of a man whose physical condition made it nearly impossible for him to fight the strong sexual tug that had always existed between them. She should feel guilt over her pretense of ignorance. But all she felt was arousal.

And power.

Power in the knowledge that she could take advantage of the sheer fabric of her dress that did little to conceal that she was completely naked beneath it. Power in her blatant awareness that the pale streetlight shining in through the open window outlined her body in soft, shadowy relief. Power in knowing that her building desire would not only feed his, but sustain it.

So she took advantage. Shamelessly, without guilt. Because she needed something more than simply to be strong tonight.

She arched her back, lifted her arms above her head in a slow, sinuous stretch, and deliberately turned so he could get a clear view of the heaviness of her breasts in silhouette.

His breath caught.

So did hers, at the visceral strength of his response. And she could no longer stay away.

She turned to him, slowly lowered her arms.

"Did I wake you?" she whispered.

He swallowed thickly, and she could see the pulse that beat strong and fast at his throat.

A rush of desire made her tremble. The shock and strength of it sobered her. Maybe this wasn't such a good idea.

She forced herself to take a step back. "How are you feeling?"

He actually looked relieved that she'd offered a reprieve from the heat blazing between them. "Like I'm getting damn tired of being asked that question."

His weary impatience told her how frustrated he was. And an underlying edginess also told her how difficult it was for him to keep from thinking about exactly what she was thinking about.

More knowledge. More power. To hell with caution.

She wasn't going to make this easy for him, she decided. Gathering her hair in one hand, she lifted it off her neck, letting the breeze cool the damp skin of her nape. Another shameless pose. Another deliberate provocation.

He clutched a handful of sheet and dragged it over his lap in a tangle that did little to conceal his reaction to her calculated seduction. He was as lost in this game she'd started as she was.

It wasn't wise. They should both rest. Tomorrow would be arduous as well as dangerous. But it had been so long. And she had been so foolish to let him go.

She let her hands fall to her sides and, all pretense of play gone, walked to the bed.

A sexual tension she recognized so well eddied through his big body, tensing muscles, heating his skin, changing the color of his eyes from a cool hazel to a smoky, shifting ash.

The cords in his neck tightened as he swallowed, never taking his eyes off hers. "What are you doing, Stephanie?"

The gruff rasp of his voice sent a shiver through her body. She stopped close to the bed, smiling. "If you haven't figured it out yet, then you're in worse shape than I thought."

He groaned, a frustrated, helpless sound. "Trust me. I got it. I just don't know why you'd want to, after—"

"Shh." She pressed a fingertip to his lips. "There is no after. No before. Only now. Let that be enough for now." She had no intention of letting him wander into that murky water.

"Only now," she whispered and, holding his gaze, slipped the straps of the dress off her shoulders, down her arms, and let the garment fall to the floor around her feet.

"Breathe," she urged huskily, and she tugged away the sheet and reached for the zipper on his shorts.

His hands covered hers. "Steph—"

"Shh." She brushed his hands away, and with gentle care slid the shorts off his legs. "I promise I won't hurt you."

She loved the strangled sound he made. The almost laugh. The inevitable smile of surrender. She leaned down and, careful of his poor split lip, kissed him. Nothing but soft, supple mouths remembering how love tasted, how love felt, how simple love could be when only the moment mattered.

When his breath mingled with hers on a moan, she leaned in closer; felt a sharp, electrical jolt surge through her body as the sensitive tips of her nipples met the muscled wall of his chest.

She deepened the kiss, indulging in the contact and the pleasure before finally lifting her head, meeting his eyes, and accepting the truth. He had the power, not her. He had always had the power over her.

"Tell me you don't want this, and I'll stop," she whispered, part promise, part plea.

She waited an eternity as his eyes searched hers. Then his hand was in her hair, dragging her mouth back down to his, and he was kissing her with a breathtaking urgency that shifted the balance of power back to her again.

Give. Take. Ebb. Flow. It had always been this way between them when they were naked and needy and lost in each other. It would always be that way.

Trembling with arousal, she climbed up on the bed and straddled his hips, then guided his hand to her center where she was already wet and swollen and pulsing with need for him.

"Touch me. *Please*, please touch me."

He slipped a finger inside, then slid it in . . . out . . . in . . . out, gliding the pad of his thumb over the swollen bud of her clitoris until she was sighing his name and riding his hand with wild abandon.

God, she'd missed this exquisite pressure that built and soared and transported her beyond herself into a realm of consuming pleasure. Everything in her wanted to let it take her, to let herself fly. But she needed to take care with him.

Even as he lifted his hips, driving her wild as he pressed the powerful length of his erection against her, even as he reached up to cup her breast and finesse her nipple into aching hardness and delicious sensitivity, she knew she had to rein herself in.

He was twenty pounds lighter than his very lean

fighting weight. He was recovering from an ordeal that would have annihilated a lesser man. He might think he was up for a vigorous tumble, but she knew different. And she was the one who needed to gain some control.

"Easy," she whispered and, taking his swollen length in her hand, guided him home.

His hands flew to her hips and he held himself there, still and deep inside her. She gasped at the feel of him, thick and sleek and hot and all Joe.

"You okay?" she whispered, leaning down and pressing her mouth against his ear.

He grunted something affirmative. Taking her cue from the rhythm he set, she slowly moved her hips up and down, bracing her hands on the mattress on either side of his shoulders for leverage, keeping as much of her body weight away from his bruised ribs as possible.

"Am I hurting you?"

"God, no," he ground out and sought her breasts with his hands again, urging her to lean farther over him as he guided one breast to his mouth.

His lips were magic, his tongue relentless as he licked and bit and played with her sensitive nipple until both of them were wild with the need for release.

"We need to finish this," she gasped, "before one of us gets hurt."

He chuckled low in his throat, gave her breast a final, lavish lick, and set her back so she was sitting totally upright astride him.

"By all means . . . do your worst."

She laughed and lifted her arms above her head,

knowing he loved looking at her that way. Loved sliding his hands up and over her belly, filling his palms with the weight of her breasts.

Finally, she started to move. Slow and steady and savoring.

"No," she whispered when he lifted his hips to meet hers. "Just lie there. Let me do this for you."

"Not a chance," he murmured and, gripping her hips in his hands, guided her into a rhythm that escalated in speed and friction, and had her digging her knees deeper into the mattress and her fingers deeper into his shoulders and her breath escaping on sharp, panting hitches.

He reached between them, found her clitoris again, and sent her over the edge. She cried out just as he tensed, bucked and spilled into her, uttering her name on a long, mindless groan as they rode out their climaxes together.

He was a long time recovering his breath. For several tense minutes, she was afraid she might have truly hurt him. When she had recovered enough to move, she rose on rubber legs and went into the bathroom. She came back with a cool wet cloth that she ran over his perspiring face, then carefully down over his ribs before he took over, cleaning himself up.

"You okay?" she asked.

He grabbed her wrist and tugged her down onto the bed beside him. "You need to stop asking me that. But for the record, I'm fan-fucking-tastic."

After that, he was quiet for so long, she decided he'd

fallen asleep, but then his thumb moved on the inside of her wrist. A gentle stroke across her pulse. A foreshadowing.

"Steph . . . about what I said—"

"No." Recognizing that leading tone, she pushed up on her arm so she could look down at him. He was about to apologize for something, and she wasn't listening. Not tonight.

"I don't want to talk about that now," she said. "I don't want to talk about what you said or didn't say. What you meant or didn't mean. Not now.

"But be ready, Joe. When this is over, when we get out of here and Dalmage pays for what he's done, then you're going to have a *lot* to say to me. Okay? A lot."

He searched her eyes, then finally nodded. She had no doubt that he'd understood.

He was going to finally open up to her. Or no matter how much she loved him, no matter how much she wanted him with her, she was going to be gone.

15

Joe sat on the edge of the bed early the next morning, scowling at the white linen suit jacket hooked over his left index finger and the blue silk shirt hooked over his right. "This is what you meant when you said you had it covered? Where did you find this stuff, anyway?"

"Rich Americans R Us," Stephanie said brightly as she shimmied into a siren red silk tank top, then tucked it into a very short, floral print silk wrap skirt. She smiled over her shoulder. "Suah knew a guy who knew a guy."

Suah always knew a guy. "A little showy, don't you think?"

She grinned. "A lot showy. They'll be looking for fugitives, not flamboyant American tourists."

He became fascinated by the lush curve of her very sexy ass as she planted a palm against the wall for balance and toed into a pair of red high-heel sandals.

"No one hiding out from the law would dare wear such bright colors for fear of attracting attention," she continued.

He dragged his gaze away, then returned to her breasts, also standouts beneath the clingy silk.

"Okay. I get it. Expensive luggage. Showy clothes. We're hiding in plain sight. Only one little problem." He pointed to the bandage on his head. "Sort of a dead giveaway."

"Got a fix for that." She dug into the big suitcase. "See if it fits."

He caught the straw colored Panama hat she tossed to him and settled it gingerly on his head, slanting it low on one side to cover the bandage.

"I give it two thumbs up." She shot him a quick smile and headed for the bathroom, snatching a bag out of the open suitcase as she went. "I've got to take care of this hair."

He watched her go in silence because, hell, he really didn't know what to say to her. Last night. Holy mother. Last night had been . . . where did he start? Amazing? Incredible? Earthmoving? All of the above. But what's more, it had been totally unexpected.

He stood and shrugged into the shirt, slowly working the buttons as he thought about the metamorphosis of Stephanie Tompkins. She'd always been this amazingly sensual woman. Still water came to mind when he thought of her. Understated. Never submissive, but *passive*, maybe? Was that the word he was searching for?

All that had changed overnight. This new Stephanie was a nuclear reactor, splitting atoms and moving matter in a take-charge, take-control, take-no-prisoners mode that just kept knocking him on his ass.

And, mercy, had she knocked him flat last night.

He supposed he ought to be a little intimidated by it all, but he wasn't. In fact, now that the smoke had cleared and his mind-fog had lifted, he was fascinated and more than a little infatuated. He was also curious as hell about what had precipitated the transformation that had taken her from amazing to off-the-charts unbelievable.

"Be ready, Joe. When this is over, when we get out of here and Dalmage pays for what he's done, then you're going to have a lot to say to me. Okay? A lot."

Okay. The message in her words *did* intimidate him. She'd put him on notice last night. Let him know in no uncertain terms that there was no future for them if he didn't give her access to that part of his soul that he didn't want anyone to have to deal with. Hell, *he* didn't even want to deal with it.

Didn't matter now. There was a day of reckoning coming. And for the life of him, he didn't know if he was up to it. Just that fast, he was back to square one. Afraid of losing her if he didn't come clean, afraid of losing part of himself if he did.

He dragged a hand over his head. When had the tables turned? And how had she managed to turn them on a proverbial dime? He'd left her, hadn't he? Left her so he could protect her?

"Look how well that worked out, dumb-ass," he grumbled and tucked his shirttails into the linen pants that matched the suit jacket. He wished he still didn't feel as used up as yesterday's dishwater.

The bathroom door opened, curtailing any more thoughts. *Holy mother of God, would you look at her.*

Brunette Stephanie, with her long, shining hair curling around her face, was girl-next-door gorgeous. Blond Stephanie, in a short, sassy wig that framed her face and made her brown eyes look as big as dessert plates, was a starving man's feast.

"What do you think?" She struck a pose with her sexy blond 'do and silk-covered curves and hot-pink lip gloss.

"I think I might like you to keep that wig for future . . . um . . . reference. The lipstick, too." If he had even half of his usual stamina, he'd back her up against the wall and see how long it took to get his hands up under that skirt.

She grinned, blushed prettily, then fell back on deflection by reaching for his jacket.

"Let's see if this fits as well as the Panama."

It did. But it felt odd wearing shoes and socks after going so long without. Just like it felt odd to sit back and let her take charge when she shifted into all-business mode and told him it was showtime. But this was her show. And so far, he couldn't find fault with any phase of it.

An old but well-kept stretch limo was waiting for them on the street. The windows were tinted so dark he couldn't see inside. Bekah relieved them of the leather luggage and stowed both pieces in the trunk. The suitcases were stuffed with clothes and touristy souvenirs, anything to give them weight and make them look legit in case they were stopped and searched.

Then Bekah went around to the limo's side and opened the rear door, holding it open for them.

Stephanie was about to step inside when a Range Rover overflowing with armed soldiers roared down the street, then skidded to a screeching stop in front of the limo.

"Fuck," Joe muttered under his breath. They were sunk. He had the KA-Bar strapped above his ankle, the Glock 17 stuck in his waistband, and Stephanie had her own Glock tucked inside her flashy purse. Their firepower against this shitload of soldiers was the equivalent of David wielding a broken slingshot in a showdown with Goliath on steroids.

"How fast can you run?" Stephanie whispered to Bekah.

"Like the wind," he said with the confidence of someone who knew his own strengths and that they were about to be tested.

"Then do it now."

Understanding even before she started screaming, "Thief! Thief! Someone stop him!" Bekah took off down the street like a Formula One racer and disappeared from sight before Stephanie launched her second wave.

"He robbed me! Why would he *do* that?" She turned big, sad eyes to Joe, playing the horror-stricken princess before turning accusatory glares on the storm troopers who had bailed out of the Rover and were approaching them with their rifles locked and loaded.

"Why aren't you going after him?" she demanded

of the soldiers in a spoiled American, rich bitch voice. "Don't just stand there—you can't let him get away with that! We were trying to help him. We only stopped because he looked so hungry, didn't he darling?" She turned those sad eyes on Joe again.

"Please calm yourself, dear," he drawled, falling back on his Georgia roots. "Just be thankful he didn't pull a knife. Or worse, a gun. Didn't I tell ya that stoppin' was a bad idea? They're all little heathens. Am I right, gentlemen?"

He turned a man-to-man smile on the soldiers, whose stances had transitioned from hostile and suspicious to barely concealed contempt for this stupid American couple, who was apparently slumming it for grins and giggles and had gotten themselves in a little trouble.

"My wallet," Stephanie said suddenly as she dug into her purse, frantically searching. Outrage whined through her words. "He got my wallet! It was a Louis Vuitton! My *favorite* Louis Vuitton, the pink one!"

She squeezed out a tear and pressed her forehead against Joe's chest. He wrapped a comforting arm around her shoulders.

"Can you do anything?" he asked over the top of her head, a humble man who knew there'd be hell to pay if the little woman didn't get her pound of flesh.

"That one is long gone. You must be more careful where you drive from now on." The pack leader's tone clearly relayed that he thought they'd gotten exactly what they deserved and he had no more interest in them.

With a hitch of his chin, he motioned the others to

follow him back to the Rover, where they would continue their search for the American fugitives.

"Jesus." Joe kept patting her back, consoling her as the soldiers sped off down the street.

"Close," she said, climbed into the limo's backseat.

Close? He swore as he followed her inside. If it got any closer, they'd both be riddled with bullets.

He slumped back into the leather seat, his heart still jackhammering at the thought of something happening to Stephanie, when the privacy glass slid down and the driver glanced over his shoulder and tipped his cap.

"You have got to be kidding," Joe said.

"At your service, boss," Suah said, and shifted into gear.

"What's he sitting on?" Joe asked as they glided down the street in the luxury vehicle. "The kid isn't big enough to see over the steering wheel without help. And when did he learn to drive?"

Stephanie pulled her top away from her body and leaned toward an air-conditioning vent, clearly enjoying the blast of cool air. "Seriously? That's your biggest concern?"

If only. "He's not going to fool anyone if we're stopped."

"We're not going to be stopped." She leaned back into the plush seat. "He's not speeding. Not running lights. Not drawing attention. Besides, we just had our 'chance' run-in with the bad guys. The odds are now in our favor. But just in case, we have a little insurance on board."

When he frowned, she said, "Under the front seat. I'll do it," she added when he started to lean forward. "No sense stressing those ribs."

She was right. Leaning forward was still a killer. Watching her drop to her knees on the floor, then point that premium, heart-shaped ass his way didn't exactly slow down his heart rate, either.

She dug around under the seat, pulled out a couple of frag grenades, half a dozen smoke grenades, and a pair of AK-47s with folding stocks, short barrels, and three extra ammo clips. Christ. Did the woman have a direct pipeline to every arms dealer in the city?

"You know," he said, dumbfounded after she'd shimmied up into the seat beside him, "I have assets all over the world. Assets who've been on the ground for years and still don't have the connections you've made in four days."

"Maybe you need to say 'pretty please' more often." She expertly set the stock, fit a full magazine into the rifle, then chambered a round and switched on the safety.

"Or maybe not." He continued to be amazed by her resourcefulness and by how accomplished she'd become with the weaponry. "When did you get so comfortable handling guns?" He nodded toward the rifles she'd laid on the floor at their feet.

"You slept a lot. Suah gave me lessons."

Joe glanced toward the privacy screen and the boy who had been so instrumental in keeping them alive and now, in getting them out of the country.

"You care about him, don't you?" she asked quietly.

He looked out the window at the crumbling façade of the city passing by. "The little shit's grown on me, yeah."

"He worships you."

He turned to look at her then, and saw in her eyes that she'd become as attached to Suah as he had.

But they couldn't take him with them. Even if they could, he'd be too stubborn to go. Suah, Bekah, the rest of the boys . . . they were among thousands whose fate had been decided long before he and Stephanie had come on the scene.

"I hate it that we can't do anything for him," she said, frustration thick in her voice.

He stared down at his clasped hands. Yeah. He hated it, too.

16

The docks teamed with civilian men, women, and children, along with a hefty contingent of city police and military when they rolled down the street fronting the pier twenty minutes later. Motor traffic was as thick as the crowds and clotted together like an army of ants.

Suah expertly ran the gauntlet and maneuvered the big limo through the crawling procession of cars, vans, trucks, and motorcycles, into one of three lines waiting to drive up the ramp onto the ferry that would take them to the airport.

Clouds as gray as Joe's mood and heavy with rain hung over the mountain range surrounding the city, and drifted down to skim the bay and mingle with the smoke from barbecues, trash fires, and car exhaust. Hundreds of shanties and Quonset huts rimmed the sloping land, virtually piled on top of each other as they spilled haphazardly down to the shore.

A disorganized crew of dock men orchestrated the boarding of vehicles and passengers. Verbal fisticuffs sporadically broke out as the motley crew worked to jockey too many vehicles into position in too little space. Straggler vehicles driving off the ferry added to the confusion and the slow progress as they approached the ramp and waited their turn to board.

"What a goatfuck," Joe muttered, his tension mounting as heavily armed military guards wearing cammos and sour looks patrolled the disorganized disaster, clearly searching for him and Stephanie.

The tinted glass privacy screen slid down. "They will make you get out soon," Suah said.

Yeah. He was dreading that. "What about you?"

"Unlike the other drivers, they will allow me to park the car on board. Limos get special passes. There have been too many damaged. The dock crew no longer wants the liability."

"And you think you can actually park this big boat in one of those little slots?"

Suah's response was a glare that managed to make Joe grin.

"Okay," he said, "you can do it. Don't get huffy."

"Once we're on board, we blend," Stephanie said, watching the action with as much concern as Joe. "We make the thirty-minute ride across the bay, get back in the limo, and Suah drives off the ferry and directly to the airport." It was as much a prayer as a statement.

At the airport, Brown would be waiting to fly them back to the States.

It was a good plan. And he knew Rafe and B.J. wouldn't let them down. This wasn't their first rodeo. They would send Brown fully equipped to make things happen.

It was exactly how he would have laid things out. But as they rolled closer to the ferry ramp and the moment where they'd have to leave the anonymity of the limo, adrenaline started mainlining through his blood like rocket fuel. Even the best plans had a way of going south, especially when there were so many variables. Like the ferry departing on time. Like the police and the military buying their tourist personas. And like Brown actually getting to Lungi, and if he made it, being able to spread around enough payola to convince the airport officials to turn a blind eye to a fudged flight plan and the addition of two undocumented passengers, without raising suspicion that those special passengers were the fugitives the police were after.

Yeah. A lot of fucking variables.

If it was just his neck on the line, it would be different. But if Stephanie and Suah got caught . . . He couldn't go there now. Now was all about execution and keeping cool.

"Better stow those," he said with a nod toward the AKs.

She tucked them under the front seat just in time. A crewman motioned for Suah to pull ahead, and onto the ferry they went.

On board, someone rapped on the window. "Out, out, out."

Stephanie's gaze flew to his.

He nodded. "Let's do this."

She drew a bracing breath. "I'm right behind you."

Joe opened the door and stepped out into the heat and the smells and the noise. He turned back to extend a hand to Stephanie, ignoring the four soldiers marching in their general direction. When she stepped onto the deck in her four-inch heels and clingy silk, and adopted a regal air, he couldn't help but grin and follow suit.

They immediately transformed into Dick and Jane American—*rich* Dick and Jane American—suffering the misfortune of having to mingle with the unwashed masses, but determined to make the best of a bad situation as they watched their driver maneuver their air-conditioned limo into the dark, congested cargo bay.

It was some relief to see that they weren't the only Caucasians and therefore didn't stick out as drastically as he had feared among the sea of locals who used the ferries on a daily basis. Since the RUF had been squashed ten years ago, the tourist trade had steadily grown. Europeans now flocked to Sierra Leone to enjoy the sandy beaches and bargain prices West Africa offered.

"Ignore them," Joe said close to her ear as he steered her away from the approaching soldiers and toward a metal walkway painted a peeling industrial orange.

"Oh, look, darling," she said, with animation. "They're not really going to jump from there, are they?"

Cool as a cucumber, she made a sun shield for her eyes with one hand and pointed with the other.

Twenty yards to the left, an old, rusted-out dredger rode low in the shallow water. Three teenage boys stood at the very tip of the bow, looking down into the water as if trying to decide whether they wanted to make the long plunge.

"They're boys," he said, guiding her toward the walkway again, "of course they'll jump."

The foot patrol drew closer, and Joe had to step out of their path to avoid getting run over as they passed.

"Nice work," he said, then grinned with her when the three boys took a flying run and leaped off the old boat, landing with a big splash and a lot of laughter.

They were bumped and jostled by their fellow passengers in the line that funneled toward the stairs leading up to the passenger deck. Except for the military presence, it could have been a party. Music played in the background, an African reggae fusion that blended with the drone of chatter, revving motors, and honking horns. A pretty, young woman wearing a white dress and a red scarf wound round her neck balanced a basket of bottled water on her head, stopping occasionally to make a sale. Old men and boys leaned on the upper rail, watching the loading process, talking and laughing while police cars patrolled.

"Quite the parade, what?"

Joe turned toward the voice. A middle-aged, overweight Brit decked out in a ridiculously close copy of the suit Joe was wearing grinned up at him, mopping the sweat from his bald head.

"A colorful culture, to be sure," Joe agreed and extended his hand. "Richard Wentworth. My wife, Jane," he added, including Stephanie in the introduction.

"Albert Pritchard. Pleasure to meet you. You're American, correct?"

"Mississippi born and raised," Stephanie said brightly. "Although for the life of me, I cannot recall ever experiencing heat like this even in our southern states. Ghastly, isn't it?"

Pritchard wholeheartedly agreed, and accepted their invitation to join them.

Another squad of soldiers marched past, searching for two disheveled Americans, dismissing the well-dressed, happily chatting threesome out of hand.

Last call was announced over the scratchy PA system, then the creak and groan of the ramp being hoisted reverberated beneath their feet. The ferry lurched, then pulled away from the dock, finally leaving Freetown behind.

"Bon voyage, darling." Stephanie smiled up at Joe.

It was too soon to breathe any sighs of relief, but the salt air smelled a little sweeter, and freedom felt a little closer, as they cleared the bay and headed out toward open water.

Suah stared at the wad of cash Stephanie tucked into his hand. "I cannot—"

She closed both hands over his, squeezed tight, and forced back tears. "Please take it. We wouldn't be alive if not for you."

They stood beside the limo in front of the Lungi International Airport after a quick and thankfully uneventful drive from the ferry.

Even though she'd tried to steel herself for this moment, she wasn't prepared for the rush of emotions that hit her. Joe stood beside her, looking as miserable as she felt.

"Watch your back," he said gruffly, then rested a hand on Suah's narrow shoulder.

"I need to get back to the docks or I'll miss the next ferry." Suah shoved the cash into his pocket.

Though his expression was as unreadable as ever, his eyes were suspiciously glassy. He did his damnedest to look anywhere but directly at them.

Unable to stop herself, Stephanie threw her arms around him and drew him close. When his slight body softened, and he gave her a clumsy pat on the back, she lost it. A soft sob escaped. "Please take care of yourself," she whispered, and forced herself to pull away before she embarrassed him further.

Looking shaken, Suah didn't waste any time reaching for the driver's door.

"You've got our cell numbers," Joe said, his expression grim as he watched the boy. "I expect you to keep in touch."

"You stand here much longer and the police will spot you," Suah grumbled, opening the door. "What good will these numbers do me then?"

Joe grinned. "Can't wait to get rid of me, huh?"

"Like I wish to be rid of that wart," Suah said with the barest trace of a smile.

Then he got in the limo, shifted into gear, and pulled out into traffic.

For a long, silent moment they both stood there, watching him go.

"What will happen to him?" Stephanie asked.

"He'll be fine. Don't worry. He can take care of himself," Joe said.

Stephanie wanted to believe him.

"I'm going to miss him." She brushed a tear from her cheek. "And I'm going to worry, no matter what."

"Yeah." Joe grabbed the handle of the larger suitcase and nodded for her to take the other. "Can't believe I'm saying this, but so am I."

He breathed deep. Squared his shoulders. "Let's go find Brown."

After a last look down the street, Stephanie turned and followed him, knowing she'd feel this hollow ache for a very, very long time.

Inside, the airport terminal was as noisy and hot and crowded as the ferry. Rows of lazy ceiling fans barely pushed the muggy air around, and the overly bright fluorescent panels in the dingy white ceiling cast harsh light on the cream and gray tiled floor.

The constant chatter of people, the static garble of called flights over an antiquated PA system, and the jet roar bleeding in from the tarmac raised the decibel level and added to their sense of urgency.

They'd been inside for ten minutes and still hadn't spotted Brown.

"He'll be here," Joe assured Stephanie, as well as himself. They turned around and started another pass through the terminal, walking past rows of metal gates where passengers were herded through security like cattle.

They were halfway through their second pass, Joe silently cursing his lack of stamina, when he spotted Mike Brown strolling toward them decked out in dress blues, a cap, and spit-and-polished black shoes, working the hell out of his professional pilot look.

"Holy crap," Brown said when he realized the man walking up to him was Joe. "Starve much?" he asked with typical irreverence.

Joe grinned, happy as hell to see him. "So the diet's working?"

Beneath the tall, tanned, broad-shouldered pilot's jovial expression was real concern. "Where'd you get that suit? Pimps R Us?"

"You're giving *me* crap? You're the one with a diamond stud in your ear."

"Hey, don't diss the bling. It's sacred. And before you ask, no, I'm not smoking again." He ran a fingertip along the cigarette tucked behind his other ear. "This is just—"

"A crutch?" Joe suggested.

Brown grinned. "Insurance. Never know when I'm going to have a really bad day."

"Yeah, well, let's hope you don't need it today. Stephanie," Joe said once the requisite insults had been passed, "meet Mike Brown."

So far they hadn't spotted any uniforms other than a smattering of airport security cops, and the terminal was so noisy, Joe wasn't afraid of being overheard.

Stephanie extended her hand. "Mr. Brown. I can't tell you how glad I am to finally meet you."

"Don't even start." Joe read Brown's mind as the pilot's gaze raked appreciatively over Stephanie, cutting off what was sure to be a come-on of epic proportions.

"Stephanie," Brown said, ignoring Joe and turning on the charm. "It's Mike. I was told to look for a blonde, but good Lord, woman, you're so much more bombshell than I pictured you."

Okay, fine. If Brown could make her laugh, as he just had, he could BS all he wanted.

"Let me take those for you." Mike relieved them both of the weight of their luggage. "Bricks?" he speculated with a grunt as he started tugging them along.

"Had to make it look real," Joe said.

"Speaking of things looking real, your passports are in my jacket pocket." He stopped and pulled them out, handed them to Joe, and started walking again.

The passports were works of art. BOI kept the best ink man in the business on retainer. He could produce documents from any country in any name in a matter of hours. Only this time there had been a little miscommunication.

"Riene and Gretchen Gruenwalt?" Joe glanced at Brown as he handed Stephanie her passport.

"You speak German, right?"

Joe shook his head.

"Good thing you don't have to do any talking, then, huh? We're greased through at the last gate. Just keep your mouths shut, smile at the nice man who relieved me of a lot of cash, and walk through to the ramp. We've already kicked the tires and lit the fires. Both engines are running, ready to spool up for takeoff. Ty's in the cockpit, ready to rock and roll."

"Ty? Your copilot is your brother?"

"The kid's grown up," Brown said with a note of pride in his voice.

"One of you had to," Joe ribbed.

"Better him than me," Brown agreed, taking no offense. "He's runs his own air cargo business out of Key West."

"Legit?" As opposed to Brown's Primetime Air Cargo business, which had a tendency to blur the line between legitimate and shady.

Again, Brown grinned. "Like I said. Better him than me." Then he got down to business. "The head honcho in the tower's gonna have a backache tonight, from sitting on that wad of bills I tucked in his wallet. As soon as I say that we're ready to rumble, he'll clear the runway and we are outta here."

"It's really that easy?" Stephanie asked, clearly stunned by the lax security and the favors money could buy.

"We'll find out soon enough." Brown headed for the gate. "Okay, lady and gent. See what you can do about looking German, would ya?"

17

Stephanie walked across the concrete toward the waiting business jet, her heart beating so fast that she seriously thought she might pass out. Heat hit the ramp from above and ricocheted back up in her face like solar flares. Add the exhaust from the planes and her concern for Joe, and it all almost brought her to her knees.

Joe hadn't been on his feet this long since they'd run to the new safe house yesterday. And today had been hard on him physically as well as emotionally. She had to concentrate on getting both her and Joe the thirty yards across the ramp to the plane that shot heat out of its twin engines, stacking wavy mirages for several yards behind it.

"God, she's a pretty sight." Joe stopped and stared at the G-550. "But those aren't our tail numbers."

"Nope," Brown said. "Had a special paint job done just for this trip before we left Buenos Aires. Wouldn't do for whoever's on your ass to find out your employer sent a plane to haul your carcass home. Might be a tip-off, don't you think?

"I filed the flight plan using the bogus tail numbers as ID. Paint's supposed to fade within forty-eight hours. If my calcs are right, that should be about three hours before we touch down in D.C., where they *are* expecting the BOI corporate jet. Don't you just love subterfuge?"

"That I do," Joe agreed.

When he started walking again, Stephanie could see that he was struggling. She hooked her arm around his waist and knew when he leaned heavily against her that he was grateful for the support.

"You gonna make it, or am I going to have to haul your candy-ass up those steps?" Brown's brows were pinched together in concern as he stopped at the bottom of the jet's air stairs.

"Don't you worry about me," Joe said, his breath labored. "I'm fine. You just worry about flying this bird outta here."

"Aye aye, Cap'n Bly." Brown gave him a smart salute, but made certain, Stephanie noticed, that he was right behind Joe as he laboriously climbed the short set of stairs.

"How bad is he?" Brown asked when he'd jogged back down to collect the luggage. He motioned Stephanie to walk up ahead of him.

"Better than he was." She stepped into the luxury cabin, grateful for the cool, conditioned air inside. Joe was up front, saying hello to Mike's brother and thanking him for signing on.

"Today's been rough. He's exhausted."

"I'm thinking he's not the only one who's had a big day."

Oh, my. When he turned those laser blue eyes on her and hit her with the full effect of that stunning bad-boy smile, Stephanie understood why the guys called him Primetime. Hollywood gorgeous, he could easily headline any prime-time show. Add in the rebel ear-ring, the tall, dark, and built component, and this guy had drool factor written all over him.

And when Joe stepped back into the cabin, a younger version of Mike following him, she couldn't help but appreciate the gene pool responsible for creating these two stunningly handsome men.

"Ma'am," Ty said, extending his hand. "Welcome aboard."

"We can chitchat once we're airborne." Brown re-tracted the air stairs, then secured the hatch, and the noise level immediately dropped. "Let's get buckled in, okay? Soon as I get clearance, we're gonna boogie out of here faster than rainwater running through a downspout."

Correctly reading the "waiting for the other shoe to fall" look on Stephanie's face, he added sweetly, "Relax, darlin'. I'm gonna get you home. Your work is officially over."

The sudden burn of tears caught her completely off guard.

"Been a rough ride, yes?" Brown laid a comforting hand on her shoulder.

She laughed, part nerves, part relief, and a whole lot of exhaustion. "It's been a piece of cake."

"Atta girl. You look like your brother, by the way," he added, his deep voice turning soft. "Great kid."

It hadn't occurred to her that Mike might have known Bryan. But if he'd provided transport for the TFM team, of course he would have known all the guys.

"Seat belt," he reminded her, and headed for the cockpit.

She eased down beside Joe, who had already collapsed into one of the plush seats. His seat belt was buckled. His eyes were closed. If he wasn't already asleep he soon would be, even though the whine of the engines was loud enough to wake a hibernating bear.

She buckled up, then sat there a moment, soaking up the realization that they'd made it, that they were finally home free. With a satisfied sigh, she looked out the window.

And did a double take, not wanting to accept what she saw.

Four Range Rovers barreled down the road that ran parallel to the terminal. One by one they braked and cut hard rights into the terminal drive.

"Oh, God," she muttered.

Joe came immediately to attention. "What?"

"I think we have a problem."

"Never trust a man who's willing to take a bribe," Brown grumbled to Joe, then opened his mike again. They were sitting on the ramp, ready to taxi into takeoff position onto the runway. "Lungi ground, I repeat, this is Gulfstream 174GG, requesting taxi for takeoff. Please advise."

Joe stood in the open cockpit door, hands braced above him on the bulkhead.

"Hold your position. Please stand by for clearance," the air traffic controller replied.

Mike swore under his breath.

"I'd say the jig is up," Ty said with a grim look.

"Someone got to him, all right," Mike agreed. "Someone who scares him more than the prospect of me storming that tower and ripping him a new asshole."

Joe searched the runway. The traffic was light to nonexistent. Two commercial jets and one corporate jet rimmed the apron, one refueling, one taxiing in, one positioning for takeoff ahead of them. The clearance hold was as bogus as a three-dollar bill.

"Tell him you'll find your own room, so they'd better clear a lane if they want to avoid a major catastrophe."

"Been there, done that already, good buddy. I'm still getting the ol' stall. Got any other ideas?"

"They're sending police out onto the ramp now," Stephanie called.

Joe turned to see her twisted around in her seat, looking out the window on the terminal side.

"At least twenty," she added, giving them a play by play. "All heavily armed."

Joe whipped his head back to the windshield and scanned the airport. "What's going on over there?" He hitched his chin toward an area cordoned off with yellow caution tape.

"New runway in progress. Looks to be about eighty

percent complete," Mike said, then grinned up over his shoulder at Joe.

"How many feet do you need?"

Brown shrugged. "We're rollin' light, so around five thousand. Maybe a little less."

Joe looked down the new construction. "What do you think? Is there enough concrete to make this happen?"

"Only one way to find out."

"Do it," Joe said.

"Ty?" Mike deferred to his brother.

"I go where the plane goes."

"Good answer." Mike glanced over his shoulder at Joe. "Make sure she's buckled in tight, then strap yourself in. It may be a rough ride."

Joe hadn't even gotten back to his seat when the jet started rolling.

"What's he going to do?" Stephanie asked, wide-eyed.

"Tower won't give us clearance. So we're going to inaugurate the new runway."

She blinked in confusion, then looked out the window. When she saw the partially completed landing strip, lined by construction equipment and fenced off with caution tape, she paled.

Joe grabbed her hand. "This is no hill for a climber, and Brown's scaled some big ones. We'll be airborne in no time."

She laced her fingers with his and turned to look out her window again. "No time is exactly what we've got.

The Range Rovers are lined up behind a padlocked gate. Looks like they're waiting for someone to unlock it and let them out onto the ramp."

"Four-wheelers on our six!" Joe yelled, letting Mike know things had just gotten more dicey.

The powerful engines whined as Mike throttled forward and they rolled faster down the ramp.

Stephanie flinched and tightened her grip on Joe's fingers. "Oh, God. Is that what I think it is?"

If she thought the green glowing tracer fire zipping past the windows meant they were under fire, she was dead right. They'd doubtless pulled out the belt-fed machine guns, too.

Joe cupped his hands and yelled toward the cockpit, "Taking fire!"

"No shit, Sherlock!" Brown made a sharp right turn toward the unfinished runway, lined them up, and shoved the power levels to max.

Joe glanced out his window as they picked up speed and saw two Range Rovers speeding toward them.

"They're getting closer!" Stephanie yelled.

They needed a minimum speed of 140 knots to get airborne, and it would take about forty-five seconds to get there. "They'll be eating our dust soon enough," he assured her.

He saw the muzzle flashes of at least four rifles pumping out on full auto, and knew that the same action was happening on Stephanie's side of the plane.

The new runway was rough but level, so the surface wasn't a problem. Length might be the problem.

He'd been aboard this bird dozens of times, and he had a pretty good idea that they might run out of runway before the twin engines reached liftoff velocity. Add the hammering they were taking from the rifle fire, and their odds of reaching critical speed before one of those yahoos hit something vital were roughly the same as Brown going five minutes without flirting with a woman.

He glanced at Stephanie. Her eyes were closed, her head was pressed back against the headrest, her entire body was wound spring-tight. She'd ditched the wig and her hair tumbled softly around her shoulders. Her breath came hard and fast, her breasts rising and falling beneath the clingy silk; her wrap skirt had hitched halfway up her thighs and fell open almost to her panties on her right side.

She was scared but steady, and the sexiest damn woman he'd ever seen. Jesus—they were spinning straight toward a disaster that might end it for all of them, and all he could think about was getting her naked.

And getting her safely home, where he could figure out how to love her the way she deserved to be loved. He glanced forward. Less and less runway and more and more mountain peaks lay dead ahead. One of those AKs could pierce a fuel tank. The machine guns could blow a tire. They could burst into flames any second, or lose control and do a rollover.

"Stephanie."

She opened her eyes and met his.

"I need you to know—"

"No," she cut in sharply. "No last words. I refuse to believe—"

She stopped mid-sentence, her eyes widening with hope. "You feel that?"

He grinned and exhaled a breath so huge it made his ribs hurt. "We're airborne."

"Oh, my God. He did it!"

Joe nodded, still smiling. "He sure as hell did."

"Hoo weee!" Brown whooped from the cockpit. "I don't know about the rest of you, but I could use a cigarette. Hot *damn*. That was almost better than sex."

The jet suddenly jolted, jerking them forward against their seat belts before leveling out again.

The oxygen masks bounced down from the ceiling, dancing on the end of their tubes. An alarm bell started clanging, then the jet took an abrupt nosedive.

Stephanie's wild gaze shot to Joe's. "What's happening?"

Joe looked toward the cockpit, saw Mike frantically pushing levers, and had a real bad feeling that he didn't want to know.

18

Greer Dalmage sat behind his desk at his suite of offices in Freetown. One hand gripped the arm of his chair. In the other he clenched the small prescription bottle of nitroglycerin, waiting for it to ease the crippling hold of the angina spasm. His shirt was damp with perspiration beneath his suit jacket. His chest burned and clutched around his heart like an iron fist.

The attacks were coming more and more frequently. His fault. He needed to control them better. He forced a calm, level breath. He could not panic. Not about the angina. Not about Bangura's ineptness. Not about what would happen to him if Joe Green escaped Freetown and ferreted out the whole truth.

He would be ruined. Everything he'd worked for, everything he'd set into play over the past fifteen years—all of it would be gone.

He would also be dead. The men he owed both money and favors wouldn't hesitate to extract payment from his flesh.

All because of one man. His only mistake, his *only*

mistake, had been keeping Green alive for too long.

A soft rap sounded on his closed door, then Ms. Foster poked her head inside. "I know you said to hold all calls, but Lieutenant Bangura is on line one for you, sir. He insists that you will want to take his call."

"Thank you Ms. Foster. Put him through."

"Excuse me, sir." She hesitated at the door, her usually dour expression softened by concern. "But are you all right?"

"I'm fine. Please close the door on your way out."

"Very good, sir." Looking unconvinced, she backed out of the room, closing the door behind her.

"Speak," he said after picking up the receiver.

"It is done." Bangura's voice brimmed with jovial conviction.

Greer slumped back in his chair. A relief so visceral, so sweet, sent a hum of excitement washing through him that was almost sexual. "How? Where?"

"We found them attempting to escape at Lungi airport. My men did not let that happen."

"They're dead, then?"

"As you specified, yes."

He hadn't succeeded this long without covering all of his bases. "I want to see the bodies."

Bangura hesitated, then cleared his throat. "I am sorry. That is not possible. There was a crash. The bodies were burned."

Greer told himself that the trace of doubt flicking in and out of his mind was a carryover from Bangura's prior mistake.

"Rest assured," Bangura continued, "there remains no trace that either of the Americans were ever here."

Saidu hung up the phone, rose stiffly from his desk, and walked across the room. He flicked off the light and locked his office door behind him. Then he left for home. Where he would sit alone in the dark. And drink.

There would be fallout from his actions today. He didn't know when. He didn't know what. But when Dalmage learned the whole truth, there would be fallout.

"Stephanie. Wake up. You need to get back in your seat and buckle up. We're going to start our approach soon."

Stephanie stretched and yawned, then forced herself to sit up. Joe sat on the edge of the seat opposite hers. The heaviness around his eyes told her he'd been resting, too.

"Did you sleep?" she asked, stretching.

"Apparently." He scrubbed both hands over the stubble shadowing his face. "Last I knew, we were less than halfway home."

Home. The word never sounded so good. Especially after the scare they'd had.

"Relax," Brown had shouted from the cockpit a few minutes after takeoff. "Bastards must have punctured the fuselage back near the equipment bay. We're good. Air cabin pressure's fine. Oxygen is fine."

They hadn't lost an engine. They hadn't lost their hydraulics. And he didn't need to turn around or make an emergency landing at another airport, he assured them after a thorough check of all of his systems.

Their relief had been outdistanced only by fatigue. And they weren't done yet. Although the direct flight on the G-550 cut the normal flight time by eight hours and they were almost home, they still were a long way from finishing what Joe had started.

"We can go to my apartment," Stephanie said as she buckled up in the seat beside Joe.

"Too far," he said.

"Hotel?" she suggested. Mike and Ty planned to book rooms at a hotel near the airport while they waited for the repairs on the G-550 to be completed.

He smiled. "I've got a better idea."

Joe looked weary and tense behind the wheel as they sped across D.C. in the black SUV that had been waiting for them in long-term parking. While Mike dealt with scheduling the G-550 for repairs—a tough trick at midnight, with skeleton crews on duty—and since it was a nippy twenty degrees and Stephanie and Joe were dressed for the heat they'd just left, Ty had trotted out to the lot and brought the car around.

She was wrapped tight in a warm winter parka— there'd been one for each of them waiting in the SUV—and still Stephanie shivered. "Rafe thought of everything. Even the parkas."

"Those were most likely B.J.'s doing," Joe said as

he checked his rearview, switched lanes, and made a right.

Stephanie recognized the neighborhood. "We're going to Gabe and Jenna's?"

He nodded.

Of all the guys on the BOI team, Joe was probably the closest with Gabe. They were both big men, both quiet men. And while they'd all been through the fire, these two probably carried the most scars: Gabe's physical— he'd lost a leg to shrapnel when he'd saved Jenna from a bomb blast in Buenos Aires—and Joe's emotional.

"I talked with Jenna last week, just before she left for Wyoming. She was going to take the baby and spend a little time with her parents."

Little Ali Lynn was two months old, had come into the world a squalling seven pounds, eleven ounces, just in time for Christmas, and had reduced one of the fiercest warriors in the Western hemisphere to Jell-O. Gabe had been pure putty the moment her tiny pink fist had clamped around his little finger.

At any rate, Jenna was out west, and they didn't know where Gabe was—only that he was out of the country and still out of touch.

"Need to make a quick stop," Joe said and pulled into the parking lot of a twenty-four-hour convenience store. "Sit tight. Get warm. I'll be right back."

Stephanie huddled deeper into the navy blue parka, steeling herself against the rush of frigid air when he opened the door and got out.

Her mind had been running at warp speed ever since

they'd landed. Mike had purchased throwaway phones for all of them and they'd exchanged numbers before they'd parted, but she still needed to get in contact with Rhonda. She needed her laptop and her software programs so she could get her search programs set up. And she was worried about B.J.

Because Dalmage had no way of knowing that she was involved—thank God she'd used a fake name at his Freetown office—they decided it was finally safe for her to turn on her own personal cell phone. When she found a message from Rafe asking her to call ASAP, she was glad she had.

Rafe had been preoccupied but eager to talk to her.

"We found odds and ends. Nothing we've been able to tie together yet," he said when she asked about their search into Dalmage's background. "And we're fresh out of time here." Rafe had sounded anxious. "B.J.'s in labor. Though she promised she wouldn't, she waited too damn long to tell me," he'd added, frustration mixed in with pride. "I swear, if she had her way, she'd be clenching a piece of leather between her teeth and squatting by a riverbank. We're on the way to the hospital now."

That was B.J. She was as tough as nails and could out-stubborn a mule. Stephanie couldn't stop a smile. "Is she doing okay?"

"She's swearing like a storm trooper, but she's not threatening to take a knife to any of my important parts yet. So I think it's safe to say she's doing okay."

Despite everything, she'd laughed. "Give her my love. And tell her to behave herself."

"Please don't make me tell her that," he pleaded. "She'll hurt me."

She'd laughed again, picturing the fiery blonde who took advice about as well as a stone floated.

When Joe had motioned for her that they had to get going, she'd sobered abruptly. "Rafe. I hate to ask you this, but when can you send me what you've got on Dalmage?"

"Already did. It's encrypted, so it's safe until you download it. Gotta go, *cara*. I'll be in touch."

That conversation had been over an hour ago. Not that she expected word anytime soon, but Stephanie was both eager and anxious for B.J. And envious. What she and Rafe had together—the give, the take, the fire, the burn—it was the kind of love that inspired songs and books and movies. For that matter, all of the BOIs seemed to have found that special connection. Gabe and Jenna, Sam and Abbie, Johnny D and Crystal, then just last year, Wyatt and Sophie had figured out the magic formula. Even Doc, formerly a confirmed bachelor, seemed well settled and deeply in love with Val. And how could she not look toward Nate and Juliana as a shining example of what love could endure and still evolve to something strong and lasting and magical?

The driver's side door opened and Joe slid back inside with another blast of cold air. He handed her a sack full of groceries.

"You okay?" he asked, pausing before shifting into reverse to search her face under the dome light.

Was she okay?

No. She was not okay. She wanted what her friends had. She didn't have any idea if Joe would ever be able to open up to her, to lay the groundwork for the kind of relationship that would sustain them both for the long haul.

"I'm fine." She tried not to let the simple, domestic act—Joe shopping for groceries and handing them to her like they were Mr. and Mrs. Couple—send her into a funk that would only feed her brief pity party.

She was not going there again. She didn't want to be the kind of woman who did.

When he kept staring, concern etched on his strong face, she said brightly, "I hope you've got a frozen pizza in here."

"Pepperoni," he said with a smile, because he knew it was her favorite, then shifted into reverse. "There's also milk, eggs, bacon, bread, OJ, ice cream bars, and cola."

"You're the best shopper ever. Let's fix some of everything."

A few minutes later, they parked in the underground garage of the high-security apartment complex. Joe punched in a series of security codes that got them into the building, then the elevator, and finally inside Gabe and Jenna's tenth-floor apartment.

Stephanie knew apartment 10C well. She and Jenna had spent a lot of time here together—many times, like now, in the wee hours of the morning—waiting anxiously for word that the guys had made it back safely from a mission.

She walked into the kitchen and set the sack of groceries on the counter as Joe turned on lights and hiked up the thermostat. The large, open loft-apartment had a spacious living area that opened directly to the dining room and angled left to a big galley kitchen filled with contemporary cherry cabinets, gleaming stainless steel appliances, and black granite countertops.

French doors behind the dining table to the left of the kitchen opened to a terrace that ran the width of the apartment. In the spring, Jenna filled every nook and cranny with potted plants and blooming flowers. This spring, Stephanie suspected, the terrace would also be home to a playpen.

But now the dark slate tile was covered with several inches of snow and the comfy lounge furniture was stored away. Stephanie settled the cold food in the fridge, then, hugging her bare arms against the chill, walked over to the terrace doors. Ten stories below only a smattering of cars braved the streets, moving at a snail's pace in the freshly plowed snow while a new shower of fluffy white flakes drifted down, intent on undermining the snowplow's best efforts.

It had been on a night like this that Joe had come to her apartment, then dropped his bombshell and left her. God. Had it only been a little less than six weeks ago? It felt like an eternity had passed.

She felt Joe's presence behind her, looked over her shoulder, and saw by the look on his face that he wanted to talk.

She didn't. Not yet.

"I'm going to go find a sweater," she said with an exaggerated shiver, and headed toward the hallway leading to the master bedroom. "Want me to find something of Gabe's for you to wear?"

He looked a little haunted but also a little relieved, and didn't press her. "No. I keep a couple of changes of clothes in the guest bedroom. I'm going to hit the shower," he added. "I've been thinking about hot water and a shave ever since we touched down."

"Good idea."

"You want to shower first?" he offered.

"We can both shower. I'll take the master bathroom. You can use the guest bath."

Gabe and Jenna's walk-in shower was large enough to accommodate a marching band, but Stephanie headed down the hall by herself.

It wasn't that she didn't want to be with him. Wasn't that she didn't ache with arousal at the thought of taking him to her bed. She wanted it fiercely. But somewhere over that sack of groceries, she'd made a decision.

No matter how badly she wanted him, no matter how badly he wanted her, she felt too vulnerable right now. She needed to leave sex off the table until they'd exposed Dalmage and ended this nightmare.

Whether she could draw that line and not cross it until there was nothing to distract them from working this through—or, she added soberly, walking away—she didn't know.

She really didn't know.

She reached into the shower, turned on the faucet, then stripped while the water warmed up. She didn't want to walk away. But she would. She stepped into the stall and tipped her face up to the steaming spray.

She would walk away and not look back if he couldn't give her what she wanted. What she deserved. What he needed to give, if he were ever to move past the darkness and into the light.

19

Joe was munching on a piece of crisp bacon and stirring a skillet full of scrambled eggs when he heard Stephanie enter the kitchen.

"Smells like cholesterol heaven," she said with a smile.

"Sorry, I started without you." He extended the plate of bacon.

She snatched up a piece like it was candy. "He who cooks, eats first—and you can use the calories."

Yeah. He could. His black T-shirt didn't exactly hang on him, but the XXL usually fit glove-tight. And even with his belt tightened a couple of notches, his cammo pants still hung a little low on his hips. Now that his gut was able to handle real food, he was going to pack in the cals like there was no tomorrow to get back up to fighting weight.

Until the ribs healed a little more, though, hitting the gym was going to have to wait.

"Oh. My. God. This is ambrosia." Stephanie's eyes were closed in ecstasy as she ate the bacon. "It's going to be a long time before I'll want to eat rice again," she added, opening a cupboard and pulling out two plates. "What can I do?"

Two pieces of toast popped out of the toaster. "You can butter those if you want."

"Hope you like it slathered. I'm in a mood for indulging."

She found a knife and went to work while he scooped eggs onto the plates, then carried them to the table he'd already set with silverware, juice, and milk.

"You're just a model of efficiency, aren't you?" She sat across from him and opened a napkin onto her lap.

"What I am is hungry. Pass the salt, would you?"

Then he dug in and tried not to think about things that would get him into trouble. Like the way she smelled, shower fresh and flowery. Or how she looked, a soft blue sweater hugging her breasts and a pair of Jenna's well-worn jeans fitting her like a second skin.

Her hair was damp and she'd woven it into a thick braid that lay over her left shoulder, its tail reaching the top of her breast. She looked wholesome and as happy as a lumberjack, digging in without an ounce of restraint, and Jesus God, it hit him right in the solar plexus how close he'd come to losing her.

A wave of light-headedness swamped him. He stood abruptly, pushed away from the table, and walked over to the terrace doors. He stood with his forehead pressed against the cold glass, his heart hammering like a battering ram, his gut knotted so tight he could barely breathe.

He closed his eyes, tried to get it the fuck together . . . but images flashed like strobes behind his eyelids.

A booted foot kicking him in the ribs as he lay curled on the floor in the stench and the filth. One hundred eighty-four iron bars. Waking in the dead of night to the hiss of a viper coiled inches from his face. The truck rolling over with him trapped inside. A pool of blood beneath a holy man's head.

And superimposed over it all was the memory of Stephanie in the jail—and God, oh, God, the things they would have done to her.

"Joe."

Her whisper jarred him back to the present.

"Joe."

The touch of her hand on his back settled him.

"It's okay. You're okay. We're okay. Come on," she said gently. "Your eggs are getting cold."

He reached for her hand; waited for her to meet his eyes. "I know you don't want to hear this. But I'm sorry, Steph. I am so, *so* sorry that I dragged you into the middle of that nightmare. Jesus. If . . . if something had happened to you—"

"Nothing did. Nothing's going to. Now come on. You need to eat. We both do."

Her fingers linked with his, and squeezed. "We'll eat, get a few hours of real sleep, and then we'll figure out how to bring Dalmage to his knees."

"I was scared to death for you!" Rhonda rushed into the apartment at seven that morning and hugged Stephanie hard before setting her away and leveling a scowl. "Don't you *ever* fucking scare me like that again, and before you ask, no, I was not followed. All this cloak-and-dagger crap is creeping me out. What is going on?"

"First of all, I love you, too, sweetie. Thanks for coming on such short notice—and for taking . . . vacation?"

"Sick leave," Rhonda said, faking a theatrical cough.

Steph squeezed her friend's shoulders as she helped her out of her coat. "And let me just say? Wow. Thanks for not making me feel like wallpaper."

"And let me just say? Wow. Thanks for not making me feel like wallpaper."

It was rare that Stephanie ever saw Rhonda when she was not turned out in full camera-ready mode. Even in her pink Juicy sweat suit, ponytail, and makeup-free face, though, she was adorable.

"This is what you get when you call at the butt crack of dawn. You want glam-shot material, you've got to give me at least two hours' prep time."

"Which we don't have," Stephanie said, picking up the two laptops Rhonda had brought with her.

Stephanie wasn't certain what had compelled her to leave her laptop, with Rhonda, but it had been a majorly insightful decision.

"Thank you, God, is that coffee I smell?"

"And improvised breakfast pizza." Stephanie headed for the kitchen and poured Rhonda a cup. "Joe scrambled a ton of eggs and fried a couple pounds of bacon last night before we turned in. I layered the leftovers onto a pepperoni pizza that should be ready any minute."

The oven timer dinged just then.

"God, I'm good." She grinned and hunted up a pair of oven mitts.

"So," Rhonda said, leaning her hips against the counter and warming her hands on her coffee mug while she watched Stephanie slice into the pizza. "Where *is* Walk-Away Joe?"

Stephanie glanced over her shoulder. "Be nice. And don't let your jaw hit the floor when you see him."

"Why? Does he have a gaping hole in his chest from where you ripped his heart out and stomped it? And I ask that with nothing but hope in my own heart."

"I said, be nice." Stephanie turned to face her friend. "He wasn't in very good shape when we got him out of that prison. He still has a way to go to recover."

"Oh." Rhonda actually looked contrite. "Is he okay?"

"He will be." She hoped. "How many slices?" she asked, shifting the conversation away from Joe.

Last night, after they'd eaten and cleaned up the kitchen together in a careful silence, Stephanie had said a quick good night and disappeared into the master bedroom.

She'd lain in bed and questioned her decision until she'd finally fallen asleep. She'd been tempted a hundred times to join him in his bed and just hold him. If anyone needed holding, it was Joe. But holding would have led to caressing, then to kissing, then to making love. And as good as it would have felt, as much as they both needed the comfort, the pleasure, the release, it would have been the wrong thing to do in the long run.

"Steph?"

She realized with a start that she'd zoned out on Rhonda. "Sorry. What?"

"So where is he?" Rhonda had taken her coffee and a plate with a slice of pizza to the dining room table and was in the process of booting up her laptop.

"Still sleeping." She hadn't heard a sound since she'd gotten up. It had been after three when they'd finally turned in. She hoped it meant he was simply catching up on some much-needed rest, and not that he'd lain awake too long last night like she had.

"Good stuff," Rhonda said digging in. "Spin class, here I come. In the meantime, why am I here? What's going on?"

"It's big," Stephanie warned. "Really, really big."

"Ho-kay." Rhonda searched her face. "Care to give me a point of reference?"

"Greer Dalmage." Stephanie's heart picked up a beat just saying his name out loud.

"The U.S. liaison to the UWAN," Rhonda said, her eyes narrowed as she dug the information out of her memory banks. "And I just heard he's on the president's short list for the sec of state position. What about him?" she prompted.

Stephanie laced her hands together on the table. "Dalmage is responsible for Bryan's death."

Rhonda inclined her head as if she hadn't heard her right. Apparently the look on Stephanie's face convinced her that she had.

"Responsible? As in, he was the one who screwed up the mission?"

"As in, there wasn't any screwup. Dalmage was a colonel on the ground when Task Force Mercy was there. He ordered the RUF attack on the guys. None of the team was supposed to survive that night."

Rhonda's face paled. She sat back in her chair, eyes wide and wary. "Whoa. Wait. A colonel in the U.S. Army ordered an attack on his own forces? Did you just hear yourself?"

Fifteen minutes later, after Stephanie spelled it out as clearly as she could, and Rhonda had pumped her with questions, Rhonda knew everything that Stephanie knew. More important, she believed her.

"Oh, honey." Rhonda reached across the table and covered Stephanie's hands with hers. "That *sonofabitch!* We can't let him get away with it," she said decisively. "What do you need from me?"

"Anything and everything you can find on Dalmage. Any activity in foreign markets, especially Sierra Leone. Any business partners. Links with foreign governments. Financials. *Anything* that you can dig up."

"Going back how far?"

Stephanie had already booted up her laptop and opened her e-mail. She waited while hundreds of messages filed into her in-box. She was looking for only one: Rafe's message. "Let's go back fifteen years. That will get us within the window of time when Task Force Mercy was deployed in Sierra Leone."

"You got it."

She forwarded Rafe's post to Rhonda. "Use this as a starting point."

"Wow. They've been busy," Rhonda said after reading the e-mail. "Dalmage is gonna fry. We're gonna make sure of it."

After an hour of digging, finessing their programs, and cajoling search engines, they knew they were on to something.

His old gray sweats felt huge and hung low on his hips when Joe walked into the kitchen on bare feet, yawning and scrubbing a hand over his head to wake himself up. The cobwebs were thick and murky; he'd be damn glad when he could get by on short combat naps again.

"Okay, not that I mind a mostly naked man in the morning, but um, you look like shit."

He stopped, blinked, and focused on the blonde in the hot-pink sweats. "Rhonda," he said with a nod and shuffled on over to the coffeepot. "And you look—"

"Don't say it. We'll both be happier for it." She leaned back in her chair and gave him another once-over—like he was a piece of meat she didn't find particularly appetizing.

He probably shouldn't admit it, but Rhonda intimidated him—just a little. She was too gorgeous, too confident, and for his money, too aggressive. But she was a good friend to Stephanie, so that made her okay with him. He just wished she wouldn't always look at him like she was the head of a hiring committee and he was on the bottom of her call-back list.

"Where's Stephanie?"

"Right here."

He turned to see her walk into the kitchen. She was dressed in the same soft blue sweater and jeans as last night, but she'd unbraided her hair. It fell over her shoulder in soft waves. Soft sweater, soft hair. But nothing about her eyes was soft this morning. She was focused, serious, and excited.

"What's up?"

"Get your coffee. Then grab some pizza and sit. We've got him, Joe. We've got Dalmage."

His heart gave a mule kick and he headed straight to the table. "Tell me."

Stephanie filled a coffee mug and scooped three pieces of pizza onto a plate, then set both down in front of him with an expectant look.

He picked up a slice and took a bite to satisfy her. "Now talk."

"You'll have to bear with us for a bit, okay? We're going to take a circular route to get you there."

He nodded and, prompted by her warning look, picked up the pizza again. "Go."

"We've discovered that a company by the name of EXnergy made a major land purchase in Sierra Leone several years ago."

"To the tune of several hundred acres in the Pampana River Valley concession," Rhonda added, her voice animated.

Joe swallowed, then wiped his mouth with a napkin. "How many years ago?"

Stephanie met his gaze, held it. "Fifteen."

Bingo. "The same time we were running our missions there."

Stephanie sat down and turned her laptop toward him so he could see the screen. "Only here's the deal. EXnergy doesn't really exist."

Didn't surprise him. "So it's a dummy company?"

"Close," Rhonda jumped in. "A dummy company is set up to serve as a cover for one or more companies. It looks real on paper but lacks the capacity to function independently, because its whole goal is to conceal true ownership and avoid taxes."

"Technically," Stephanie explained, "EXnergy is a *front* company. It was set up to look indy when, in fact, it's controlled by an actual company that doesn't want to be associated or identified as being associated with it. The real company can use the front company to act for it without the actions being attributed back to the true owners."

"So you're saying the CIA has their fingers in this pie?" The CIA set up front companies all the time. They'd want people on the ground in someplace like Libya or Pakistan, so they'd set up a legit charity there and put operatives in place with a plausible background story, occupations, whatever.

"*Like* the CIA," Stephanie said, glancing at Rhonda. "But *not* the CIA." She looked at him expectantly.

"Dalmage," he said, reading between the lines. "Dalmage is EXnergy?"

"We're pretty certain, yeah. We have to dig a little deeper to tie it up with a pretty pink bow, but yeah, Dalmage is EXnergy."

He forgot all about the pizza. "So what's on this land? Have you been able to nail that down?"

"Oh, yeah." Rhonda looked like a cat that had swallowed the entire contents of a goldfish bowl. "Huge deposits of large scale REEs."

"Rare earth elements," Stephanie clarified. "Lanthanum, scandium, thulium, cerium, dysprosium, hafnium, lutetium, niobium, neodymium, praesodymium, tantalum, and zircon. Seventeen in all. All in commercially exploitable grades."

"Exploitable for making what?" he asked, feeding off their excitement.

"REEs are critical in making green technology—like the batteries that power hybrid cars, eco-friendly wind turbines, low-energy lightbulbs—even fiber-optic cable and missile guidance systems, and many other energy technologies," Stephanie said.

"What makes the Pampana River Valley deposits so valuable," Rhonda went on, "is that China produces ninety-seven percent of the entire world's supply . . . and guess what? They aren't selling their REEs to anyone. They're using them all themselves."

"Which leaves a green energy world in need of another supply," Stephanie said unnecessarily.

"So," Joe said, thinking out loud, "Dalmage's foresight, in the face of China's global domination, makes the Sierra Leone property limitless in value."

"In the trillions of dollars, at least. Dalmage is holding the proverbial golden goose in his hands," Rhonda agreed.

"Only one problem for him," Stephanie said. "Ethically, morally, and legally, since Dalmage was a representative of the U.S. government at the time of the purchase, and he's now a U.S. diplomat, it's strictly forbidden for him to profit from his position."

"Which means he had to hide his involvement," Rhonda summed it up.

"So EXnergy was born." Joe met Stephanie's eyes, the fire of revenge burning hot in his gut. "And Bryan died."

20

Stephanie watched Joe push away from the table and walk over to the terrace doors. He'd grown very quiet. As it always did, the tattoo running down the center of his back moved her. Even more, the lingering bruises and the very obvious fact of his barbaric treatment made her chest ache. He'd risked all to avenge Bryan's death, and had almost lost all. And for far too long, she hadn't believed him.

"I'm so sorry, Joe. I should have believed you long ago."

"You weren't the only one with doubts," he said, and slowly turned and met her eyes. "I had them, too."

She saw forgiveness there. And understanding, and other emotions she couldn't let herself explore until she was on more solid ground herself.

"You always knew it was Dalmage?" Rhonda asked.

"No." Joe glanced at her. "Not until last year, when I saw his picture on the wall in Marcus Chamberlin's office."

"And from that you pieced it together?"

"Something like that. Where did Dalmage come up with the cash to fund this purchase?"

"That was our question, too." Her cheeks flushed, Rhonda leaned forward in her chair. "This kind of money excites me," she said with a grin. "And we're talking tons of money. Dalmage had to pony up millions in up-front capital. His family has a certain amount of wealth, but not anywhere near enough to back him on this. And nothing we turned up in his financials says he could have gathered that kind of dough, either."

"So it seems he found himself some backers," Stephanie continued. "We haven't nailed it down yet, but we've been back-tracing several money trails that lead to some pretty bad guys in pretty rogue nations. Qaddafi-type bad guys. Kim Jong Il bad guys.

"And that's not all. We got access to satellite data on the mining site. They're trying to hide it, but the mines are active. They're set to start mass production of REEs possibly within a year."

"So, Dalmage is heavily indebted to these nations. Nations that, among other things, support Islamic extremists in their terrorist activities." Joe mulled it over aloud as he paced back to the coffeepot. "The question then becomes, how does he intend to settle his debts?"

Joe supposed he should feel relief. He wasn't crazy. He'd been right.

But all he felt was numb as he silently left Stephanie and Rhonda clicking away on their laptops. Shouldn't there be more than this?

For fifteen years he'd carried the weight of Bry's death on his shoulders. For fifteen years, he'd questioned his actions, his decisions, his failures. He hadn't saved Bryan. He hadn't saved his brother, Bobby.

He wasn't even sure that he'd saved himself.

He'd been right about Dalmage, yet he felt nothing but empty.

He stripped off his clothes and hit the shower again, turning the water as hot as it would go, driven by an overwhelming compulsion to wash away the stench of Dalmage's treachery that had dragged him down for most of his adult life.

He wanted to feel righteous, soul-cleansing anger. He wanted to swear and roar and punch his fist into something deliciously solid and destructible . . . but all he felt was weary.

Jesus, he felt so fucking weary.

He planted his palms against the shower wall, hung his head between his arms, and willed the steaming water pouring over his body to cleanse him. To heal him. To make him feel like he was more than a used-up, burned-out shell of a man.

He stood there until the water ran cold, until he was shivering beneath the icy spray. Head down. Eyes closed. Eyes burning. Eyes wet.

He didn't hear her come into the bathroom.

He didn't react when she reached in and turned off the water.

And he sure as hell didn't look at her. Couldn't look at her when she wrapped a towel around his shoulders and gently guided him out of the shower stall, then silently eased him down onto the edge of the tub.

He couldn't *do* anything but acquiesce as she stood between his thighs, laid her cheek on top of his lowered head, and held him while his shoulders shook. While he shed hot, raging tears for his brother whom he couldn't save, for *her* brother, whom Dalmage killed, for the years he'd lost, for the lives he'd taken. For the love he had no right to expect from this woman, who held him together while every force in the universe tried to rip him apart.

Rhonda stretched and yawned and worked the kinks out of her neck after several hours spent bending over her laptop. All the while, Stephanie had felt her friends curious glances.

"So what happened to wonder boy?" Rhonda asked.

Stephanie scrolled slowly through several news releases concerning the upcoming presidential appointment for the secretary of state position, which Dalmage seemed destined to receive. Something was orbiting around in the back of her mind—something to do with that appointment, something that hadn't quite jelled.

"He's sleeping," she said absently.

Rhonda cleared her throat. "Just how sick is he?"

Stephanie's shoulders sagged as she exhaled and leaned back in her chair.

"He's not sick," she said. Not physically. But his heart and his soul needed intensive care. As painful as it had been to witness his anguish, she knew that it was the first step in his healing process.

"He was starved and beaten daily. The conditions were beyond barbaric."

Rhonda didn't press for details. "This hasn't exactly been a piece of cake for you, either, sweetie," her friend said softly.

Stephanie loved Rhonda for her concern. "I was only there for a few days. He thought he was going to die there. When I saw him the first time, I was amazed that he hadn't already."

She became lost in memories of a beaten, ravaged Joe curled into himself on that filthy cell floor.

"It's going to be okay now." Rhonda placed a hand over hers and squeezed gently.

"Yeah," Stephanie agreed and gave Rhonda a bracing smile. "It's going to be fine. We just need to figure out the rest of this puzzle."

Rhonda made a big show of flexing her fingers over the keyboard. "With these babies on the job, Dalmage doesn't stand a chance."

Speaking of babies, Rafe had called. B.J.'s labor had stopped, so they were back home on hold again, waiting for the blessed event.

"You want more coffee?" Stephanie pushed away from the table with her empty mug and headed for the coffeepot.

"Nah, I'd better back off the caffeine for a while. Whoa," Rhonda added, leaning in close to her screen. "This is interesting."

Stephanie filled her mug and returned to look over Rhonda's shoulder. Her heart started pounding as she read the obituary Rhonda had uncovered, and that nebulous cloud of an idea that had been swirling around in her mind suddenly took shape and form.

"Hold on. Look at this." She scrambled back to her laptop, clicked around until she found what she was looking for, and turned the screen so Rhonda could see it.

"Holy shit. Co-inki-dink, Sherlock?"

Stephanie shook her head. "No way in hell is that a coincidence."

"Joe's going to want to see this."

"Not yet." Stephanie started a search on all names recently mentioned as potential candidates for the secretary of state appointment. "Let's make sure we're really on to something."

"We are *totally* on to something."

"I still want a little more proof."

"Proof of what?" Joe asked.

Stephanie's head whipped around. He was wearing those sexy, low-hanging sweatpants and tugging a T-shirt over his head. When his head popped through, his eyes were on her. Softly slumberous. A little tentative. One hundred percent male.

He looked rested. And gorgeous. And she might be imagining it, but she swore that some of his ghosts had flown off for parts unknown.

"We're not sure yet," she said as he crossed to the table and pulled up a chair beside her.

"Tell me what you're not yet sure of."

He leaned in close, smelling of sleep and soap and an indefinable essence she'd always secretly thought of as Mo-Joe. He had the mojo, all right. Just the scent of him made her heart fluttery.

And when he laid his arm across the back of her chair, then casually rested his hand on her burning shoulder muscles, kneading softly, she was damn glad she was sitting down.

"Patience," she insisted and forced herself to concentrate on her search. "Give us ten more minutes and we'll have something you're really going to want to hear."

He stood up again. "Might as well make myself useful. Who's hungry?"

Rhonda shot him a quick grin. "Are you taking orders?"

"The menu's a little limited, but if it's for bacon and cheese omelets, then yeah."

"Works for me," Rhonda said.

"Which is a good thing, since eggs are pretty much the extent of my culinary skills."

"It's a BOI thing," Stephanie told Rhonda, and noticed that her friend's appreciative gaze was locked on Joe's butt as he ambled toward the kitchen on bare feet.

"Need I mention I already called dibs?" Stephanie asked in a low voice.

Rhonda sighed theatrically, then whispered, "Just lookin'. Does this mean you two are a thing again?"

Stephanie tightened her lips. "The jury's still out on that."

"For you, maybe. Not for him. He is totally, uncategorically in love with you." Rhonda glanced back at her laptop.

Stephanie's curiosity got the best of her. "And you know this how?"

Rhonda cut a quick look toward the kitchen. "Maybe you haven't been paying attention to the way he looks at you, but I have."

Oh, she'd been paying attention all right. To the way he'd touched her shoulder. To the vulnerability she saw in his eyes when he met hers. The signs were good, but the truth would be in the telling.

"Read it and weep." Rhonda shoved the list of names she and Stephanie had compiled in front of Joe as he joined them at the table, his plate heaped with a steaming, aromatic concoction of eggs, cheese, and bacon.

He'd already served them their omelets, buttered toast, and orange juice. Stephanie watched him intently as he picked up the sheet of paper, brought a forkful of eggs halfway to his mouth, then set it back on his plate.

"What's this?" he asked without looking up from the list.

"Recognize any of the names?" Stephanie's pulse jumped as she watched him.

"All of them. Carson: senator from Ohio. Arms committee. Krenshaw: past Majority Whip. Alberts . . ." He closed his eyes, trying to remember. "Budget oversight and then foreign affairs. But, wait—Carson is dead, right?"

"Car accident several months ago," Stephanie confirmed, then dropped her bomb. "Krenshaw and Alberts are also dead."

He sat forward in his chair, the tension in his big body palpable. "What?"

"Krenshaw died just last month. Mugging turned to murder. Alberts had a heart attack—or so the obit says."

He narrowed his eyes and glanced at the list again. "And the others?"

"Dead. Dead. And dead," Rhonda said flatly. "Except for Williams and Jacobson. Both were recently admitted to long-term care facilities in the veggie unit."

He frowned. "This says Williams is forty-seven. Jacobson is fifty-eight. And you're telling me they're in nursing homes?"

"Williams had a paralyzing stroke. Jacobson had a sudden onset of dementia."

The temperature in the apartment seemed to drop to an icy chill as Stephanie waited for Joe to make the connection.

"Jesus." He dragged a hand over his jaw. "They were all once on the short list for secretary of state, weren't they?"

"Yeah," she said quietly. "And now there's only one front-runner."

Stephanie knew the moment the answer to all their questions finally rose to the surface.

"That's how Dalmage plans to repay his debts," he concluded. "He takes all viable candidates out of the running, becomes sec of state, then grants certain favors to his backers—like turning a blind eye to their genocidal rampages. He lets his despot bankers run roughshod over U.S. interests overseas, and a good time is had by all."

Stephanie stood to pace, her anger filling her with

restless energy. "He's been planning and positioning himself for years."

"So there may be even more dead senators who would still be alive if Dalmage hadn't targeted them," Joe said.

"And no one has any reason to suspect Dalmage," Stephanie stated grimly, "let alone be able to prove that he had a hand in the murders."

"Or to prove that any of them *were* murdered." Joe grabbed her hand as she went by, settling her with a look.

"He's good, no doubt about it. One of the potential nominees died in a 'freak' accident at his home," Rhonda said. "Just last week, a scandal broke about another one of the potential nominees, linking him to a child pornography ring. He ended up supposedly committing suicide."

"One by one, Dalmage has taken them out," Stephanie said quietly.

"And we prove this, how?" asked Rhonda.

"We need to talk to the families of the victims," Joe said decisively. "Find out what they know, if anything. Someone's got to have seen something. Heard something."

They each picked up a phone and started making calls.

21

Dalmage checked his watch as the commercial jet approached Dulles Airport. It was closing in on 3:30 p.m. It would be dark in another two hours. A light layer of snow covered the runway below, and toy-size plows and trucks scurried back and forth shoving snow into piles.

He thought about Saidu Bangura. The way the fat man's face had swelled, the way his eyes had bulged, the way his pork sausage fingers had gripped at the garrote Dalmage had slipped around his throat while his paid attendant stood guard with an assault rifle leveled point-blank at Bangura's chest.

His men had found Bangura's wife. He'd made the police lieutenant watch them kill her first, of course. Dalmage had watched unblinking as she had screamed for mercy, and Bangura had pleaded for her life. He'd felt a satisfying sense of retribution when the bullet had blown her brains all over Bangura's garishly furnished living room. He regretted that the children had managed to escape. Bangura would no doubt have promised to do any number of humiliating things to spare them.

They were better off orphans.

And he was better off with the inept officer dead and gone.

Bangura had lied. A fatal mistake. He'd been a dead man the moment Green and his accomplice had escaped the country, but to lie? To tell him that Green and company were dead? That deception could not go unpunished. So of course the wife had had to die, too.

"Mr. Dalmage?"

The flight attendant's voice drew him out of his thoughts.

"We've landed, sir. Do you need assistance with your carry-on?"

"I'm fine," he said gruffly, unbuckled his seat belt, and stood.

First order of business: locate Joseph Green.

Second order of business: eliminate him.

"It's all about order, right, son?"

He could still hear his father's voice in his head. Would always hear his father's voice. Always feel his belt against his back.

"There is no room for failure. There is only one acceptable outcome: victory. So suck it up, boy. Quit your whimpering. One day you'll thank me for making a man out of you. A man I can be proud of."

"I'll show that warped son of a bitch," he muttered under his breath as he retrieved his attaché case from the overhead bin. Just like he'd show Green, who had become an albatross around his neck.

Green couldn't have discovered that he was behind

the Task Force Mercy ambush. But on the off chance he had figured it out, there was no way in hell he could prove it. No way Green could tie him to anything incriminating. Green could squawk but he couldn't prove a damn thing.

Green's integrity quotient would have the credibility of Bernie Madoff by the time Dalmage was finished with his smear campaign against the rogue former CIA agent who had gone off the deep end.

So he was not concerned about Green as he walked down the Jetway toward the terminal.

The TV news report that greeted him after his arrival at his Georgetown brownstone, however, *did* concern him. "No. This couldn't be happening." He stared at the TV, paralyzed with shock.

He felt his face grow hot as the report ended. Felt his heart muscles constrict so quickly he didn't have time to pop a nitro. Excruciating pain lanced through his chest.

His knees buckled and he dropped into an armchair. His shaking fingers fumbled around inside his chest pocket for his nitro—and dropped the bottle.

"Goddamnit!" he roared to the cold, empty house.

He fell to his hands and knees as the tiny tablets scattered all over the polished hardwood floor. He was whimpering by the time he managed to find one and tuck it under his tongue, and sobbing by the time the clutching grip of angina pain finally let go of his chest.

"Goddamnit," he muttered over and over, fighting the encroaching sense that his carefully laid plans teetered on the edge of an abyss.

It took the better part of fifteen minutes to get himself back together, to rally his resolve, to devise a plan for dealing with this latest setback.

"There is only one acceptable outcome."

He had to find Ann Tompkins, fast.

He had fifteen minutes before the offices at the Department of Justice closed for the day. He picked up his phone. A congratulatory call was in order, after all. A personal call, directly from him.

After maneuvering the maze of automated prompts, he cursed viciously when he was sent straight to voice mail.

"You've reached the desk of Ann Tompkins. I'll be out of the office until Monday the twenty-eighth, but will return your call as soon as I can. If this is an emergency, please dial extension 5032 and ask for my assistant, Erin Clemons."

He punched in the number. A young, perky, looking-for-advancement voice answered on the second ring.

"Yes, Ms. Clemons. I'm trying to reach Ann Tompkins and was given your extension. I'm hoping you can help me out and tell me how to get in touch with her."

"May I ask who's calling, please?" the judicious Ms. Clemons chirped.

"Forgive me. Matthew Bridgefield. Ann's doctor."

"Oh. Her *doctor?*"

"I don't mean to be abrupt, Ms. Clemons, but I really need to get in touch with her. I've tried both her home and the cell number she gave me and all I'm getting is voice mail. I'm hoping someone at her office can help."

"Dr. Bridgefield, I'm sorry. I'm not at liberty to give out private information regarding Mrs. Tompkins."

"Of course." He made a show of sounding defeated. "I understand and frankly, I anticipated you wouldn't be able to help me. I'm under strict confidentiality restrictions myself." He paused for dramatic effect. "In this case, however, I need to make an exception. This is a bit of a medical emergency. I really do need to get in touch with Ann regarding her test results."

"Oh. Oh, dear. I hope . . . goodness. Is she okay?"

He smiled. She was hooked. "I'm not at liberty to discuss her medical condition, but it is of the utmost urgency that I reach her. I know you can't help, but can you think of anyone else . . . anyone who might not be bound by the same confidentiality restrictions?"

"Have you tried her daughter?"

"No, you're my first call. But I think that Ann may have given me her daughter's number. Hold on, let me check. I'm not much of a note taker, I'm afraid. Oh. Here it is. Two-oh-two area code, correct?"

"No, Stephanie lives near New Carrolton. That's a 301 code."

"Damn," he muttered. "If this isn't her number then it must be at home somewhere. I hope my wife didn't figure it for a scrap and toss it."

He got silence. A silence that he hoped meant she was reconsidering.

"You didn't get this from me, okay?" she said, finally giving in, knowing she shouldn't yet wanting to help. "I have Stephanie's cell phone number."

"Thank you, Erin," he said after she gave him the number. "You did a good thing. Good night."

He disconnected, then let himself have one brief moment to gloat. He was back on his game.

"I have something for you," he said when he reached Carl Wilson on one of the many throwaway cells he kept on hand to ensure his calls couldn't be traced back to him. Stephanie Tompkins would have no need for such precautions. He was banking on her personal cell phone to lead him to her mother. Calling her was out of the question, of course, but finding her was essential.

Wilson had been on his payroll since the beginning. He was loyal, efficient, got results, and didn't ask questions. Wilson was loyal because Dalmage paid him a king's ransom for his allegiance. He was efficient because he had been trained by the U.S. military's elite forces to be the best at what he did. He got results because he enjoyed killing. And he didn't ask questions because he felt no need for justification. Wilson was a machine. Brutal, heartless, without conscience.

He gave Wilson Stephanie Tompkins's cell phone number, knowing the former CIA operative would be able to track the phone and pin down her exact location.

"She is the key to locating her mother. And Ann Tompkins's unfortunate death has become key in ensuring the endgame. Place your team on standby. You'll need to deploy at a moment's notice once you locate her."

"Consider it done."

"And Carl, I want you leading this operation. No one but the best—this is the money shot. Neither of us can afford for this mission to fail."

"Understood."

"Report when you have news I want to hear."

Stephanie, Rhonda, and Joe spent several long, disturbing hours making long, disturbing phone calls. By the end of the day Stephanie was heartsick, and 100 percent convinced that Dalmage was as dirty as atomic waste.

Most heartbreaking was her conversation with the wife of Rick Wagoner, the representative from Indiana who'd been named in a child pornography scandal. His family was adamant that it was all a lie and that his unexpected suicide wasn't a suicide at all. They just couldn't prove it.

"Dalmage has no limits." Stephanie's stomach churned with a sickening mix of shock and disgust. "He'll go to any extent to secure that appointment."

No one said a word for a long moment. Finally, Rhonda drummed her fingers on the table. "So now what?"

Stephanie looked at the clock. It was almost midnight. "Now I think we need to sleep on it." They were all drained. "We'll decide how to proceed in the morning."

Joe's jaw was clenched tight. It was clear that sleeping was the last thing on his mind.

"We're going to nail him," she said, the conviction in her tone forcing him to meet her eyes. "But we're going to do it right. We *have* to do it right," she reminded him.

He breathed deep, finally gave her a clipped nod, then walked to the terrace doors and stared silently outside.

"I'm going to hit the road." Rhonda sounded as exhausted as Stephanie felt.

"You should stay here tonight. It's late."

"Thanks, sweetie, but me and my bed . . . we have this special relationship. And I heart my *own* pillow."

Stephanie walked her to the door and hugged her hard. "Thank you. We'd still be at this if not for you."

"Is he going to be all right?" Rhonda glanced back toward Joe as she shrugged into her coat.

"I hope so."

Joe watched Stephanie give Rhonda a warm embrace, then lock the door behind her.

She looked wrung out and sad as she walked back to the dining area. But the set of her chin and her erect posture said she wasn't letting this thing beat her.

The way it had beaten him.

Humiliation washed through him. He'd bawled like a fucking baby. His face flushed hot at the memory. He'd bawled like he hadn't bawled since he'd been fifteen, sitting in that stark white hospital room wearing a sterile surgical gown, latex gloves on his hands, and a mask on his face, and lied to his kid brother, promising him that he would not let him die.

He'd been running from Bobby's ghost ever since.

He'd been running from Bry's for far too long, as well.

Bry was finally going to get retribution. Bobby . . . Bobby was just gone.

"Leave them," he said when Stephanie started clearing the dirty dishes. "I'll take care of the mess."

"You cooked," she pointed out.

"And I can clean up after myself."

"How about we do it together?"

Short of his yanking away the plates—and he had so much rage bottled up inside that he didn't dare touch her right now—she was going to have her way.

"Fine," he finally conceded. "I wash. You dry."

"Deal."

For the next several minutes the only sounds in the apartment were of water running, dishes clinking, drawers opening, pans rattling. The elephant in the room waited in the corner, rocking back and forth, trunk swinging, making it clear that no matter how hard Joe tried to ignore it, it wasn't going away.

He pulled the stopper, grabbed a dish towel, and dried his hands. All the while, he watched Stephanie avoid eye contact, give him space, give him the silence she'd decided that he needed.

"About . . . earlier . . . in the shower," he began hesitantly.

She shook her head. "Don't apologize, Joe. Not for that. Not ever for that."

Yeah. She always gave him what he needed. Even when it wasn't in her best interest.

And when he touched a hand to her hair, brushed it back away from her face, and gently turned her toward him, he couldn't stop himself from asking her for more.

She lifted her head slowly, almost shyly.

And didn't make him ask.

Didn't make him beg or plead, or spill his guts or his blood, or the part of himself that he hadn't yet figured out how to heal.

Her mouth welcomed his on a sigh when he lowered his head. Her hand reached out to his and led him to the bedroom.

Where she let him lay her down.

Where she let him slowly undress her and press his lips against the welcoming softness of each inch of satin skin he revealed.

Where he sank into the bed, then sank into her, and without making him feel guilt or regret or even wonder at the gift of her giving, she took him to a place where nothing but soft breasts, sleek limbs, and her wildly racing heart existed.

A black panel van pulled up a block away from the D.C. apartment building and parked in an empty alley. A man dressed in black got out, looped a coil of rope over his shoulder, double-checked his tool belt, and headed down the snow-covered street. Stephanie Tompkins's cell phone signal had been pinging off towers and led him straight to this address.

The target building was ten stories. His target apartment was on the ninth floor. He wasted no time scaling the building by climbing from terrace to terrace—he wasn't known as the best second-story man on the east coast for nothing—until he landed soundless on the ninth-floor balcony.

By feel, he removed his specialized tools and quickly disabled the alarm system. He taped a neat circle in the glass door near the handle, pulled his rubber mallet out of the loop in his coveralls, and gave the glass a sharp rap. The glass shattered almost soundlessly and he reached a gloved hand inside, undid the lock, and let himself in.

Once inside apartment 9C, he waited, letting his eyes adjust to the darkness cut only by a low-wattage night-light on the refrigerator door. It was enough light to guide him to the hallway. A clock ticked rhythmically in the background as he made his way across plush white carpeting to a closed door. The master bedroom.

The door opened with a soft *snick*. A man snored heavily from the right side of a king-size bed. He crept to the man's side, inserted the needle swiftly into his neck. The man's struggle was brief and quiet. He would sleep for a good twenty-four hours. Or he would die. Didn't matter. He just needed to buy some quiet time.

It took him less than five minutes to affix the contact microphones to the ceilings in each room. The mikes would pick up every nuance of conversation from apartment 10C above.

Satisfied that everything was in working order, he let himself out of the apartment through the front door and walked out of the building. All any security video would pick up was a man dressed in black with his face turned away from the camera.

In and out and back to the van in fifteen minutes.

Once he was behind the wheel, he dialed the cell number, turned on the microphone receiver, and started listening.

"It's done," he said when the man who paid him answered.

"And you were undetected?" Carl Wilson asked.

Because he was paid promptly and well, the man forgave the slur on his competence. "I was not detected. I'll be back in touch as soon as I have actionable information."

Wilson disconnected, then went back to cleaning his Kninkov, his new traveling weapon of choice. The AK-74SU had a collapsible stock and fired a smaller cartridge than the AK-47. It was compact, concealable, and controllable. Just like he suspected Ann Tompkins would be controllable when her own daughter unknowingly led him straight to her door.

22

Stephanie awoke to the sound of the wind howling outside the dark bedroom window, the weight of Joe's thigh on hers, and a massive bicep caging her in with gentle possessiveness.

So much for her line of demarcation.

But what they'd shared in this bed hadn't really been about sex. It had been about connecting. About caring. About needs that transcended the physical and delved into far stickier stuff.

Would he always be this wounded, she wondered, worried for him.

Would she always feel the need to heal him, she thought, worried for herself.

She turned her head on the pillow, still feeling stunned at the depth of his need, still feeling a love so deep and abiding, she questioned if she'd have the courage of her convictions when push came to shove.

Because she loved him, she had to stay strong. Because she loved him, she had to stay firm. He was worth the struggle. So was she. She just hoped he would realize it when the showdown came.

Tomorrow's problems would supersede everything else. Tomorrow they needed to figure out what to do about Dalmage.

Exhaustion finally tugged her back to sleep . . . until her cell phone woke her again. She turned her head deeper into the pillow, determined to let it ring.

Beside her, Joe stirred. "What the hell is that?" he mumbled.

"My cell." She snuggled closer to his side. "Ignore it."

"Not an option in my playbook." With a grunt, he pushed himself up and out of bed.

She heard him walk out of the room. Walk back. The bed dipped when he sat down and folded the cell phone into her hand.

She forced herself up on an elbow as he turned on a bedside lamp. "Hello?"

"It's a girl! Finally." It was Rafe. He sounded exalted, exhausted, and stunned. "She's beautiful, Steph. Just . . . oh, my God, screaming, squalling, immaculately beautiful."

She smiled, caught up in Rafe's joy. "Of course she's beautiful. Look at her parents. How is B.J.?"

"Amazing. She's a goddess. A warrior."

"And now a mother," Steph said softly and gave Joe a thumbs up. "Do we have a name yet?"

"We want to get to know her a little better first. But it will be something strong. Something beautiful."

She laughed. "I think I'm hearing a theme here. I'm so happy for you, Rafe. Give them both a kiss for me.

There's someone else here who wants to congratulate you. Hold on."

She handed Joe her phone, then pulled the covers up to her chin again. B.J. was a momma, she thought, smiling as Joe softly congratulated his friend. She'd be lying if she didn't admit that she'd always hoped to become a mother someday. She loved babies. Loved children. Loved the idea of creating a life so unique and magical. A little girl who might have her eyes. Or a boy who would have Joe's.

She stopped herself right there, as she always did when her thoughts strayed in that direction. Joe had never spoken about kids. Joe had never spoken about a future.

She glanced at him now, realizing that somewhere during her woolgathering, the subject had changed. She felt victorious for Joe as he filled Rafe in on Dalmage's involvement in Bryan's death, and their theory that he'd been behind the murders of so many potential sec of state candidates.

"Yeah. I know. It's a lot to process," Joe said gravely. "Don't worry about it, man," he added, and she understood that Rafe had just apologized for doubting him. Everyone had doubted him.

A long silence filled the room as Joe listened, nodded, made sounds of understanding.

"Let me know when the guys surface," he said finally. "In the meantime, we've got it covered. You just take care of your woman and your baby, okay?"

Another silence, then Joe handed her the phone.

"He wants to talk to you again. No doubt he plans to warn you to warn me to reel myself in."

"Smart man," she said, then told Rafe she was back on the line.

"Don't let him go off half-cocked, *cara*. Now that he's safe, now that you're *both* safe," he added with a good dose of censure to remind her he was still upset with her for striking out on her own, "he needs to sit tight and wait for the team to get back. I expect them any day now. We'll all figure out how to deal with Dalmage together. Nate will have some ideas."

"Exactly what I've been thinking," she agreed. Nate Black was not only an amazing strategist, he also had contacts in high places. Much higher than her mother's in the Department of Justice.

"And I don't think you have to worry about Joe going off half-cocked," she added, meeting his scowling face and holding his gaze. "He knows you all want justice for Bryan. He knows this is a team mission." After another round of well wishes, she disconnected.

"Message received," Joe said, lying down beside her again. "We wait."

"Thanks—"

Before he could turn off the lamp her phone rang again.

"Steph, it's Rhonda. Turn on the TV," she said with an edge in her voice that had Stephanie sitting straight up.

"What's wrong?"

"It's your mom. Go turn on the TV," she repeated, sounding agitated and anxious.

"My mom? Oh, God. Something happened to my mom?" In full-blown panic mode, she flew out of bed and rushed into the living room, barely aware that Joe was following her.

She searched frantically for the TV remote.

"No. No. I didn't mean to scare you. Nothing's happened—not yet. Just turn it on. I'll wait."

She found the remote, clicked on the set with trembling fingers, and started flipping through the channels. Blindly shoving the phone in Joe's hand, she punched in a news channel, then stood shaking in front of the screen.

"What's going on?"

"I don't know." She glanced over her shoulder at Joe. He'd pulled on sweatpants. "Rhonda said Mom was on the news."

Her mom most definitely *was* on the news.

"Oh, my God," she whispered when she found the footage that had apparently been playing since early evening yesterday when the news report had first broken.

Joe's big hands gripped her shoulders, supporting her as they watched.

"While Ann Tompkins is a relative unknown in the D.C. political arena," a weekend anchor reported from behind her desk, her long blond hair perfectly coiffed, her red dress stylish and vivid, "she's no stranger to the bureaucracy or the political machine.

"Tompkins—whose husband, Robert Tompkins, was a member of President Billings's cabinet—has been in a power position at the Department of Justice since her appointment several years ago. Hers is the latest viable name tossed into the mix of potential replacements for Secretary of State Rydell, who will be stepping down at the end of the month. The only other true contender still in the running is Greer Dalmage, the current UWAN liaison, who has repeatedly made it clear that if appointed, he will be honored to serve.

"Mrs. Tompkins is currently unavailable for comment, but sources who work with her speculate that she is worthy of the post and would make a fine appointee."

"Dalmage will go after her." Stephanie could hardly get the words out. Her fingers had gone numb; her heart felt like it had short-wired. They should have turned on the TV yesterday. But they'd worked all day, so mired in uncovering Dalmage's dirty laundry she'd never given the news a thought.

She turned terrified eyes to Joe. "We have to warn her!"

"Get her on the phone."

"I can't. She and Dad are out of touch. No cell service, no land lines. They wanted complete privacy."

Which meant complete isolation. Total vulnerability.

"Where the hell are they?"

She told him about the remote cabin on Lake Kabetogama in northern Minnesota and he swore under his breath. The bleak look on his face pretty much summed up her feelings.

"What are we going to do?" she asked.

"Call the local police up there. Explain what's going on."

"Explain *what*?" she asked, panicked. "That we have no way to prove it, but we *think* a high-level government official might order a hit squad to go to Minnesota and kill my mother? They'll figure me for a whack job and hang up on me."

"Tell them it's a medical emergency. Tell them to find your mom and dad and bring them into town and hang on to them until we get there."

"And what if they don't buy it?"

"Be convincing, Steph. I'll call Brown and get him filing a flight plan."

Dalmage leaned back from his desk stunned into silence after listening to the taped conversations Wilson had provided. Not only was the content jarring; the fact that Joe Green was holed up with Ann Tompkins's daughter was unbelievably opportune.

Life was a study in ironies. Ann Tompkins's daughter had been Green's accomplice in Freetown. How absolutely fascinating. And now they were together in D.C. The tapes Wilson had procured were highly informational. They'd figured things out, right down to EXnergy, his carefully orchestrated culling of the secretary of state candidates, and his collusion with certain enemies of the state. He felt admiration for them for piecing it together, but Green was going to die anyway. Now the daughter would have to die, as well.

He propped his elbow on the arm of his desk chair and rubbed his index finger back and forth over his upper lip, thinking . . . thinking . . . thinking. Everything he'd worked for—the power, the money, his legacy—was riding on how he handled this new twist in the game.

He could have Wilson and his team move in now. Take Green and the daughter out immediately, here in D.C. But there were risks in such a blatant assassination. Questions would be raised. Conclusions could be drawn. Stephanie Tompkins had been in Freetown at the exact same time he had. She and Green had been making phone calls, digging into his life. Those records could be traced if their deaths prompted an investigation.

He rose, paced to the window, and stared outside at the snow lying heavy on the shrubs bordering his front stoop. A plan began to formulate. Why not gather all the little chicks in the same roost? Why not let Stephanie Tompkins and Green go ahead and travel to Minnesota, reunite with her parents, and do away with them all at the same time? It would be a touching end.

He envisioned the news lead: "The tragic accidental deaths of Ann and Robert Tompkins, their daughter, and a family friend in the wilderness of Minnesota, in a Northern weather-related accident, has shocked and saddened the Washington, D.C., community."

Yes, he liked the sound of that. Wilson was the master at creating "accidental" deaths, was he not? Perhaps they would break through the ice on their snowmobiles and drown. Perhaps they'd become lost and disoriented while cross-country skiing and die of exposure in subzero temperatures. Perhaps their wilderness cabin would catch fire and all would die inside.

He had confidence that Wilson could handle it. Just as he had confidence that Green and Stephanie Tompkins's discoveries would go to their grave with them, and he would emerge unscathed.

But time was critical. Wilson needed to move out. His team had to be in place and contain Ann and Robert Tompkins before the lovebirds went north. Law enforcement officials had to be diverted. A murder in Duluth, perhaps? He'd leave the details up to Wilson, who was paid handsomely to think of these things for him.

He glanced at his watch. Not yet seven a.m. There was still plenty of time.

23

⟨ornament⟩

"I'm only going to say this one more time." Mike Brown's face burned red; the anger in his voice reverberated through the small office in the maintenance hangar. "I am not asking you to drive to outer-fucking-Mongolia. It's thirty freaking miles. Now get in your truck and bring that repair part over here pronto, because so help me God, if I have to drive over there and get it myself, you are *not* going to like my method of payment. Are we clear?"

He paused for a heartbeat. "Good. You've got an hour." He slammed down the receiver.

"So glad you opted to use the catch-more-flies-with-honey approach," Joe said dryly.

"Oh, we are way past sweet talk." Mike rocked back in the manager's chair and crossed his feet on top of the desk. "First they told me they didn't have the part. Then they said it was on the way. Then they said it was back-ordered. Then they *miraculously* found out they had it in stock after all! The bird could have been patched up and cleared for flight hours ago, if not for their total screwup."

Stephanie barely heard Mike's tirade. She hugged her arms around herself and paced back and forth in the small office, feeling helpless and scared.

First they couldn't get the jet repaired. Now weather reports of a coming storm threatened to shut down all airports between Denver and D.C. And three hours after making contact with the International Falls police department, a deputy had finally called her back, apologetically explaining that since the lake where her parents were staying was in Voyageurs National Park, it was out of their jurisdiction and they couldn't dispatch a car.

"Let me give you the number of the St. Louis County sheriff's office, ma'am," the officer had said. "Give 'em a call. See if they can help you."

So she'd called. And yes, they could help. But since the St. Louis County seat was in Duluth, two and a half hours south of Lake Kabetogama in good weather conditions, it was going to be a while until they could make it. They were sorry. She was sorry. And half out of her mind with worry.

She glanced out the office window at several small planes in various stages of repair. The tail section of the G-550's fuselage gaped open, waiting for the part to arrive.

"Flight plan's filed and an FAA inspector is on standby," Mike said, attempting to reassure her. "Once that part arrives it'll take twenty minutes tops to install, another five for the inspector to okay it, and we'll be ready to roll."

"What about the storm moving in?" she asked. "Can you even land at the airport up there?"

"Not a problem. The International Falls airport has plenty of runway—7400 feet—and instrument approaches are good down to a two-hundred-foot ceiling and a half mile of visibility. This bird has EVS—an enhanced vision system—sort of like night vision goggles. It'll let me drop to one hundred feet without actually seeing the runway."

Playing devil's advocate, Joe asked, "And are they going to give us clearance here for takeoff, knowing a major storm is moving in?"

"Yes, darlin'. As long as we've got an alternate with suitable weather within range of our fuel load—and with this bird, that's most of the country and Canada—they'll let us take off."

"And what if it is bad when we get there? What then?" Joe asked.

"Jesus. When'd you get so mother-henny?" Brown groused. "Look—those guys on the ground crew know how to handle snow on the runway. It's the frickin' ice capital of the world up there, for God's sake. As long as I can see the runway lights, I can land it.

"Of course," he added with his patented Primetime grin, "with a slippery runway and side winds, it can make stopping straight ahead a bit dicey. The most fun part of flying is landing in a twenty-five-knot crosswind and thirty-five-knot gusts. Throw in a snowstorm? Hell, it's party time.

"And before you even ask, our anti-icing system can handle most anything in-flight."

Ty walked into the office just then, his arms full of shopping bags. "He bragging again?"

"Just telling it straight, little bro. What'd you bring me?"

"Parka. Gloves and boots all around. I guessed on sizes."

Stephanie might have felt reassured by Brown's banter and Ty's foresight, but this lack of action was making her crazy. Not knowing if her mom and dad were safe was killing her.

Joe, who was leaning against a wall, pushed away and reached for her hand when she paced by. "Look, Steph, we don't even know if Dalmage is aware that Ann's on the list," he said, stopping her.

"You don't believe that," she snapped. "Why else would he come back from Sierra Leone so quickly?"

Rhonda had supplied them with that information earlier this morning: Dalmage had arrived in D.C. around four o'clock yesterday afternoon.

"Because he's looking for me?" Joe suggested.

"Of course he's looking for you. But you know he's coming. You know what he's capable of. Mom and Dad have no clue that their lives are in danger."

"Easy, Steph." Joe rubbed his hand soothingly up and down her arm. "We're not going to let anything happen to them."

"You can't know that. You can't promise that!"

She stopped when she realized how high her voice had risen. Feeling horrible for acting so bitchy, she took a breath and got control of the panic that had knotted in her chest.

"I'm sorry. I'm just . . ."

"Afraid for them," he finished, his eyes dark with empathy.

She nodded, glanced at the wall clock, and barely suppressed a howl of frustration. It was 1:35 p.m.

"We should have booked a commercial flight," she muttered.

"And we'd get there at ten tonight, if we're lucky," Mike pointed out. "International Falls is way off any main flight path—only one flight in and out a day this time of year. You'd have to connect in Minneapolis and wait out a five-hour layover—I checked. And with this snowstorm moving in, that flight could easily be canceled."

The airport in International Falls, Minnesota, was their only option. The town was set smack on the U.S.-Canadian border and was the closest airport to Lake Kabetogama, where her parents were staying in a secluded cabin, blissfully unaware that their lives could be in danger.

"Look at it this way," Mike said in an encouraging tone. "If we haven't been able to get to them yet, no one else is going to be able to, either."

"Maybe they didn't have repair issues and they're already there," she said bleakly.

"Easy." Joe took her into his arms and pulled her against his chest. "It's going to be okay," he assured her.

"In the meantime, don't take a hike on me, Steph. You need to keep it together."

She let the heat of his big body work its magic and settle her.

"I'm sorry. It's . . . just so frustrating."

"And scary," he said with understanding.

Yeah. It was. But she had a bad feeling that the really scary part hadn't even started.

"For the record," Brown bellowed four hours later, "just once, I'd like to fly a mission with you Black Ops boys that didn't involve gunfire, explosives, or impossible takeoff or landing conditions."

"You weren't singing that song on the ground," Joe yelled back from the cabin, bracing as the jet descended through major turbulence and Brown attempted to line them up with the runway.

"That's because I didn't know 'snowstorm' meant 'epic fucking blizzard,'" Brown countered.

The jet was taking a pounding. Beside him, Stephanie looked pale and shaken in the dim cabin lights.

He hadn't wanted her to come along. He hadn't wanted her anywhere near the action they might face, and he'd told her so.

She, of course, hadn't wanted to listen.

"He *can* land this plane, right?" she asked now.

Joe heaved a huge breath. "He can land it," he said, then held on when the wheels hit the icy tarmac and Brown reversed thrust with a G-force that sucked his breath from his lungs.

The jet engines roared, inertia fought velocity. Ice and wind joined the party with a vengeance as the plane bumped and skidded, finally coming to a sliding stop just fifty yards from the end of the runway.

For a long moment, silence filled the cabin.

Brown turned in the pilot's seat, a broad grin on his face. "Can I get a 'yee-haw,' pilgrim?"

Joe flipped his good friend the bird.

Brown chuckled. "And you, my friend, are very welcome."

While the guys finished up the paperwork for the four-wheel-drive truck they'd arranged to have ready for them, and Mike did some checking on other incoming flights, Stephanie called the St. Louis County sheriff's office.

"What's happening?" Joe joined her by the pay phone a few minutes later.

"The deputies didn't make it to the cabin. They didn't even get out of Duluth. There was some bizarre murder/suicide, and a string of snow-related accidents and emergencies."

Her anxiety level was off the charts, but she made herself keep it together. "Did you find anything out?"

"Brown schmoozed the air traffic controller. There were no commercial flights in or out today."

"But?" She knew that look; there was more.

"A small corporate jet arrived a couple hours ago. Pilot and four passengers."

Her heart skidded. "Oh, God. That means Dalmage knows she's up here."

"Don't jump to conclusions, Steph. We don't know that yet."

"What *do* we know?"

"Brown said that according to the receptionist, they rented a black Suburban. Told her they were here on business with Boise Cascade. Biggest employer in the area," he added in response to her questioning look. "Exec types fly in and out on a regular basis."

"So you think their story was legit?" Stephanie asked hopefully.

He shrugged. "Apparently the receptionist did— although she thought it was unusual that none of them had any luggage—only large attaché cases."

"Large enough for disassembled assault rifles?" she asked. From the grim set of his mouth, he was thinking the same thing.

"Mike talked the air traffic guy into letting him check out the plane. We'll see if he learns anything suspicious."

"I did." Mike walked up behind them, looking sober. "Their flight log shows they flew here out of D.C."

"Oh, God." Stephanie turned to Joe. "We have to find my parents before they do."

"Come on." Joe took her by the elbow as Ty pulled up in front of the terminal doors in a club cab Chevy pickup.

They all scooted inside, Joe up front riding shotgun and Mike and Stephanie in the back.

"According to this," Joe said studying a map, "the lake is twenty-five miles south of here. We've got a good hour-long trip in this weather, and we need to hit a sporting goods store before we leave town."

Because they had no weapons, Stephanie realized grimly. It took days to arrange for weapons permits out of D.C., and the strict security inspections of every pilot, passenger, and crew member had made it impossible for them to bring anything on board.

Yet Dalmage's men—and Stephanie knew by the look on Joe's face that he agreed, they *were* Dalmage's men—were most likely carrying weapons in their attaché cases. Weapons that could easily be broken down for transport.

"Hurry," she said swamped by a renewed sense of urgency. Ty stepped on the gas.

"For the tenth time, can you crank the heat up? I'm getting frostbite back here," Mike grumbled. "What kind of idiots voluntarily live in this icebox, anyway?"

Ty snorted. "We grew up in Colorado. When did you turn into such a candy-ass?"

He got a jab in his shoulder for his disrespect. "When my blood reset for South America."

"We need more weapons." Joe was driving now, drumming his gloved fingers on the wheel. Stephanie sat tensely in the front seat beside him.

Due to a stop at a sporting goods store they weren't completely unarmed, but guns had been out of the question. The store clerk made references to IDs and state gun regs when Joe had tested the waters by checking out a rifle. They was no way they could legally walk out of there with guns.

They'd settled for two compound bows, plus arrows with razor-sharp tips big enough to take down a bear.

"Gifts for my dad," Mike had said, flashing the clerk a good-ol'-boy grin. "He's going to love these. Toss these bad boys in, too," he'd added, pointing to a pair of hunting knives beneath the glass countertop.

After a five-minute shopping spree, they'd walked out of the store with two compound bows, two dozen arrows, three knives, two coils of rope, a pair of high-powered binoculars, four pairs of white hooded coveralls and matching gloves, and two sets of walkie-talkies. It was the biggest sale the clerk had made all winter.

"We should have lifted a couple rifles," Mike lamented as the wipers whipped back and forth, swiping the rapidly accumulating snow from the windshield.

"Not a risk I wanted to take," Joe said. "That little town was crawling with patrol cars on the prowl for snow-related accidents. If we'd gotten caught we'd be no use to Ann and Robert."

"According to this," Stephanie said, "there's a general store right when you turn off the main highway to go to the lake." She had flipped on the dome light to study a brochure featuring Lake Kabetogama she'd picked up at the airport. The lake was a popular tourist destination for its fishing, snowmobiling, and scenery. "Maybe someone there will recognize the cabin from the photos."

She'd printed out the magazine article with photos

of the cabin that her father had e-mailed her. Other than the name of the lake, the article was the only thing they had to go on. No one at the airport had been able to help.

Luckily, someone at the store did.

24

The Gateway General Store was out in the middle of nowhere, at the junction of Highway 53 and a county road that led to the lake. The lights over its three gas pumps cast ghostly beacons through the rapidly thickening snow.

Other than the four of them, there were few signs of life at 6:30 p.m. on this storm-whipped night. A red neon OPEN sign blinked on and off in the center of the windowed door and a light burned in what appeared to be an apartment above the store.

"Somebody's home." Joe shouldered open the driver's side door and got out.

They left the truck running, the heater on full blast, high beams shining into a front window peppered with signs that announced: LOTTERY TICKETS SOLD HERE, GROCERIES, TACKLE, and LIQUOR. A buzzer sounded as they rushed inside, slamming the door against the swirling snow and frigid air.

They were stomping snow from their boots when they heard footsteps on creaking stairs. A door opened and a lean, attractive woman wearing worn jeans, a blue and brown–plaid flannel shirt, and soft leather moccasins entered the store.

"You folks lost?" she asked with a curious smile. "Or just crazy to be out on a night like this?"

"A little bit of both." Stephanie forced a smile. "I'm Stephanie Tompkins. This is Joe, Mike, and Ty."

"Jess Albert."

She had a pleasant face and a kind but slightly wary expression. Short brown hair curled prettily around her face.

"What can I do for you tonight?" She moved behind a tall service counter loaded with everything from lottery tickets to hunting and fishing licenses to candy bars to tackle.

"We're trying to find my parents. They flew up here a week ago." Stephanie pulled the folded article out of her coat pocket. "We know the cabin is on the lake but don't have an address. Do you recognize this place?"

Jess glanced at the pictures. "Sure. That's the Nelson place."

Stephanie breathed her first breath of relief since she'd seen the TV news report. "Can you give us directions?"

"I can do better than that." Jess found a notepad under the counter and drew them a quick map. "Left on Gamma Road, right on State Point. It's about five miles, give or take, at the end of a dead-end road. You hit the lake, you've gone too far." She paused. "It's one popular destination today."

Stephanie's senses jumped into overdrive. "How so?"

"You're the second wave to come in here looking for that cabin."

"Oh, God." Stephanie felt her knees go weak.

"Five men?" Joe asked while Stephanie struggled for a breath.

"Yeah." Jess narrowed her eyes, clearly disconcerted by the edge in his voice. "Friends of yours?"

"How long ago were they here?" Mike's tone let Jess know that, no, they were not friends.

"Couple hours. Maybe a little less."

A shotgun suddenly materialized from behind the counter. Jess expertly pumped the forearm, making it clear that she knew how to use it. "You want to tell me what's going on?"

Stephanie looked from the gun to the other woman's face.

"Tell her," Joe said.

So she did, trusting this stranger with her parents' lives.

"I knew there was a reason I played dumb."

"You didn't direct them to the cabin?"

Jess shook her head. "No. But Russ Cramston did. He stopped in for a cup of coffee. I saw him talking to them out by the gas pumps, pointing in the direction of the lake, then drawing a map in the snow."

Stephanie's heart sank.

"Sorry, hon," Jess added with an apologetic look before addressing the guys. "You boys armed?"

"Against rabbits and raccoons," Ty said grimly.

After a moment of indecision, Jess moved out from behind the counter. "Follow me. I have something in the back room you might be able to use."

She led them around the empty bait tanks and several shelves of groceries to a storage room; a massive gun safe took up the bulk of the 10 x 10 foot area.

"Motherlode," Ty muttered after Jess had spun the combination and opened it up. A pair of AR-15s sat alongside several hunting rifles, shotguns, and handguns.

"They were my husband's." Jess crossed her arms, stood back, and invited them to take whatever they wanted.

Ty, who Stephanie had noticed seemed interested in Jess, asked quietly, "What happened to your husband?"

"IED in Afghanistan two years ago. Jeff was Spec Ops, too," she added with a sad smile. "I can spot one of you guys a mile away."

"What kind of a read did you get on the other guys?" Mike asked.

"A bad one," she said. "They were not boy scouts."

"Don't suppose you've got any body armor or flash bangs." Mike was only half joking. "Every former SFer I've ever known has a stash of stuff that 'fell off a truck.'"

Meaning things they'd brought back that they probably shouldn't have.

"No body armor," she said with a wistful look, and Stephanie wondered if Jess was thinking that body armor hadn't saved her husband. "No flash bangs, either. But I do have some bear bangers. Hold on a sec."

She dug around on a lower shelf until she came up

with a box containing half a dozen exploding flares and a launcher. "Every once in a while, I'll get a pesky black bear or a couple of cubs who think my Dumpsters are their smorgasbord. Lotta bang, lotta smoke, but nothing lethal."

Ty tucked the box of bangers under his arm along with the launcher. Their eyes held for a long moment before he thanked her with a nod.

Stephanie reached out and laid a hand on Jess's arm and thanked her for her help.

"That's okay," Jess said. "Just don't make me sorry I gave you those guns."

"Call the police," Joe told her as they gathered ammo for the rifles and shotguns, then headed for the door. "Tell them jurisdiction or not, they need to haul ass out here ASAP. And tell 'em they'd better bring an ambulance with them."

"In a storm like this you're not going to get any help from them anytime soon."

"We don't need their help," Mike said with a warrior look on his face that Stephanie had never seen before. "We need them for cleanup."

"Please. If it's money you want, we can get it. Just tell me what you want. None of this is necessary."

Carl Wilson scowled at the two bound, hooded captives. They'd been here almost two hours and he'd grown weary of Ann Tompkins's attempts to invoke reason.

"Gag her," he told Simpson.

His second-in-command walked over to the woman, pulled a roll of duct tape out of his pocket, and jerked the hood off her head. He roughly slapped a piece over her mouth and replaced the hood.

Finally. Quiet.

These people were pathetic. The husband had made a decent attempt to stop them, but really. It had been over before it started.

Robert Tompkins may have once been former president Billings's right-hand man, but his situational awareness was for shit. So were his self-preservation instincts. That's why he was now slumped in a wooden chair back-to-back with his wife, and both of them bound with their hands behind their backs. It was also why Tompkins was bleeding from a sharp rap to his temple.

The cabin had been lit up like Times Square when they'd pulled up. He'd give one point to that hick town. The rental car agency knew what kind of horsepower a man needed to get around in this weather.

Fuck, he hated the cold. Give him camels and sand fleas any day. Just spare him the snow and the deep freeze. Despite the weather and his aversion to it, it had been a textbook siege. Kill the Suburban lights a quarter mile away. Gear up and approach the cabin, assault rifles shouldered. Split up and block all exits. In this case, there were three. The front door, a back door that led out to a deck, and the door to the attached garage.

A look inside had revealed a Christmas card–perfect scene. A blazing fire in the hearth. Husband and wife snuggled together on an overstuffed sofa in front of it, reading books. Mugs of steaming hot chocolate sitting on the low pine table in front of them. A checkers board laid out and ready for the next game.

How cozy.

And how rude, he thought with a smug grin, that he had blasted into the little love nest and turned paradise into the Tompkins's worst nightmare.

The Suburban was now hidden out of sight, parked beside the Tompkins's vehicle in the garage. His men were positioned for optimum observation and defensive positioning.

He flicked on his commo mike and raised Benson. "Anything?"

Benson and Janikowski were on lookout outside. Benson was positioned a quarter of a mile down the drive, concealed by trees and snow. Janikowski was perched on the garage roof, his sniper rifle aimed at the only vehicle approach.

"Negative," Benson, an L.A. transplant, responded through chattering teeth. It was their third shift in the cold, and even though Wilson had been cycling them in and out at twenty-minute intervals, the weather was starting to take a toll.

"Same," said Janikowski.

Ski was a short, stocky Pol from Milwaukee. He was handling the sub-zero temps better than Benson. Still, it wouldn't do to lose two of his best men to frostbite.

"Relieve them," he told Simpson and Duvall.

Neither man said a word. They just zipped into their

heavy parkas, boots, and gloves and, grabbing their weapons, headed for the door.

"Don't fall off the ladder this time," he warned Duvall, who would scale the fourteen-foot extension ladder at the back of the cabin to get to their rooftop perch.

"I only make a mistake once." Duvall was a former recon Marine who'd become disenchanted with the system. He walked outside, limping. His shin had taken a beating in the fall.

Five minutes later, Benson and Janikowski walked stiffly inside, snow swirling in their wake. They wore the frigid air on their coats. Their cheeks glowed red with cold. And he could tell by the way they moved that their feet were half frozen.

Neither said a word. They just shrugged out of their heavy outerwear and headed straight for the coffeepot in the kitchen.

Tough bastards, Wilson thought with satisfaction. He'd chosen well.

He'd give them twenty minutes to thaw out and warm up, then the shift would change again. Company would be here soon. In the meantime, everyone had to be in tip-top shape for the big party.

He'd planned for two—the daughter and Green, who couldn't anticipate that Dalmage was aware he'd been found out. They'd be as clueless as the hostages bound and gagged in the middle of the great room.

Or not. He was prepared for not, just as he was prepared for the possibility of accomplices.

Success was all about contingencies, and all he cared

about was the win. He didn't give a fuck about these people. Didn't give a fuck about Dalmage. It was the game. It was the money. You won the game, you got the prize. That was enough for him. But he found himself hoping that Green, who he'd been told was a warrior, might give him a bit of a challenge.

25

"This is as far as we go in the truck." Joe killed the Chevy's lights and rolled to a stop in the middle of the road. "According to the map Jess drew, the cabin is about a half a mile up this road."

They'd been creeping through over a foot of snow for the last several miles. Several inches had accumulated on the hood. Everywhere they looked, all they could see was snow. Trees standing in snow. Trees covered in snow. Drifts filled the ditches. It was a night sky of black, a landscape of white, broken only by snow-laden trees.

"Are you sure you're strong enough to do this?" Stephanie asked as he zipped up his white coveralls, then pulled a thick stocking cap over his head before flipping up the hood.

"I'm sure."

He wasn't sure of anything. But his adrenaline burn would go a long way toward getting him through whatever lay ahead.

He was in full-out battle mode now. Mind, body, and spirit.

"You ready?" he asked Mike.

"Born that way." Mike jammed his fingers into thick white gloves and shouldered open the door.

The wind slashed inside, frosting the seats with snow.

"Be careful," Stephanie whispered, touching his arm.

"Don't leave the truck," Joe warned her. "Whatever happens, do *not* leave the truck."

She could die out here on a night like this. Hell, they all could. A cold this brittle would reach the very marrow of your bones, freeze your blood into Popsicles. Add the blowing snow, the dark, and almost zero visibility factor, and a man could get lost in a heartbeat. The fact that he'd aced land navigation meant exactly *nada*. NVGs, if they had them, would be useless. Same for sensors. A herd of elephants could stampede through these woods tonight and no one would ever know. He seriously doubted the bad guys had messed with sensors or trip wires, given the storm and the time limits.

"Stay with her, Ty," he said and joined Mike out in the elements.

Working as fast as they could against the wind and cold, he opened the tailgate and dug through the snow-filled truck bed for their weapons.

"As long as we don't veer off the road, we should be all right," Joe said, turning his face away from the wind. Once they ducked into the trees, however, they were going to need a rope to guide them back.

Mike gave him a thumbs-up. They were already

armed with handguns and knives, and helped each other tie the coils of rope at their waists and fix the bows across their chests before slinging their rifles onto their shoulders.

It took less than a minute to get geared up, and already Joe was feeling the bite of the cold in his fingers.

He pulled a walkie-talkie out of the breast pocket of his coveralls. "Commo check one."

"Check, check," Ty replied.

"Check three," Mike said behind him.

Joe tucked his head and, aware of Mike falling in behind him, started wading through the drifts toward the cabin.

Joe lay on his belly, elbows dug into the snow, a deadfall log providing cover. Beside him Mike lay on his back, digging into his coveralls for the binoculars. Fifteen yards ahead of them stood the cabin. Less than a quarter of a mile behind them lay a dead man.

They'd been almost on top of the sentry before they'd spotted him. Only because the lookout had dropped his guard and leaned his rifle against a tree to remove his gloves and blow on his frozen fingers had they gotten the drop on him.

Crouching low, they'd split up, Mike to the left, Joe to the right. Then they jumped him like fleas on a dog.

Mike went in low; Joe hit him high and toppled him facedown on the ground. He jammed a knee between the man's shoulder blades, gripped his jaw in one hand

and the back of his head in the other, and snapped his neck.

The adrenaline rush had shot heat into his freezing extremities, but that was five long minutes ago. Now the frozen ground seeped through his clothes in icy waves. The brutal wind burned his eyes, swept snow crystals cutting into his cheeks.

"Up there." Mike lowered the binoculars, handed them to Joe, and pointed to the garage roof.

"Got him," Joe said after finding him in the binoculars. "Best guess?"

"Stoner SR-25 sniper rifle. And you can bet he knows how to use it."

Joe reached above his head and worked the bow from around his chest.

"Seriously?" Mike asked when he realized what Joe planned to do.

"A rifle shot will alert the boys inside. Don't worry. I shot my first deer with a compound bow when I was fifteen," Joe said, removing an arrow from a quiver.

"That ain't no deer," Mike pointed out unnecessarily.

No, it wasn't. And now it got dicey.

At the very least, he wanted to be five yards closer. And he was going to have to stand up to get a good line on the target.

"Cover me." He left the rifle with Mike, crawled over the log and, crouching low, crept toward the cabin.

Moving at a snail's pace he finally arrived at the base of a substantial white pine less than ten yards away from the garage. Careful not to draw the sniper's attention with any sudden movement, he rose to his feet.

His knees ached. His blood felt just this side of freezing. And he was still at less than full strength after his ordeal, compliments of Greer Dalmage, in that fucking prison.

Thinking about Dalmage and Freetown got anger boiling hot inside him. Just enough to give him the burst of energy he needed to fix the notch of an arrow in the rocking point of the bowstring and draw it back.

The shooter lay like a slug on the peak of the roof, his left eye snugged against his rifle scope, searching, searching, searching the night.

Joe waited, waited, waited. Breathing deep and slow. The shaft of the arrow aligned against his cheek. His biceps burned from holding tension on the bow.

Finally, the sniper lifted his head a few inches. Just enough.

He let the arrow fly. Felt the fletching slice across his cheek. Saw the shooter's hands jerk away from the rifle and clutch frantically at his throat before he went limp, then slid slowly down the metal roof, his rifle going along for the ride.

He landed like a sack of cement in a snowdrift behind the garage.

"Jesus," Mike muttered beside him. "You are Robin fuckin' Hood."

Joe lowered the bow, his arms trembling from the exertion. His heart had ratcheted up several beats.

He motioned for Mike to follow him. "Recon."

He didn't want to go into this final phase blind. Yeah, some of their intel would have to be SWAG—a Scientific Wild Assed Guess. But he needed a clue so they didn't walk into a flat-out ambush.

There was no time to waste. They'd been out in the cold too long. The sentries would be expected to check in, and when they didn't the men inside would go ape shit.

Ann and Robert were now more vulnerable than they had been before Joe and company had arrived.

"I swear to God." Mike shivered in the backseat, rubbing his hands briskly together to get the circulation back. "People who live and work in this icebox are tougher than woodpecker lips."

Joe and Mike had quickly scouted the cabin by peeking in through a window. His heart had almost given out on him when he'd seen Ann and Robert tied back-to-back, hoods over their heads.

He'd counted three men. Lots of weaponry—no surprise. The surprise, he hoped, was going to be on them.

Using the ropes they'd tied from tree to tree to guide them, they'd hightailed it back to the truck as fast as their frozen feet could carry them. They were going to need Ty to pull this off.

Joe hadn't whitewashed it when he'd told Stephanie about Ann and Robert. He'd have given anything to spare her from the knowledge that her mom and dad would be in the direct line of fire when this went down, but he knew she would want the truth. She deserved the truth.

She'd handled it like a soldier.

"Here's how we see it going down," Joe said, recounting the plan he and Mike had devised on the jog back to the truck. "There's a ladder propped up against the back of the garage. One of us needs to climb it, get up on the main roof, and cover the chimney so the smoke will back up in the cabin."

"Sounds like a job for a copilot," Ty said without hesitation.

"Get back on the ground ASAP," Joe told him.

"And don't break your neck in the process." There was more brotherly concern in Mike's voice than he would probably admit to.

"It won't take them long to figure out something's up. By that time they'll be choking and coughing and their eyes will be watering, but they'll be hyperalert.

"Mike, take the back door from the deck. Ty, you come in through the garage door. I'll be at the front entrance."

"Where do you want me?" Stephanie's warrior face almost broke Joe's heart.

"In the truck," all three men said in unison.

"Look," Joe said, at her crestfallen expression. "If this goes FUBAR, you need to haul ass out and get help."

"It'll be too late for help," she pointed out unnecessarily.

"Someone's gotta hang Dalmage." Joe gave her a hard look. "You're the only one who can do it."

She finally nodded. He squeezed her hand, then turned back to the guys. "When I toss the bear banger through the window, that's your cue. I don't need to tell you what has to happen next."

And it had better be damn good, Joe thought as he chambered a round in the 30-06 rifle. Because during that small window of time, every aspect of their plan had the best chance of going really, really bad.

Wilson coughed, wiped his burning eyes, and spoke into his commo mike. "Lookout one. What's your status? Over." He'd made repeated attempts to raise Duvall and was starting to get a really bad feeling about this. In case they did have company he'd kept the line clear, not wanting to reveal their location with too much chatter. So it had been ten minutes since he'd asked for a radio check, and neither Duvall nor Simpson were responding.

His only answer was static-filled silence. A tingle of unease went up his spine, his situational awareness humming in warning.

Across the room Benson alternately sipped coffee, did push-ups, and rubbed his arms to increase the circulation.

Janikowski fiddled ineffectively with the fireplace damper.

"What's wrong with that thing?" Benson growled, coughing as a sudden influx of smoke poured into the room.

"Fuck if I know." Janikowski was coughing, too, waving one arm in front of him to push away the billowing smoke while fiddling with the flue with his other hand. "Something's blocking the chimney."

He staggered away from the hearth, choking and rubbing his burning eyes. "Jesus. Open a door."

Robert Tompkins had started to stir. His wife made muffled choking sounds beneath the hood.

Benson headed across the room toward the front door, covering his nose with a cupped palm but failing to avoid breathing the acrid smoke into his lungs.

"Stop!" Wilson held a hand in the air, his gut telling him they had company. "Someone's out there."

This was it. Joe jammed his elbow through the window; glass shattered. He fired a bear banger into the cabin. The flare whistled and hit the floor spinning, then exploded with a reverberating *boom!*

He crashed in right behind it, dove straight for Robert and Ann and tumbled them to the floor, out of the line of fire that suddenly ricocheted through the room.

Mike and Ty burst in right on his heels. He couldn't see them through the smoke, but over the din of gunfire he recognized the *strike, strike, strike* concussion of the AR-15s and knew they were following orders to shoot anything above waist level that moved.

A man groaned; a body hit the floor.

He lay on top of Ann and Robert. "It's Joe," he yelled above the melee. "Lie still. Don't try to get up."

Then he pushed to his knees, drew his rifle to his shoulder and searched for targets.

A white shadow moved across the kitchen. Ty.

Another white shape dropped and rolled, the muzzle flash of his rifle blasting in sharp, blinding beats. Mike.

Directly across from him another figure, crouching low, shouldered his rifle and took a bead on Mike.

Joe fired the 30-06, aiming dead center at his throat.

The man spun like a top and dropped to his back on the floor, the concussion from the shot reverberating through the night.

"Duck and cover!" Joe yelled, and Ty scrambled behind the kitchen counter. Mike dove behind a heavy wooden chest.

"Hold fire!" Joe yelled.

An echoing silence filled the cabin. From his position on his knees behind the sofa, Joe listened. Other than Ann's labored breathing, there was silence.

"Clear right?"

Ty responded with an immediate "Yo."

"Clear left?"

Mike confirmed with a "Yo yo."

"Let's be careful out there." With his rifle shouldered and sweeping the room, Joe slowly rose to his feet. From their positions, Mike and Ty did the same.

The open doors had helped clear out the smoke. The furniture and log walls and cabinetry were riddled with bullet holes. Window glass lay shattered and broken everywhere.

The wind whipped gusts of snow inside, where it melted as soon as it hit the floor.

"Give me a body count," Joe said, sweeping the room.

"One down over here." Ty knelt to feel a pulse. "Dead tango."

"Same goes," Mike said, checking the pulse at another shooter's neck.

"Ann? Bob?"

"I'm okay," Robert Tompkins said, his voice weak when Joe reached down and pulled off his hood. He did the same for Ann, then carefully removed the duct tape.

"Thank God," she whispered, and started crying.

Joe squeezed her shoulder and stood, his gaze sweeping the room and coming up one body short.

Shit. "Where's the other one?"

"Right here."

He swung around.

And there stood a man dressed in black. The unnatural bulk of his chest made it clear he was wearing body armor beneath his clothes.

His shouldered assault rifle was pointed dead center at Joe's head. "Tell them to drop the weapons. Now."

His finger tightened on the trigger.

Mike and Ty stood frozen, stunned and indecisive.

"There are three of us and one of you," Joe pointed out, all of his focus locked on the gunman's eyes. "With a world of luck, you might get one of us before we double your weight with lead."

The shooter's rifle swung toward the Tompkinses. "True, but I can probably get both of them before you get me. Pretty high breakage for a hostage rescue. Your call," he said without lifting his aim from Robert's head.

Joe had no choice. He gave the guys a clipped nod.

Behind him, he heard first one AR-15 then the other hit the floor.

"Kick them over here," the man snapped.

Heavy metal skidded across polished pine.

The shooter kicked the guns behind him, never taking his finger off the trigger, and swung the rifle back toward Joe. "You picked a bad night to piss me off."

He sighted down the barrel and drew a bead.

A shot cracked through the icy stillness.

The shooter lurched clumsily forward, one step, then two, before his knees folded and he fell face-first on the floor.

"What the hell?" Mike rushed across the room, then stopped, his jaw dropping.

Joe was frozen in place, staring at the woman in the open doorway, snow swirling around her slender shoulders, the howling wind whipping her dark hair around her expressionless face.

Stephanie.

Her feet were braced wide apart, her arms stretched out straight in front of her.

And her grip on the Glock was rock-solid steady as a thin curl of smoke spiraled from the muzzle of a fallen U.S. soldier's pistol.

26

The first lady was fond of throwing parties. Dalmage believed he could become fond of the first lady—and she of him—when his appointment inevitably went through.

He watched her now, standing across the room in front of the three windows that overlooked the south lawn, stunning in a red power dress as she greeted her guests. She was a bright light in the White House's Blue room with its soft, muted colors and delicate French Empire décor.

Yes, he knew these things. He'd made it a point early on in his career to be well versed on all things associated with the government, including the White House, where this reception was taking place. The furniture was for the most part original to the room. European beech, compliments of James Monroe. A seventeenth-century French Empire clock with a figure of Hannibal sat on the mantel. Opulent and tasteful.

It was a heady pleasure to have this knowledge. To be

on the guest list for events such as these. And soon, to be a member of the president's cabinet. The downside was that he had to suffer fools like Bernard Muldoon.

"Clichés work for a reason," Senator Muldoon said, dragging Dalmage back to the conversation he'd managed to tune out for a few moments. "To that end, make sure you keep your friends close and your enemies closer."

Greer smiled, indulging the senior senator from Maryland, who laughed as though he'd invented the line. Christ, the man was a bore. But he knew how to play this game. It was a necessary evil to glad-hand and backslap and feed the monster egos that always snarled for fresh meat on Capitol Hill.

"I'll make sure I keep that in mind, Muldoon. Now, excuse me, would you? I need to have a word with Margaret Harris."

Extricating himself from that tight little knot of pompous windbags, he cut a direct path toward the defense secretary, pausing momentarily to pull out his phone and check for messages.

Nothing. Wilson should have reported in by now. He was determined, however, not to let his concern ruin his evening. Accidental deaths took time to orchestrate. And the weather had no doubt caused some travel delays.

He smiled distractedly as a young woman excused herself to squeeze by him. It was a bit of a crush with all the cabinet members, close personal friends of the president and first lady, and a few honored guests, such as himself, who had caught the president's eye with their loyalty and dedication to service.

No one had dedicated themselves more than he had. For that reason, he resented the president greatly for keeping him on the string so long. For constantly dangling the secretary of state cabinet appointment, then jerking it away from him when it was all but sewn up, adding yet another name to his precious list.

But that game was now over. Rydell had turned in his resignation yesterday. Greer had heard the announcement right after Wilson had notified him that he'd located "the package" and was en route to tie up the loose ends. Greer halfway expected the president to pull him aside tonight and confide that he would make the formal public announcement of Greer's appointment tomorrow.

Barely suppressing a smile, he started across the room again—then stopped, thunderstruck, when he spotted the woman walking through the door.

His chest suddenly seized; pain shot through his left arm and jaw.

It couldn't be. His eyes were playing tricks.

The woman just *looked* like Ann Tompkins—it couldn't be her. Ann Tompkins was dead by now. She *had* to be dead.

He had almost convinced himself when Robert Tompkins stepped next to her—and then a young woman whose resemblance indisputably identified her as Ann's daughter, flanked Ann on the other side.

The pain in his chest was now breathtaking, and he

spun around. He had to get out of this room. He had to think. He had to—

He took two faltering steps, and ran straight into the solid wall of a man's chest.

"Out of my way!" he roared, fighting for breath as his chest continued to seize, weakening him with blinding, consuming pain. "I have to . . . leave. I have to—"

"But the party's just getting started," the man said, gripping his arm when he frantically attempted to bull his way around him. "I'd hate to see you go before I had a chance to introduce myself."

The grip on his arm tightened like a vise. Gasping for air, Dalmage reached out, gripped the man's shirt, and peered up into eyes as cold as gunmetal.

"The name's Green. Joe Green."

Fireballs exploded in his chest like hand grenades. He couldn't bear it. He clutched at his throat. Felt his eyes bulge. His knees buckle.

The collective gasps in the room barely registered as he dropped to his knees. He was aware only of pain. Layers on layers of pain, wave on unyielding wave.

"Help . . . me," he gasped, pleading into those cold hard eyes that stared down at him without an ounce of pity or compassion.

He collapsed on his back on the floor, his world ending as blackness sucked him into the cold, dark deep.

"Come on, you sonofabitch," Joe muttered as he administered CPR to the man who had killed his friend, altered the course of his life, and plotted to sell out his own nation.

"Joe."

He shook Stephanie's hand off his shoulder and doggedly continued his compressions.

"Joe," Stephanie repeated more firmly, then got down on her knees beside him. "It's over. He's dead. There's nothing more you can do."

The gravity of her tone finally got to him. He sat back on his heels, pressed his fists against his thighs, and tried to catch his breath.

Dalmage was dead.

It was what he'd wanted, what he'd lived for. But when he'd realized what was happening, instinct had taken over and he'd applied CPR.

Because he'd realized Stephanie was right: Dalmage should pay publicly for what he'd done. Joe wanted him alive to stand trial before the American public. He wanted the world to know that this bastard was responsible for Bryan's death.

But Dalmage lay dead on the floor, his lifeless eyes staring sightlessly at the ceiling.

He felt cheated. He felt betrayed.

"Come on, Joe." Stephanie gently pulled him to his feet. "Time to let it go."

"Love you, too. I'll talk to you again tomorrow, Mom." Stephanie disconnected, then tossed her cell phone on her coffee table and leaned her head back against the plush sofa. She didn't know who needed the daily contact more, her or her mother. She hugged her arms around herself, feeling a sudden chill despite the warmth of her heavy sweater, warm fuzzy socks, and her favorite jeans.

Her dad had needed medical treatment before they could leave Minnesota. He had a concussion and needed several stitches in his head, but fortunately he was doing fine now.

Dealing with the law enforcement in Minnesota had been another story. It had taken every weapon in Ann's bag of DOJ tricks to convince them to keep a lid on the crime scene long enough to let them confront Dalmage. No one had imagined that less than twenty-four hours later, Dalmage would be dead.

Joe's big hand reached out, squeezed her thigh. "So . . . they're doing okay?"

She turned her face up to his and smiled. Tonight was the first night they'd been able to grab some time alone together since they'd returned to D.C.

"They're good." She was proud of the strength both her mom and dad had shown through this entire ordeal. "Happy to be home, and happy to start putting this all behind them."

It had been three days since Dalmage had died of a massive heart attack. Three days of giving statements to the attorney general's office and to the Department of Justice attorneys, turning over their theories and their findings, and explaining five dead bodies and a destroyed cabin in the wilds of Minnesota. It had taken a toll on all of them.

She was exhausted. So was Joe, who still hadn't recovered all of his strength. Unfortunately, the situation was far from over. The first news story had leaked yesterday, detailing a startlingly accurate account of Dalmage's corruption—from his traitorous acts in Sierra Leone that had begun all those years ago; to EXnergy; to the murders of potential secretary of state appointments, and finally to her parents' abduction and near miss with death. There would be more testimony over the next few weeks. Months of sorting out REE rights in Sierra Leone. Only because Nate Black was held in such high regard by the United States government for the covert work he and the BOIs performed were the names of the individuals responsible for uncovering Dalmage's crimes and saving Ann and Robert's lives withheld.

Joe had dodged a bullet. Mike and Ty had also been spared. The president himself had leveled a mandate that their names would not be linked with the case under any circumstances. Because she was Ann and Robert's daughter, Stephanie had been tied to the Dalmage affair, but her direct involvement in uncovering his crimes remained a secret.

She became aware that Joe had grown very quiet beside her. "What?" she asked when she realized he was watching her.

He brushed her hair away from her forehead and tucked it behind her ear. "How about you? Are you going to be able to put this all behind you?"

She knew exactly what he was asking. She'd killed a

man. It had been necessary and justified. But that didn't mean there wasn't going to be fallout. It didn't mean she wasn't going to spend many sleepless nights figuring out how to handle it.

"I'll be fine," she assured him, because he didn't need the weight of her issues on top of his own.

She rose abruptly. "And right now I'm beyond starved. I think I'll heat up that lasagna Rhonda sent over. Want some?" She turned toward the kitchen.

He reached out and caught her hand, stopping her. He wanted to talk about it. She didn't. The memory was still too raw. She wasn't ready to face it yet.

"Really, really hungry," she said with a teasing grin, resisting the concern in his eyes that she knew would soon result in a "come to Jesus" talk about dealing with those feelings.

He tugged harder, but she was literally saved by the bell. The doorbell.

"Hello, gorgeous." Mike Brown caught her up in his arms when she opened the door to him and Ty. "How about you and I run off into the sunset together? Blow this joint and that big ugly dude sitting like a stain on your pretty sofa. Hey, big ugly dude." Mike waved to Joe, who flipped him the bird.

Stephanie laughed and hugged Mike back. "I'm going to miss you."

"I'm not," Joe said. He walked across the room and shook Ty's hand. "Hey, bud. How's it going?"

"It's all good," Ty said, then hugged Stephanie hello.

"You guys want a beer?" Stephanie asked.

"Can't," Ty said. "I've got a plane to catch. Some of us have to work for a living."

Mike looked wounded. "I bring you on board for a really excellent adventure, and you diss me? That is not cool, bro."

"Not to split hairs," Ty said, giving back as good as Mike gave, "but you brought me on board for a—let's see, how did you put it? Oh yeah: 'a simple little copilot gig to West Africa and back.' You never said a word about bullets, bad guys, or frostbite."

"You loved it," Mike said confidently.

Ty grinned. "Yeah," he admitted, crossing his arms over his chest and widening his stance. "I did. Felt good to be back in action again."

"There was something *else* you loved," Mike teased, and winked at Stephanie.

Ty frowned at his brother. "What are you talking about?"

"Seriously?" Mike made a sound of disbelief, then sing-songed, *"Tyler and Jessie sittin' in a tree, K-I-S-S-I-N-G."*

Ty, trying to look unaffected, made a sound of disgust. "What are you, twelve?"

Mike looked at his brother with a maddening smile. "Hey, I'm not the one who was crushing on the pretty little Minnesota widow lady."

"I was not *crushing*, for Christsake," Ty grumbled.

"Like hell. I know that look. You were smitten."

"Show her a little respect." Ty's face turned red. "She saved our bacon when she gave us those guns."

Mike pressed a hand against his chest. "I've got nothing but respect and gratitude for that woman. I just don't want to show my gratitude the same way you do. So when are you headed back up north, Nanook?"

Ty set his jaw and glared. "Shut up, Mikey. Just . . . shut up."

Stephanie was still grinning when the brothers left a few minutes later, still lobbing insults at each other.

"I thought Laurel and Hardy would never leave," Joe said, closing the door behind them.

"They *are* a pair," she agreed.

"And I'd have either one watch my back any day."

Yeah, she thought. The BOI team—who had returned from their mission just yesterday and had all been on the phone with Joe since—hadn't been able to help but Mike and Ty had stepped up to the plate like pros.

"I knew Mike was a Navy pilot in another life, but I hadn't realized Ty also had a military background." She headed for the kitchen to finally heat up the lasagna.

"Followed his big brother's footsteps," Joe said, trailing her. "Pretty awesome, when you think about it."

Yeah. It was pretty awesome. But the way he said it made it sound a little sad.

Or maybe it was just her. Her big brother, Bryan, had been on her mind a lot these past harrowing days.

"Steph?"

Joe's voice made her realize she'd zoned out. Apparently it wasn't the first time he'd tried to get her attention.

"Sorry. What?"

"I'm going to go take a shower while that heats up, okay?"

"Yeah, sure. I'll have everything ready by the time you're finished."

While the microwave hummed quietly in the background, she leaned her forearms on the counter, lowered her head between them, and closed her eyes.

And saw Carl Wilson fall dead on the floor again.

I killed a man.

She lifted her head abruptly and drove the memory from her mind. She thought about her parents instead. About how she'd almost lost them. About the blood, and bruises.

Okay—not the best deterrent.

She was just going to have to live with those images for a while, she conceded as the bloody scene in the cabin flashed through her mind again. The horror of finding Joe in that Freetown jail. The look in Suah's eyes when they'd left him.

She was going to live with a lot of things, for a very long time.

27

They ate dinner in silence, then she shooed him into the living area while she cleaned up.

Joe sat on the sofa, flipping through the news channels, stealing covert glances as she made work of nothing. How long did it take to tidy up the kitchen? A long time, apparently, when you were determined to avoid a very specific conversation.

He'd had enough of her stalling. He turned the TV off and tossed the remote on the coffee table.

"Stephanie. Come here."

"Almost finished," she said, wiping down the counter for the third time. He knew it was the third time because he'd counted. "Then I want to give Rhonda a call."

He pushed to his feet and stalked barefoot across the cool wood floor into the kitchen.

"With me." He latched on to her wrist, dragged her into the living area, and sank back down on the sofa with her on his lap. "I want you to talk to me."

She didn't pretend not to understand. But she had

no intention of having this conversation. "Joe, give it a rest. And give me some credit. I'm fine. There's nothing—"

"Stop it."

He hadn't meant to snap. And he hadn't expected to see that beautiful poker face crumble.

Damn. He sucked at this.

"Look," he said when she looked down, her hair hiding her face. He reached up and tucked it behind her ear. "You're dealing with the Grand Poobah of denial here, okay? You think I can't see that things are eating you up inside?"

A single tear landed on her folded hands. Still she wouldn't look at him.

Hell.

He felt heartsick for her and the unjustified guilt she was feeling. "It's never easy to take a life, Steph. Sometimes, it's just necessary."

Her shoulders sagged and she just sort of folded, leaning against him, her cheek on his chest, her hand on his shoulder. "He was going to kill you. He was going to kill Mom and Dad. So why do I feel this horrible remorse?"

"Because you hold life precious. Because you're trying to attribute your values, your heart, to a cold-blooded killer. But it doesn't work that way, Steph. People like Dalmage, like Carl Wilson and his team, they've got something missing. They're defective."

"They're human beings."

"They're not. Not in the way normal people are human. They're sharks, Stephanie. Predators. Put you in a room with a goldfish, you'll nurture it. Put a shark in a tank with that goldfish and he'll eat it. Without a thought to what it means to the goldfish. That's the difference between them and us."

He curled a finger under her chin and tipped her face to his. "You can't pity them. You can't fix them. You can't inject them with a dose of humanity or compassion or whatever it is that makes us different from them. They're unredeemable. So you eliminate them. And the world's a better, safer place without them."

She tucked her head back under his jaw, was quiet for a very long time. Finally, she exhaled deeply then looked up at him again.

"Why is it, that a man who has such difficulty expressing his own feelings, knows so much about how to help me with mine?"

This was the part he'd been dreading. When he'd forced her to open up to him, to help her sort things out, he'd known she'd expect the same in return.

Didn't mean it was going to be easy.

He stared at the ceiling, knowing she was waiting. Knowing what she deserved from him.

"Soldiers aren't supposed to talk about . . . things, you know?" He glanced at her, saw in her eyes that she did know. "From the time you enlist to the time you get out, it's all about sucking it up, shoving it back, locking it inside."

"It's not healthy."

"In the real world, no, it's not healthy," he agreed. "But it serves a purpose in the military. In covert ops.

It makes you strong. Keeps you focused. One enemy. One goal. One-track mind. If you're weak, if you falter, somebody dies."

"Sometimes they die anyway," she said softly, and he knew she was thinking of her brother.

Would he always feel that he could have prevented Bry's death? Probably. He would always wonder if there was something he could have done. But the guilt . . . he wasn't going to carry that any longer. Dalmage was responsible. And Dalmage had paid. Now he had to let it go.

When it came to Bobby's death, though, there was nowhere to shift the blame. He owned that one, lock, stock, and barrel.

He needed to tell her. His heart slammed out a couple of beats at double time. She was waiting. This was going to be so fucking hard.

"My little brother," he began, but had to stop because his mouth had gone bone dry.

Long moments passed, his heart pounding, his breath shallow, before he worked up the courage to meet the eyes that were focused on him with shock and concern.

"You have a brother?"

She was trying not to sound hurt. What kind of a man, after all, withheld something like that from the woman he loved? From the woman who loved him?

"Had a brother," he said hoarsely. He looked away. Clenched his jaw. "Bobby was ten when he died."

"Oh, Joe." The compassion in her voice was humbling. But compassion was totally misplaced on him.

"I killed him," he said flat out before he lost his nerve and bailed on her.

The harsh, stark words hung in the air while he waited for compassion to change to horror and disgust.

But apparently she didn't get it. Tears welled in her eyes. Tears he could barely see through the mist that suddenly burned in his.

He couldn't sit still any longer. He set her aside, pushed himself off the sofa, and paced. Eyes down. Shoulders stooped with the weight of the secret he'd carried all these years.

He'd never told anyone. Not Nate. Not the guys. Didn't talk about it with his parents. Not when it happened, and not after the funeral.

Sweep it under the rug. Let the sleeping dog lie. Lock the door. Don't ever let it out.

But now he had to.

"I was fifteen. Bobby"—*God it hurt to say his name*—"he was always wanting to tag along with me," he said, remembering Bobby's wiry grin, his freckled face, and gangly gait. "Bobby was . . . hell, he was Opie, walking barefoot down a dirt road with a fishing pole. Earnest and honest and a persistent little pest. Always begging to go with me. Always promising he'd be my wingman. Always trusting me to have his back. "

He stopped pacing. "Sometimes I'd let him have his way. I'd take him along. Hunting. Fishing. Just being boys.

"One day . . ." He stopped again, closed his eyes, "One day was the wrong day to give in."

He'd replayed this scene a thousand times in his head. What if he'd said no? What if he hadn't seen that big buck and chased after it? What if . . . what if . . .

"We took off on the three-wheeler," he finally said, forcing himself out of the spin cycle of could-have-beens and should-have-beens. "I was going too fast—Bobby always wanted me to go fast. I . . . I didn't see the washout on the side of the creek. I swerved too late. The ATV flipped and rolled and . . . and ran over him."

His breath felt like it had backed up in his lungs for a decade. He let it out, feeling weighted by the mistake of a lifetime. "His chest was crushed. I didn't even have a scratch."

He dropped back down onto the edge of the sofa, propped his elbows on his thighs, and stared at his clasped hands. "He hung on for three weeks. On a ventilator. In isolation, because of the infection that set into his lungs. Every day, I promised him I wouldn't let him die. Every single day."

Silence.

Ringing.

Hollow.

"So much for my promises."

Her hand touched his shoulder; her face pressed against his neck. And then she was curling her body around him, loving and giving and warm. "I'm so, so sorry."

He hung his head. Yeah. He was so, so sorry, too.

For a long time, she simply held him. Then she turned her face to his and kissed him.

"Tell me about him," she urged gently, just as she urged him gently back onto the sofa, and climbed back onto his lap.

He wrapped his arms around her; hung on tight. Silence ticked by like the lost years since Bobby had died. Long, bleak silence while she waited, and he stalled—then finally, haltingly, began to talk. About his little brother. About his quirky little smile. About how he could always make his dad laugh, his mother beam. How he could eat his weight in fried chicken, then stuff down half a peach pie without breaking a sweat.

He told her about his father, the stoic, keep-it-all-bottled-up-inside former Army staff sergeant who had never looked at him the same way again after Bobby died. About his mother, and how she'd promised him they didn't blame him. How the laughter had left her life from that moment on.

He told her about his guilt, his grieving, how he'd become completely, despondently disillusioned with life. So he'd joined the Army, so he could cope like his dad. So he could shut down, zone out, and just do the job, and not have to think about Bobby or his mom's sad face.

"And the CIA?"

"Upped the stakes. Required even more of me."

"Yet you left it to work with Nate."

"Didn't leave willingly," he said, a small smile tilting one corner of his mouth. "I was recruited for Task Force Mercy, like Wyatt. He embraced it. I went kicking and screaming."

"But Nate eventually won you over."

"Yeah. Nate and the guys."

"Your *other* brothers," she said, reminding him of their unbreakable bond.

Yeah. His other brothers. Men he'd fought beside, lived with, would die for. Men who would now die for the women who stood by their sides.

"I get it now," he said reflectively.

"Get what?"

"How they do it. How they separate what they do from who they are. How they compartmentalize and compromise, and live *in* life instead of avoiding it. How they stay sane in the face of insanity. How they stay human doing a job that could suck out your soul."

"And how do they do that?" Her eyes were full of understanding and hope that he was going to give her the right answer. The one she'd figured out a long time ago.

"They found their true north," he said, shifting her so she was straddling his thighs with her arms looped around his neck. "Like I found mine when I found you."

Tears brimmed in her eyes. Spilled down her cheeks. He tenderly kissed them away. He would never fully recover from Bobby's death. He'd always feel the loss. And the guilt. But with Stephanie in his corner, he knew he would someday stop beating himself up. Because of her, he was ready to start looking ahead, instead of always looking behind.

"I'm sorry I shut you out for so long."

"I'm sorry that I let you," she murmured, pressing her lips to his, then slowly, deliciously, kissing the corner of his mouth. The fading bruise on his temple. The hollow beneath his jaw where his heartbeat quickened.

"How could I ever have thought you were fragile?" he asked, leaning deeper into the sofa, giving her access to his throat, to his collarbone, as she scattered increasingly hungry kisses along his rapidly heating skin.

"How could you not?" she whispered, her warm breath stirring the embers of arousal into licking flames. "What had I ever shown you that would make you believe I wouldn't fall apart like a tissue if life got too messy?" The tip of her tongue grazed the curve of his ear. "Or too scary." Her teeth tugged ever so sweetly on his lobe. "Or too tough."

"Well, you've shown me now. You have definitely shown me now."

She pushed away from his chest so she could look into his eyes. "So we're squared away, then? No more secrets? No more of you protecting me from your big bad self?"

"Yeah," he said softly. "We are definitely squared away. Thank you, Stephanie."

She cupped his cheeks between her palms and looked deep into his eyes, making certain his full attention was riveted on her next words. "I love you, Joe. I want to marry you."

Enormous, uncontainable happiness filled his chest.

"I love you, Stephanie. I don't deserve you, but I love you, and there is no way on earth that you're not going to become my wife."

She smiled joyously, and if he didn't miss his guess, a little smugly. "Took you long enough to ask."

He laughed, something he didn't do easily. He had a feeling that was going to change. "So that's what I just did?"

"Close enough. So," she said, her eyes sparkling. "Looks like we're getting married."

He cupped her sweet, sexy ass in his palms. "Looks like."

They shared an insanely giddy look.

"Something this big . . . something this special," she said, leaning in and bussing her nose against his, "it seems like we should celebrate. Do something special to commemorate the occasion."

Oh, he knew that look. And he knew where this was leading. God, he was a lucky man.

"Seems like we should," he agreed, sliding his hands up under her sweater and unhooking her bra. "What'd you have in mind?"

She reached between them and pressed the flat of her palm over the ridge of his zipper. "Let's give it a little thought. I'm sure we'll come up with something."

He laughed again as "something" came up beneath her hand.

"You're such a guy," she said, biting his lower lip. "I was thinking of something more along the lines of a party."

"The hell you were."

She shrieked and laughed when he flipped her on her back. He leaned over her, his hands braced on either side of her head, fun and games suddenly transitioning to something deep and needy. "Take your clothes off."

"I'm a little busy right now."

He sucked in a sharp breath because yes, her *very* busy hands were making quick work of his zipper.

"Fine. I'll"—he groaned when she freed him and took him in her hands—"do it myself."

"That's one of the things I love about you. You're a can-do kind of guy."

He stood abruptly, because if he didn't, he was going to be finished before she even got started. He loved the look in her eyes as she lay sprawled wantonly on her back and watched him shuck his jeans then whip his shirt over his head and toss it to the floor. Loved the sounds she made when he pulled her sweater up and over her head, her bra going with it.

And God, oh, God, he *loved* the look of her, naked to the waist, her arms above her head, her eyes sensual and alive and aroused.

He dropped to his knees beside the sofa. Cupped the generous weight of a pale, creamy breast in his hand, lowered his head, and nuzzled. "You have the most beautiful breasts," he whispered against her flesh, then covered her nipple with his mouth, sucking and sipping and indulging his senses in her heady response.

Her nipple hardened. Her hand flew to his head, pressing him closer, begging for more attention. More of his mouth. More of his tongue. And more, he gladly gave. He bit her gently, tugged and teased, then pulled back to see the results of his work.

The tight bud of her nipple glistened and quivered as she arched her back and offered herself completely.

"Touch me. Please touch me," she begged, taking his hand in hers and guiding it to the snap at her waist. "Please," she sighed, breathless, yearning, as he slipped his fingers under her jeans, glided inside her panties, and cupped her where she was wet and pulsing and ready for him.

She gasped and he drove his fingers lower. Teased her. Enticed her enough to make her writhe against his hand, lift her hips off the sofa, and shove her jeans down and off.

She whispered his name, whimpered a prayer when he slipped a finger inside and stroked her. Once. Twice, and *sweet mother*, she came in his hand.

Her breath stalled. Her back arched. And her shocked exhalation of breath came out on a cry.

"Oh, God," she murmured, and dropped a hand heavily on the back of his head when he bent to kiss her stomach. "I didn't want . . . didn't want that . . . to happen yet. I'm sorry."

"Sorry? That was beautiful, Steph," he whispered, nuzzling her navel, spreading butterfly kisses where her ribs gave way to the softer, pliant flesh of her waist. "Beautiful." He lightly bit her hip point, felt a rush of arousal when she shivered. "And I'm so not through with you yet."

So not through.

He ran his hands along the inside of her knees, asking her with gentle pressure to part them. Never taking his gaze from hers, he kissed the silky skin of her inner thighs. First the left. Then the right. Back and forth between them, nuzzling, nipping, moving leisurely toward her center and the part of her he could never get enough of.

She was hot and wet, swollen and slick. She tasted like woman and sex and the essence of life and love and everything good and giving. He burrowed a hand beneath her hips and tilted her toward his mouth. Then he worshiped at the altar of her sexuality, delving deep into her silken folds with his tongue, parting her with his fingers and opening her wider to the relentless attention of his mouth.

Her response was wanton and lush as she dug her heels into the sofa and pressed herself against him. Her fingers dug into his shoulders. The sounds she made ... God, the sounds she made had desire coiling tight and hot in his belly.

He could wait. She couldn't. He didn't want to merely make this good for her. He wanted to destroy her with sensation, make her scream out in pleasure, make her incapable of looking at him, at his mouth, at his hands, without thinking of them together this way.

She was frantically begging him to *stop, I can't take any more*. Then begging him to *please, please, don't ever stop*, until finally her entire body stiffened. She cried out. And wept. And laughed as her release pulsed through her.

He lifted his head, pressed loving kisses to the inside of her trembling thighs, then watched her ride it out, her breasts heaving, her body flushed and tender and drained.

"Hello," he said with a soft smile when she finally opened her eyes. "Welcome back."

A limp hand landed on his cheek. "Come up here."

He crawled slowly up her body, loving that place she made for him between her thighs.

"You have totally ruined me."

"God, I hope so."

She drew his head down to hers and kissed him with such sweet, open love that he swore he felt his heart swell. Nothing else could explain the sensation that made his chest hurt because it felt so full.

"I love you," she whispered, then reached between them. She found him thick and pulsing and aching for her, and finally guided him home.

Home. With this woman for the rest of his life.

Epilogue

"Babies and bad boys. A pretty appealing combination, wouldn't you agree?"

Yeah. Stephanie agreed wholeheartedly with her mother as she scooped a bowl of chips and a plate of pickles off the kitchen counter and followed her into the great room where, indeed, the array of babies and bad boys inside and just outside the terrace doors was darn near irresistible.

The entire boisterous team and all their wives and offspring had gathered at her parents' Virginia home to celebrate Selena Rossella Janine Mendoza's happy and healthy entry into the world six weeks ago.

And they were celebrating so much more.

Her mother's thrilling appointment to the secretary of state position, for one. Stephanie and Joe's engagement for another.

And in an unexpected turn of events, they were also celebrating Nate's announcement that Black Ops, Inc. would not only be relocating to an as-yet-undisclosed location in the States, but would also soon become a recognized entity under the Department of Defense and enjoy all the protection that the U.S. military machine had at its disposal. They were officially no longer unofficial.

With most of the BOIs married now and producing babies at a steady rate, the commuting had started to take a toll, so this had been most welcome news to everyone. Even Sam Lang, who had settled in Vegas and opted out of active duty a while ago, was considering coming back into the fold.

Stephanie caught Joe's eye where he stood talking with her dad across the room, looking relaxed and happy and healthy six weeks after his imprisonment in Freetown. He smiled and winked at her—Joe Green *winked*—and her heart got all swishy and light.

Life was very, very good.

Joe was back in fighting form. She was on the way to getting fairly ripped herself. No more desk jockeying for her. As the newest member of the BOI team—joining Crystal and B.J. among the BOIs who were GIRLS— she had to be in shape. So she and Joe had trained together the past four weeks. And she'd found out what kind of stuff she was really made of.

Setting the chips and dill spears on the sideboard with the rest of the lunch spread, Stephanie stood there a moment taking it all in.

Jenna, Gabe's wife and a highly acclaimed journalist, sat in a relatively quiet corner with Wyatt's wife, Sophie, who had founded a school in San Salvador for underprivileged children. With Ali asleep in Jenna's arms, and little Mariah scooting around near her mother, Sophie's, feet, the two women were discussing an article Jenna was pulling together on education in the Central American country.

Stephanie couldn't hear everything they were saying because the noise, as always when they all got together, was joyously deafening. Even with some of the big boys and little girls outside.

Her mom looped an arm through hers and nodded toward the terrace doors where a take-no-prisoners snowball fight was in progress.

"I thought they were building a snowman," Ann said, grinning.

"Looks like Reed may have preempted that idea."

The accusatory shouts and jeers that petite, red-headed Crystal, aka Tinkerbelle, was launching at her laughing husband, Johnny Reed, pretty much confirmed that he was the culprit. Aided and abetted by Wyatt and Sophie Savage's fourteen-year-old daughter, Hope, and by Sam and Abbie Lang's ten-year-old niece, Tina, the three of them had apparently staged a sneak attack against Rafe, Tink, and Nate Black's wife, Juliana, of all people. The sophisticated, demure Argentina native, Dr. Juliana Flores-Black, was joyously enamored by the white stuff.

"We never got snow where I lived growing up," she'd said earlier as she'd gazed out the window at the fluffy white flakes drifting down. "Sometimes we'd drive to the mountains just to see and touch it, but I've never actually been in a snowstorm."

Stephanie hadn't wanted to break it to her that this wasn't a snowstorm. What they'd lived through in Minnesota more than a month ago . . . *that* had been a snowstorm, she thought with a shiver. This was an anomalous stalled front that had dumped an unprecedented eight inches of snow throughout the day.

Most of it would melt away by tomorrow; the sun was already peeking out to help the thaw along. But in the meantime, Rafe—Colombian born and Miami raised, and apparently snow deprived like Juliana—had also fallen victim to the lure of a romp in the snow. The gorgeous Latino was laughing like a kid as he dodged a missile Reed fired that barely missed Rafe's head.

"Whoa." Gabe Jones winced as he watched the action. "Reed just got nailed. Juliana's got one helluvan arm."

Luke "Doc Holliday" Colter, the BOI team medic, straightened from the pool table where he and Wyatt Savage were squared off in a game of eight ball. "Everything she learned, she learned from you, right, boss?" He grinned at Nate Black.

"Reed's mistake was underestimating her," Nate said, watching his wife with quiet pride. "I learned not to do that a long time ago."

It was good seeing the BOI founder this relaxed, Stephanie thought. Nate carried a lot on his shoulders. She was glad that he took advantage of these infrequent gatherings and let himself unwind a bit.

"Your shot, Colter." Wyatt Savage leaned a hip against the pool table, studying the balls scattered over green felt.

Doc took his time chalking his cue, his Indiana Jones fedora tilted rakishly on his head. "Papa Bear, are you *really* that anxious to part with your money?"

With this crew, no game—be it poker, pool, or a push-up competition—ever got played without a bet.

Wyatt, a mellow, slow-talking, Georgia boy, just smiled. "You're going down, Doctorman. It's just a matter of time."

Unperturbed, Luke called, "Three ball, corner pocket." He eyeballed the angle, and took his shot.

Wyatt snorted when Luke missed.

"You're off your stride, Colter." Sam Lang watched the table action with interest, arms folded over his chest, legs wide.

"He didn't get much sleep last night." Valentina walked up to Luke's side and handed him a bottle of beer.

"The baby kept kicking me in the back." He laid a hand lovingly on his wife's swelling abdomen, then bent down and whispered against her round stomach. "Hey, little guy. Daddy's gonna win you a horsey."

Val relieved him of the fedora. "Little *girl*," she corrected, setting the hat at a jaunty angle on top of her own head.

"You changed your mind and found out the baby's sex?" Stephanie asked, sitting on the arm of the nearby sofa.

"No, we still don't want to know. But you know Luke. There has to be a bet on the outcome."

"If I win," Luke said, watching Wyatt line up his shot,

"she's going to buy me a fifty-four-inch flat screen. If Val wins, I'm going to buy her a Diaper Genie. What?" he asked, acting clueless when eyes rolled in collective disbelief. "She *wants* a Diaper Genie, don't you, baby?" He grinned at his wife.

Val patted him on the cheek. "Absolutely," she agreed, playing along.

Even six months pregnant, Valentina was astoundingly beautiful. The internationally famous model wore her pregnancy well, just as she wore her celebrity well. The fee she'd earned from a recent spread in *Vogue*, showcasing Val in all her pregnant glory, was earmarked for Save the Children, Sierra Leone.

"Val looks like a goddess," Abbie Lang groused goodnaturedly as she and her two boys joined Stephanie on the sofa. "All I get are swollen ankles."

Stephanie lifted little Bryan, her brother's namesake, onto her lap and kissed the top of his head, while Abbie corralled Thomas, who had just woken up from his nap and was firing on all cylinders.

"You look beautiful," Sam assured her, taking Thomas off her hands.

"For a blimp." Abbie was due in two weeks. She sighed heavily. "I'll be so happy when I can see my feet again."

Stephanie smiled down at Bryan. "So what do you want Mommy to bring home from the hospital?"

"A puppy," the three year old said.

Abbie made a face. "Reed taught him to say that."

Bryan wriggled off Stephanie's lap and ran up to

B.J. when she walked into the room, carrying baby Selena.

"Can I hold her?" Bryan asked.

"Let's both hold her." B.J., who had blossomed with motherhood, sat down in an oversize wing chair. "Come sit beside me, sweetheart."

"She's so little." Bryan looked awestruck when B.J. placed the sleeping baby in his arms. "Does she cry a lot? Daddy says babies cry all the time and that I'd better get used to it."

"Babies cry when they're hungry, or when they're tired, or when they need their diapers changed."

B.J.'s explanation seemed to satisfy Bryan, who had apparently grown tired of talking about babies. He carefully handed Selena back to her mother, then slipped off the chair in search of more interesting stuff.

"You're a natural at this." Stephanie admired both B.J.'s relaxed ease and the beautiful child. Little Selena had coal-black hair just like her daddy that lay in tiny little corkscrews very reminiscent of B.J.'s curly blond hair.

"You wouldn't have said that if you'd seen me the first week we brought her home."

Reed breezed in through the door just then, brushing snow from his hair and bringing a cool breeze with him. Crystal raced in after him, laughing and stuffing a handful of snow down his shirt. He grabbed her around the waist, lifted her off her feet, and kissed her. "You are really pressing your luck here, Tinkerbelle.

"Whoa," he added as the rest of the snow crew piled

inside after him. "You can't swing a dead cat around here without running into a pregnant woman or a tadpole." He touched a curled finger to little Selena's cheek, his eyes going soft before he addressed the room at large. "Do you people *not* know how to contain this?"

Tink slipped out of her jacket, then quietly cleared her throat. "Maybe we'd better have a little talk, Johnny."

He glanced at his wife. "About where babies come from? Tink, darlin', I read the book."

"You read a book?" Doc asked with a startled look.

"Shut up, Colter. And *I'm* not the one pollinating the flowers around here."

"Um . . . yeah, actually you are. You *did*," Crystal amended, her green eyes watchful and waiting.

Distracted as Sophie and Wyatt's little girl latched on to his leg, Johnny picked her up, then laughed when her pudgy little hand started pulling his earlobe. "Lookie there. Even the little girls find me irresistible."

He was the last one to realize that all the adults in the room had gone quiet. When he finally tuned in, his confused gaze swept the room. "What did I miss?"

Everyone turned their eyes to Crystal. They were all smiling.

He whipped his head toward his wife. And suddenly he got it.

"Wait a minute. Rewind."

He handed Mariah off to her mother. "You said I did something. I did *what*?"

"You pollinated your flower," Crystal said, then

watched his expression go from confused to stunned to helpless disbelief.

"I . . . seriously?"

She nodded.

He dragged a hand over his head. "How . . . how did that happen?"

Tink laughed. "I thought you said you read the book."

He searched his wife's green eyes. "A baby? Seriously, Tink?" he asked again, his voice soft and tender. His eyes were questioning and hopeful. "We're going to have a *baby*?"

She nodded, a huge smile lighting her face.

Joy, disbelief, panic, and love raced through Johnny's eyes. Then he dropped to his knees in front of his wife, and carefully positioned his big rough hands, fingers splayed wide, over her flat abdomen. Awestruck, he looked up at her. "There's a baby in there."

She touched a hand to his cheek, the love shining in her eyes as blinding as the sunlight refracting through the window. "Yup."

He drew her hips against his face and kissed her there, reverent, happy, and clearly a little afraid.

Gabe was the first to break the happy silence that had Stephanie and the rest of the women near tears. "Please, God, let it be a girl. The world can't handle another Johnny Duane Reed."

"And let her look like her mother," Sam added, giving Crystal a congratulatory peck on the cheek as Johnny rose shakily to his feet.

"You should sit down," Johnny told her, ignoring them. Serious as a judge, he took Crystal's hands in his and led her to the nearest empty chair. Full-out panic had set in. "And you should *not* have been outside in the snow. What if . . . what if, oh, God—I can't even say it. Juliana. You're a doctor. Tell her she has to be more careful. And Nate. You're her boss. Put her on the D.L. right now."

"Guys," Crystal appealed to the men, cutting Johnny off before he could start construction on a protective cage. "Help me out here, would you?"

As one, the men converged. Nate, Luke, Wyatt, and Rafe attacked Reed's left flank; Gabe, Sam, and Joe honed in on his right. Reed was tough and he was wiry, but he was no match for the collective muscle of his BOI teammates. They bodily picked him up and headed across the room.

Robert held the double doors open wide as they marched outside, and on the count of three, heaved him into a snowdrift.

Reed was swearing a blue streak and promising some really creative payback when the *whop, whop, whop* of a helicopter drowned him out.

All eyes turned to the small Bell chopper as it descended, then set down gracefully on the lawn.

Joe was the first one to recognize the pilot.

"It's Brown," he said, as Stephanie joined him by the terrace door.

"What the hell is he up to now?" Rafe asked as Mike shouldered open the cockpit door and stepped out into the snow.

"Oh, my God," Stephanie cried, covering her mouth with her hands when she saw who climbed out behind him.

She felt her mother's arm around her shoulders. "Go ahead, honey. Go to him."

Tears blurred her eyes as she met Ann's gentle smile. "You did this?"

"Your father and I did, yes. Someone had to. We couldn't bear the look in your eyes when you talked about him."

She hugged her mother hard, then ran outside to where Joe was already waiting as Suah Korama walked hesitantly toward them.

"So," Joe said, only his eyes relaying what he dared not say for fear of embarrassing the boy, who was a man, who had come so far on blind faith. "I guess you missed me."

Suah reached out, shook Joe's extended hand, and delivered his signature line. "Like a wart." A ghost of a smile touched his lips and Stephanie simply melted.

She folded the boy in her arms, while the man she loved looked on, smiling.

"Welcome, Suah. Welcome home."

The house was quiet and mostly dark when Stephanie headed toward the great room, looking for Joe. The party had broken up over an hour ago. Some of the guys and their wives were upstairs in the spare bedrooms; the overflow had booked rooms in a nearby hotel. Tomorrow morning, they'd be back for breakfast before everyone headed their separate ways.

Suah was sound asleep in Bryan's old room, exhausted from the long flight. Most likely, he was also having second thoughts about coming. Most certainly, he was overwhelmed by the personalities and the sheer volume of people who were now going to be a part of his new, very different life.

Her heart had fractured a hundred times since he'd stepped off that helicopter. At the way his eyes had widened at the abundance of food, the opulence of her parents' home. At the idea of a room that was all his own. With a bed. And clean sheets.

She'd tried to see it all through his eyes, but realized there was no way she ever could. She realized also that they were all going to be making compromises to make this work. Suah was a resilient kid. He'd adjust. They all would. Most important, he now had a chance at a life, not merely an existence.

She saw Joe the moment she walked into the family room. He stood with his back to her in front of the fireplace, where a mellow fire spread warmth through the room. His focus was above the white marble mantel, on the life-size oil portrait of Staff Sergeant Bryan Tompkins in full dress blues. Forever young. Forever brave.

Forever gone.

"You okay?" Stephanie slipped up beside him.

He drew her against him, pressed a kiss to the top of her head. And said nothing.

"He'd be so proud, Joe." She touched his jaw and urged him to look at her. "He'd be so proud of you."

He swallowed hard. "I still remember the first day I met him. A real smart-ass."

She smiled. "He had his moments."

"He did," Joe agreed. "He absolutely did."

And now, Bryan finally had his justice. And peace. All of them did.

"So much for a quiet farewell breakfast." Stephanie grinned as Joe found a spot near the window so he could grab a moment with her.

"You know Doc. No BOI gathering is complete without a rip-roaring, wild west poker game."

A war whoop came from the poker table. Crystal had just cleaned house on Doc and Primetime was rubbing it in with unbridled glee. Jenna high-fived Crystal over the stack of chips.

"Hoisted by my own petard," Luke grumbled as Crystal raked in her winnings.

"If that's something like smashed by your own tank, then yeah, you've been hoisted. And by an itty-bitty pregnant girl." Reed kissed his wife smack on the mouth.

This was his family, Joe thought. They laughed together, they loved together, they had each other's backs.

In a world where chaos threatened to take over, where darkness constantly opposed light, the Tompkinses' home provided refuge. Peace. An atmosphere of hope and home and family.

Ann and Robert's words came back to him from that long-ago day when the team had first gathered here to mourn their fallen brother.

"Remember, you're Bry's brothers . . . consider us your second family . . . so come home, boys. Anytime. When you need to recharge. When you need a soft place to land. Whenever you need to . . . just come home."

So here he was. Home with the family they had all become.

"How do you think Suah's doing?" He glanced across the room, where Ann and Robert were shepherding Suah through the buffet line.

"He's a little shell-shocked," Stephanie said, "but he's doing okay. I still can't believe he's here."

Joe couldn't take his eyes off her face. She was so animated and happy and beautiful. The BOIs were his family, but Stephanie was his life.

"Let's have a baby," he said abruptly.

She did a double take, a startled smile playing at the corners of her mouth. "That's . . . sudden."

He traced a fingertip down her cheek. "I see the way you look at those babies. You think I don't know how much you want one of your own?"

"I'm that transparent?"

"A little, yeah," he said, smiling softly. "You're a lot of things, Steph. Beautiful. Smart. Kick-ass brave." He turned her toward him, looping his arms around her waist. "But most of all, you're mine. And I'm never going to be stupid enough to let you go."

"Together, we can survive anything," she said.

"Anything," he agreed.

In the arms of this woman he loved, he *could* do anything. Be anything. Conquer anything. Even his guilt over Bobby.

He looked over Stephanie's shoulder at Suah, saw the fear and the hope and the resilience squaring his narrow shoulders.

Bobby was gone, and Bryan was gone.

But for Joe, Stephanie, and Suah, life was just beginning.

**If you enjoyed
this last book in the Black Ops, Inc. series,
turn the page
for excerpts from all the previous books!**

SHOW NO MERCY
Gabriel Jones's and Jenna McMillan's story

"Tonight? Are you crazy?" Jenna shook her head at Gabe. "I'm not flying anywhere. And I'm sure not going home."

"For the last time, you need to back away from Maxim and get out of Argentina."

"Okay. Let's get something straight. In the first place, you don't tell me what to do. In the second place, I came here to do a job and I will do it. And in the third place, it's not like *I'm* being threatened here or anything. I mean, that bomb wasn't meant for me. You're not talking, but I think it's pretty safe to assume that Maxim was the target."

"Yeah, and you're just itching to get caught in the crossfire if someone goes after him again, aren't you? Damn it, Jenna. You're being stupid about this."

She stopped. Turned on him. "No, I'm being professional. I walked away from a story because of you the last time I was here. I'm not walking away from this one."

He reeled slightly. Fatigue could have been the cause, but she knew the moment she saw his face that fatigue had nothing to do with his reaction.

In that same moment she knew something else. This battle-hardened warrior, this professional soldier wasn't as immune to death and destruction as he'd like everyone to think. He struggled with the same images she did. He saw the same charred bodies, the same bloodied corpses.

He felt the same kind of horror. The only difference was she could afford the luxury of regret. He couldn't, and there was nothing she could say to make him know she understood.

Key in hand, she eased around him toward the door to her room.

"Wait!" His voice was sharp as he grabbed her wrist and kept her from inserting the key in the lock. "Let me check it first."

"Oh, for God's sake. You know what?" She was tired. Of everything. Of him thinking he could tell her what to do, of him making it clear that he didn't want or need anyone—specifically her—in his life. "You've lived too long on the 'dark side,'" she said, putting a lot of theatrical woo-woo in the last two words. "I'm tired, I'm hungry, and all I want to do is eat, shower, write my story, and go to bed."

She jerked her hand away from his, shoved the key in the lock and pushed the door open—and came face-to-face with three gunmen.

Before she could react, Gabe hit her from the side, tackling her to the ground as the blast of a gun echoed into the hallway.

She waited for the pain, visualized her own blood, then realized that nothing hurt. Nothing but her hip where she'd landed on the floor with Gabe on top of her—again.

She struggled to get up.

"Stay down!" he ordered. "And roll! Get the hell away from the door!" he choked out through a hacking cough.

"Wha—" *Oh God.*

A horrible odor hit her olfactory senses then and she realized why he was choking. She gagged on a mouthful of air. Her eyes started burning. Her gut convulsed into dry heaves.

Gabe gagged, too, as he half-dragged, half-pushed her back toward the elevator, where the air was blessedly fresh.

Jenna lay facedown on the floor. She squinted toward the sound of Gabe's tortured breathing, barely able to make him out through the tears. He'd rolled to his side facing her door, using his body as a shield between her and whatever or whoever might still be in that room. He'd wedged the hilt of his Butterfly firmly between his teeth and he'd drawn a pistol she hadn't even been aware he'd been carrying. The barrel was trained on her open hotel room door.

"Cell phone," he gritted around the knife. "Pocket."

With her eyes pinched shut against the lingering burn and streaming tears, Jenna attacked his pants, searching pockets, and finally found the one with his cell phone.

Later, she'd think about the lean hips and flat gut and all that male heat she'd encountered. Right now, she was shaking too badly to even be embarrassed that she might have grabbed something that definitely wasn't his phone.

"Punch one," he ordered.

She did.

"Lang." Sam answered on the first ring.

She could take it from here. "Men with guns. In my room."

A split second of silence. "Anyone hurt?"

"I . . . I don't know. I don't think so."

"On my way up." He disconnected.

She closed the phone, lowered her head to rest against Gabe's back, right between his shoulder blades. Right where he was solid and strong, and his deep breaths were proof that he was alive and that he planned to keep them both that way.

Finally she drew a breath that didn't feel like it dragged over razor blades. She braved peeking over his shoulder. A buckshot pattern, roughly the size of a softball, had shattered the top of the door.

"Where are they? And not that I'm complaining, but why aren't they still shooting at us?"

"Because they're probably long gone. Are you hurt?" Gabe asked with enough urgency that she realized he must have felt her shiver in delayed reaction to the hole in the door.

"No. No, I'm okay. What about you? Are you hurt?"

"Only if you count the fact that you damn near ripped off my plumbing groping around for my phone."

She made a sound of exasperation. "Now? You pick *now* to become a comedian?"

"It's all about timing," he whispered back.

TAKE NO PRISONERS
Sam Lang's and Abbie Hughes's story

Abbie spotted the gay cop cowboy the minute she came back from break. It was hard not to. The guy was incredible looking. While she felt a little kernel of unease that he'd turned up again—at the casino where she worked this time—she wasn't going to let it throw her off her stride. The Vegas Strip wasn't all that big. Not really. There were only so many places for people to eat, sleep, and gamble.

When he drifted off twenty minutes or so later without so much as looking her way, she chalked it up to coincidence. Just as she found it coincidental that the tall, dark man who'd been playing the slot beside the golden boy ambled over to the blackjack tables.

Big guy. The western-cut white shirt and slim, crisp Wrangler jeans told her he was a real cowboy. The kind who made his living in the saddle, not the kind who just dressed the part. He was confident but quiet with it, she decided, as she dealt all around to her full table, then cut another glance the big guy's way.

He stood a few feet back from the tables, arms crossed over a broad chest, long legs planted about shoulder-width apart, eyes intent on the action on the blackjack table next to hers. On any given night there were a lot of spectators in a casino, so it wasn't unusual that he stood back from the crowd and just watched. What was unusual was that between deals, her gaze kept gravitating back to him.

What was even more curious was that when one of her players scooped up his chips and wandered off, leaving the third-base chair empty, Abbie found herself wishing the tall cowboy would take his place.

What was up with that? And what was up with the little stutter-step of her heart when he ambled over, nodded hello, and eased his lean hips onto the chair?

"Howdy," she said with what she told herself was a standard, welcoming smile.

He answered with a polite nod as he reached into his hip pocket and dug out his wallet. When she'd paid and collected bets all around, he tossed a hundred-dollar bill onto the table.

Abbie scooped it up, counted out one hundred in chips from the chip tray, then spread them on the green felt tabletop for him to see. After he'd gathered them in and stacked them in front of him, she tucked the hundred into the slot in front of her.

"Place your bets," she said to the table of seven, then dealt the first round faceup from the shoe. When all players had two cards faceup, she announced her own total. "Dealer has thirteen."

Her first-base player asked for a hit, which busted him. When she got to the cute quiet cowboy, he waved his hand over his cards, standing pat with eighteen.

You could tell a lot about a person from their hands. Abbie saw a lot of hands—polished and manicured, dirty and rough, thin and arthritic. The cowboy's hands were big, like he was. His fingers were tan and long with blunt, clean nails—not buffed. Buffed, in her book, said pretentious. His were not. They were capable hands, a working man's hands, with the occasional scar to show he was more than a gentleman rancher. Plenty of calluses. He dug in.

She liked him for that. Was happy for him when she drew a king, which busted her. "Luck's running your way," she said with a smile as she paid him.

He looked up at her then and for the first time she was hit with the full force of his smile. Shy and sweet, yet she got the distinct impression there was something dark and dangerous about him.

Whoa. Where had that come from? And what the heck was going on with her?

Hundreds—hell, thousands—of players sat at her table in any given month. Some were serious, some were fun and funny, some sad. And yeah, some of them deserved a second look. But none of them flipped her switches or tripped her triggers like this man was flipping and tripping them right now. It was unsettling as all get-out.

"Place your bets," she announced again, then dealt around the table when all players had slid chips into their betting boxes.

Whereas the blond poster boy had been bad-boy gorgeous, there wasn't one thing about this man that suggested a boy. Abbie pegged him for midthirties—maybe closer to forty, but it wasn't anything physical that gave her that impression. He was rock-solid and sort of rough-and-tumble looking. Dark brown hair, close cut, dark, *dark* brown eyes, all-seeing. Nice face. Hard face. All edgy angles and bold lines.

Maybe that was where the dangerous part came in. He had a look about him that was both disconcerting and compelling. A presence suggesting experience and intelligence and a core-solid confidence that needed no outward display or action to reinforce it.

Clint Eastwood without the swagger. Matthew McConaughey without the long hair and boyish charm—and *with* a shirt on, something McConaughey was generally filmed without. Although, the cowboy *did* have his own brand of charisma going on because sure as the world, he was throwing *her* for a loop.

"Cards?" she asked him now.

"Double down."

Smart player, she thought, and split his pair of eights. She grinned again when he eventually beat the table and her on both cards.

"I think maybe *you're* my luck." He tossed a token in the form of a red chip her way.

"Tip," she said loud enough for her pit boss to hear, showed him the five-dollar chip before she pocketed it. "Thanks," she said smiling at him.

"My pleasure."

He spoke so softly that the only reason she understood what he said was because she was looking right at him. The din of the casino drowned out his words to anyone else at the table as the rest of the players talked and joked or commiserated with each other.

The next words out of his mouth—"What time do you get off?"—stopped her cold.

She averted her gaze. "Place your bets," she told the table at large, thinking, *Hokay. Quiet doesn't necessarily mean shy.*

The man moved fast. Which both surprised and pleased her because it meant that all this "awareness," for lack of a better word, wasn't one-sided. It also made her a little nervous. Her first instinct was to give him her standard "Sorry. No fraternizing with the customers" speech.

But then she got an image of a devil sitting on her shoulder—a red-haired pixie devil with a remarkable resemblance to her friend Crystal. *"Don't you dare brush him off. Look at him. Look! At! Him!"*

She chanced meeting his eyes again—his expression was expectant but not pressuring—and found herself mouthing, "Midnight."

A hint of a smile tugged at one corner of his mouth. "Where?"

She didn't hesitate nearly long enough. "Here." *God, what am I doing?*

"Cards?" she asked the table.

He gave her the "hit me" signal when she came around to him.

He broke twenty-one, shrugged.

"Sorry," she said, liking the easy way he took the loss. "Better luck next time."

"Counting on it." He stood. "Later," he said for her ears only; then he strolled away from the table.

"Dealer pays sixteen," she said absently as she paid all winners and surreptitiously watched what was arguably one of the finest Wrangler butts she'd ever seen get lost in a sea of gamblers.

WHISPER NO LIES
Johnny Duane Reed's and Crystal Debrowski's story

Crystal knew she was in deep trouble and she didn't have one single clue how it had come to this.

First the counterfeit chips had shown up on the floor, then one of her sections came up short for the evening shift's take. Tens of thousands of dollars short. Computer security codes were breached by hackers. Dozens of other little yet vital security glitches—all on her watch—had her pulling her hair out.

So yeah, she became a subject of intense scrutiny. And no. She had no explanation, just a lot of sleepless nights trying to figure out how this was happening on her shift.

Then the unthinkable happened. Last night, twelve of the thirteen gaming tables under her direct supervision had been flooded with counterfeit twenty-dollar bills. Whoever distributed them had taken the casino for close to two hundred K.

Now here she was, standing in her boss's office. "You don't seriously believe I'm stealing from you?"

Gilbert sat behind his massive mahogany desk. "I don't want to, no. But given the circumstances, Miss Debrowski, we have no choice but to place you on leave without pay."

She swallowed back anger and frustration and tears. "I understand." Actually, she didn't, but given the fact that the only case she had to plead was ignorance, what else could she say?

Gilbert pressed the intercom button on his phone. "Send them in."

The door opened. Crystal looked over her shoulder to see two uniformed LVPD officers walk in.

She turned back to Gilbert, her heart pounding. "You're having me arrested?"

Her boss had the decency to look remorseful. "I'm sorry."

"And here I thought I was the only one who got to use handcuffs on you."

Crystal looked up from the corner of the jail cell four hours later to see Johnny Duane Reed grinning at her from the other side of the bars.

Perfect.

Grinning and gorgeous, Reed was the last person she wanted to see, specifically because until today he *had* been the only one who had ever gotten to use handcuffs on her.

A vivid memory of her naked and cuffed to her own bed while Reed had hovered over her was not the diversion she needed at this point in time.

She'd ask him what he was doing here but figured she already knew. "Abbie called you."

"I was visiting the ranch," Reed said. "I was there when you called her."

It figured that Reed would be back in Vegas and not bother to come and see her. Not that she wanted him to. Not that she cared.

"I need a lawyer, not a . . ." She paused, groping for the word that best described him.

"Lover?" he suggested with that cocky grin.

"Not the word I was searching for," she grumbled, but let it go at that.

"If you don't want him, sugar, I'll be happy to take him."

Her cell mate shot Reed her best come-hither hooker smile. Reed, of course, couldn't help himself. He winked at her.

Jesus, would you look at him. Hair too long and too blond. Eyes too sexy and too blue. Body too buff, ego too healthy. Standing there in his tight, faded jeans, painted-on T-shirt, and snakeskin boots, he looked like God's guilty gift—and he knew it.

So did Crystal. What she didn't know was why she was so glad to see a man who played at life, at love, and at caring about her. That was the sum total of Reed's commitment quotient. He played at everything.

"How you holding up, Tinkerbell?" he asked gently.

Oh God. He actually sounded like he cared.

"Careful, Reed. You might get me thinking you give a rip."

He had the gall to look wounded. "Now you've gone and hurt my feelings."

"Just get me out of here," she said, rising and meeting him at the heavy, barred door.

"Working on it," he said. "Abbie and Sam are right behind me. They'll arrange bail."

"Bail's already made."

Reed looked over his shoulder at the jailer, who sauntered slowly toward them with a set of keys.

Crystal backed away from the bars when the barrel-chested and balding deputy slipped the lock and slid open the door with a hollow, heavy clink. "Someone made my bail? Who?"

He shrugged. "You'll have to ask at processing. I just do what I'm told."

"I've always had this prison-chick fantasy," Reed said confidentially as Crystal slipped out of the cell. "You know—sex-starved, man-hungry."

"Stow it." Crystal marched past him, ignoring his warped sense of humor. She was tired and terrified and doing her damnedest not to let either show.

"Hey, hey," he said gently and caught her by the arm. "Looks like someone could use a hug."

Yeah. She could use a hug. She could use a hundred hugs but now was not the time, this was not the place, and Reed was not the man she wanted to show the slightest bit of weakness to. "What I need is fresh air."

"Sure. But first, do a guy a favor. Make my fantasy complete. Tell me that you and the sister there had a hair-pulling, nail-scratching catfight and I'll die a happy man."

"Screw you, Reed."

He dropped a hand on her shoulder. Squeezed. "Now you're talkin'."

FEEL THE HEAT
Raphael Mendoza's and B.J. Chase's story

A man dressed in a black wife-beater and dark camo cargo pants and wielding the AK stepped out from behind him. He gestured with the business end of the rifle for her to raise her hands, too. "Up high. Let's see 'em, *cara*."

The look on Eduardo's face told her that he was as surprised as she was. And that they were both as good as dead if she didn't do what she was told.

Stall, she thought, as adrenaline zipped through her blood like rocket fuel. She needed to make something happen until her backup took charge of the situation.

Very slowly, she lifted her hands, all the while inching closer to the open door of the Jeep and the shotgun that lay just out of reach on the floor.

Where were they—?

Oh God. Her runaway heart rate plummeted when she saw Maynard, Hogan, and Collins suddenly illuminated by the beams of three powerful Maglites, marching slowly toward her.

Their hands were linked on top of their heads. Three men walking behind them pointed assault rifles at their backs, prodding them forward. The lot of them looked ready to chew nails. They were pissed and embarrassed that they'd been caught with their pants down. Join the club.

What kind of men were they dealing with that they could get the drop on experienced DIA field officers?

She quickly decided the men either had known they were coming or had skills the DIA officers lacked.

She cut a cautious glance toward the Jeep. Knew that if she was going to make a move, it had to be now.

She dove toward the 12-gauge.

The man with the AK struck like a viper. He grabbed her arm, yanked her away from the door, then slammed her up against the vehicle.

"Not smart." He pinned her against the Jeep with the weight of his body. "Now I'll tell you again. Keep your hands where I can see them. That way no one gets hurt."

He could hurt her, she had no doubt about that. Hell, he could have killed her by now, she thought as he turned Eduardo over to one of his men. One bullet. Close range. Clean and simple.

For whatever reason, she was still fit and fine. The others were fine, too, which gave her reason to hope that they still had a prayer of getting out of this alive. To do that, she had to play heads-up ball, which meant she had to work through the adrenaline rush that mixed with fear and made her shaky, and quickly assess her adversary.

This close, it wasn't that difficult. The face that was mere inches away from hers was not a face she would expect to meet in a dark alley on the wrong side of a mission that was rapidly heading south. *Wholesome* was the word that came to mind. Altar-boy angelic — providing she overlooked the assault rifle.

She'd caught a glimpse of a tattoo on his upper arm that appeared to be a cross of some sort. It did not, however, put her in mind of altars or boys. Neither did the gold crucifix that hung from his neck and lay against a broad chest so smooth it could have been waxed.

The bright beams of the Maglites lit up the alley. She could see that his eyes were dark, almost black, like the hair that he wore cut military close. His skin was caramel toned, his face clean shaven and flawless but for a small, triangular scar that rode at the left corner of a full, sensuous mouth. She was used to assessing and cataloging adversaries on the fly. What she wasn't used to was thinking of the enemy as disarmingly handsome—or that she would be ultra-sensitive to the fact that he was plastered so tightly against her she could feel the heat radiating from his body like a pulse.

He wasn't a big man—maybe five nine, five ten—but the body pressed against hers was as lean and hard as the Jeep at her back. The steely grip on her arm was capable of inflicting pain, yet he only used it to restrain her.

Even though his English bore a Spanish accent, something about him made her think he'd spent some time in the States. He was clean, his bearing disciplined and practiced. He knew exactly what he was doing, where his men were, and how to take control. Situational awareness. Like a soldier. Like a merc, she thought, and knew that alive or not, they were still in deep trouble.

RISK NO SECRETS
Wyatt Savage's and Sophie Baylor's story

"It's unfortunate that you picked such a difficult time in Sophie's life to visit San Salvador," Montoya said as he walked Sophie back to Wyatt's side, effectively reminding Wyatt of his outsider position.

"Wyatt's here because I asked him to come," Sophie explained, which told Wyatt that none of their private conversation had been about him. "He's helping me search for Lola."

That's right, asshole, Wyatt thought when a knowing look crawled across Montoya's face. *I'm the lowly hired muscle ready to take the heat so nancy boys like you don't have to worry about getting their hair messed up.*

"Señora."

A uniformed waiter appeared at Sophie's side, surprising her. "*Sí?*"

He gave an apologetic bow of his head and extended a silver tray holding a sealed envelope bearing Sophie's name. "I am sorry to intrude, but my manager directed me to deliver this to you."

Puzzled, Sophie reached for the envelope. "*Gracias.*"

"Wait." Wyatt stopped the waiter when he started to walk away. "Who sent this?"

"I'm sorry, sir. I do not know. Apparently, it was left on the reception table. As I told you, the manager asked that I deliver it to Señora Weber. Now, if you will excuse me, I have other guests I must tend to."

Wyatt decided the waiter was either in the dark, as he stated, or a damn fine actor. Either way, he couldn't question him further without making a scene, so he let him go as Sophie unfolded the note and scanned it. She shot Wyatt a quick glance and slipped it back into the envelope.

"From an admirer?" Montoya suggested with a teasing tone. "Tell me, *cara*, do I have competition?"

Wyatt had seen the swift flash of alarm in Sophie's eyes. She recovered quickly with a smile that answered Montoya's playful look as she tucked the envelope into her small purse.

"As if anyone could compete with you. Someone found a bracelet and recognized it as mine," she said.

Wyatt knew she was lying through her perfect white teeth. She hadn't been wearing a bracelet when they'd left the house. He would have noticed, because he had noticed every minute detail of her appearance.

He found it interesting that she felt the necessity of hiding the contents of the note from Montoya.

"The clasp must have broken," she continued smoothly. "I can't believe I didn't miss it. Anyway, they're holding it for me at the reception desk. I'm afraid you'll have to excuse me for a moment, Diego."

"I'll accompany you," Montoya said.

"Thank you, but there's no need. I know you have many hands to shake tonight. Wyatt will go with me."

Just try and stop me, Wyatt thought, directing a hard look Montoya's way.

Montoya got the message and conceded with a forced smile. "Save a dance for me, *querida*. I will find you later."

She gave him a brilliant smile. "Count on it."

"What?" Wyatt asked when they were out of earshot.

She glanced around, then pulled him into an empty alcove. "Looks like you were right about coming tonight."

Her eyes were wide with excitement as she dug the note out of her purse and handed it to him.

South side of the rear terrace. 10:45. Tell no one. Come alone. Make certain you're not followed.

"This *has* to be about Lola," she said, clutching his arm.

Wyatt figured it was, or there wouldn't be a need for all the cloak-and-dagger crap. It also explained why she hadn't wanted Montoya to know. The instructions were explicit that she tell no one.

He checked his watch. It was ten sixteen. "Come on, let's walk toward reception in case Montoya's tracking you. Tell me about the layout of the terrace."

"Let me think. It's . . . it's a big open area. No roof. Surrounded by palms and, I don't know, flowering shrubs and vines, if I remember right. It's been a while since I've been here, let alone wandered around the grounds. What are you thinking?"

"I'm thinking that I don't like the 'Come alone' part of this invitation."

She stopped walking. "What choice do we have? I can't take a chance that whoever sent this will bolt if you come with me."

"And I can't take a chance that it's a setup and you end up with a hood over your head, carried off, and thrown into the back of a van."

"So what do we do?"

"Hedge our bets," he said, and told her how it was going to go down.

WITH NO REMORSE
Luke Colter's and Valentina's story

They probably should get moving again but, damn, he still couldn't catch his breath. The thin air at this altitude was a killer. She was having the same problem. Five more minutes—then they were out of here while their luck held.

"Why are you helping me?" she asked.

He couldn't stop a confused blink. "Are you for real?"

She blinked right back.

"Because you need help, for God's sake," he said when her silence demanded an answer. "Well, not *you*, as in Valentina, but *you*, as in a kid who looked scared to death. Was I supposed to just sit there and watch them do whatever they planned to do with you?"

"So, *you're* what . . . a natural-born hero?" The sarcasm in her tone was outdistanced only by her doubt.

He was surprised by the sarcasm; not so much by the doubt. Hell, he doubted himself. "Actually, I have to work at it these days," he admitted. Until those bastards had shot that defenseless man, he'd been determined to save his own ass and to hell with anyone else's.

But back to the sarcasm. WTF? Was there a raving shrew lurking beneath the goddess façade?

Please, God, no. Don't burst my bubble.

He studied her perfect angel face. No, he told himself decisively. No way. He couldn't have been wrong all these years. She was just scared; he got that.

"Who exactly are you?"

The last time Luke had been given the third degree, he'd been tied to a chair with a gun pressed against his temple. He hadn't liked it then. He didn't much like it now. But because she was scared, because she *should* be wary, because she was Valentina, he cut her some slack.

"Luke. Luke Colter. But my friends call me Doc. And I guess now's as good a time as any to confess that I'm a huge fan."

Crap. That had sounded *so* much better in his head. From the way she scooted a few inches away from him, it was pretty clear that not only had he sounded like a dumbass of epic proportions, but he'd also spooked her.

He raised his hands to show her he was absolutely no threat. "Let's take a little time out, okay?" he suggested, still keeping his voice to a whisper. "Don't interpret *fan* to mean *stalker*. I'm just aware of who you are. Thought it might reassure you. My bad."

Her gaze darted away, and he could see that she was thinking about running.

Yep, he'd spooked her good. Hell, she'd just been chased off a train at gunpoint. She'd seen him slit one man's throat and bash in another one's head. And in his grubby jeans and two-day beard, he looked more like a derelict than a Boy Scout.

She didn't know him from the Unabomber, so from her perspective, what was to say he *wasn't* the biggest danger in these mountains?

"Valentina," he said quietly, shifting to look her in the eye.

Her head went down, but not before he saw the full-out terror on her face.

Aww, hell.

"I know you're scared, but you have nothing to fear from me. I'm one of the good guys."

She still didn't look at him.

"Let's try this," he suggested. "What do you want to know about me? Just ask. I'm an open book." Sort of. Right now she probably couldn't handle the full truth about The Book of Luke.

She still didn't say a word, which meant that *spooked* didn't begin to cover it.

Man, he was blowing this.

"Okay. How 'bout I cover the basics for you? I'm an Aquarius. I love long walks on the beach, soft cuddly kittens, and my red Jimmy Choos. Fave movie—*The Sound of Music*. Favorite food—"

Her narrow-eyed glare was as good as a stop sign. Okay, humor wasn't going to work, either. So how the hell was he supposed to make her relax?

"I'm from Montana," he said, shifting into earnest mode as he swept another glance around them. "Grew up on a ranch, just like John Wayne. Cows. Horses. Big dumb dog who loved me."

He left out the part about being voted "most likely to kiss the girls and make them cry" his senior year.

"John Wayne didn't grow up on a ranch. He was born in Iowa," she said, sounding accusatory.

"I know that," he said, working for reasonable, but it came out sounding testy. "*You* weren't supposed to, though. Give me a break here; I was just trying to find some level ground. So. Seriously. What do you want to know?"

She looked away, then back, her eyes narrowed. "You're a doctor?" she asked, sounding doubtful.

"Doctor?" He rolled back the tape on his clumsy introduction. "Oh. No. Not a doc—a medic. Corpsman, if you want to pick nits. In the Navy. SEALs, actually."

"For real? You're a SEAL?" She didn't want to be impressed but he could see that she was, marginally—if she believed him.

"I *was* a SEAL."

"And now you do . . . what?"

How did he explain that he worked for a private contractor whose business was taking out terrorists, and not lose the little ground he'd gained?

"A little of this. A little of that." He flashed his brightest smile, a tactic that had distracted a helluva lot of women over the years.

He should have known it wouldn't work on her. "Your open book has a lot of blank pages."

**Turn the page
for a sneak peek
at the exciting first book
in Cindy Gerard's new series!**

Coming soon from Pocket Books

Mike "Primetime" Brown's story

El Tocón Sangriento—the Bloody Stump—was a back-alley, low-rent cantina that hadn't changed in clientele or decor since he'd set foot in the dump eight years ago. The class of women, however, seemed to have catapulted to new levels.

Mike Brown turned his back to the bar, a shot of *pisco* in one hand, and watched one particular woman move sensuously on the dance floor to the beat of a slow, Spanish guitar.

He squinted through the tobacco and ganja haze at the dark-haired beauty stirring up trouble and testosterone with the sultry, seductive sway of her hips. She was way too hot for this dive. And he didn't have a clue why she was directing her flirty smile his way, but he wasn't going to question his good luck. Just like he wasn't questioning the reason he was tying one on like there was no tomorrow.

He tossed back the shot and grabbed another from the neat row of soldiers lined up on the bar behind him. Screw the fact that he'd been clean and sober for 364 consecutive days—a record he never seemed to beat. Tonight, like every other May fifteenth since Operation Slam Dunk had gone south, he was getting flat-ass drunk.

The end of days. That's how he thought of the debacle in Afghanistan eight years ago.

Sobrietious interruptus. That's how he thought of his annual commune with alcohol and self-pity. He was holding a post mortem. Conducting a wake for the friends who'd lost their lives. For the life and career *he'd* lost.

Call it whatever you wanted—a guilt trip, grief, suppressed rage, self-destruction—he didn't give a rip. The only new wrinkle in his annual bender was that it was starting to look like he might also get laid.

Talk about poetic justice. He was already fucked-up in the head . . . might as well make it a clean sweep.

Eyes on the prize, he slammed back one more shot, pocketed the bullet-ridden playing card, and pushed away from the bar. Then he tried like hell not to stumble as he crossed the room toward the hot little tamale who seemed to only have eyes for him. Big, dark eyes. A little sleepy, a little slutty, a lot interested.

Damn, she was something. Centerfold something. Long, satin black hair escaped in sleek, bed-mussed strands from the silver clip she'd used to secure it in a loose knot on top of her head. Elegant neck, smooth, bare shoulders, and a lot of soft, caramel skin. And that red bustier—its B cups not having a lot of luck harnessing a generous pair of C's—worn with black spandex pants that stopped at her ankles where the straps of her four-inch stilettos took over, was playing hell with the fit of his pants.

"Hey, gorgeous," he said. Because she was. And because he was too wasted to come up with anything original. He moved in close. Smelled sweet musk and raw sexuality.

"Hey," she said with a demure smile and pressed those amazing breasts against his chest. "Nice bling."

A long-nailed fingertip—slick, shiny, red—tapped the diamond stud in his left ear, then lingered at the tip of his lobe.

"Nice, um . . ." He let his gaze slide down to that magnificent cleavage before easing back to her face. ". . . smile."

She laughed and tilted her head to the side in blatant invitation, giving him an even better view of all that dewy, soft flesh.

"Wanna take this outside?" he asked, cutting straight to the chase.

The lady knew what she wanted. "Thought you'd never ask."

Her hand was small and warm when she took his and led him toward the back door. He followed like a love-struck puppy, mesmerized by the smell of her hair, the sway of her hips, and the way her sparkly bag hung from a silver chain looped over her shoulder and rhythmically bumped her gorgeous ass with every step she took.

Outside, the alley was as shadowy and dark as the desire that ripped recklessly through his groin. Somewhere in the back of his mind, a warning bled through his lust-induced fog, telling him to slow the hell down, reminding him that if he hadn't been so drunk, he might have asked a few more questions. That maybe, if he added two and two together he might come up with something other than *four*-nicate.

Just because he wanted her to be a working girl, didn't negate the fact that she had way too much class for that gig. And just because he was drunk, didn't mean he should let his guard down. He was starting to rethink this entire thing . . . but then she leaned back against the wall, gripped his T-shirt with both hands, and pulled him flush against her.

Good-bye presence of mind.

She was all hot wet open mouth and ripe breasts rubbing up against him, her left leg wedged super sweet between his thighs and moving up and down over his rapidly expanding package.

He groaned and scrabbled for a hold on his sanity. "Maybe we should take this someplace private, wild thing."

She laughed a husky, naughty purr and bit his lower lip. "That comes later . . . but *you're* gonna come right now."

Holy mother.

When she reached into her purse, he experienced another flicker of alarm.

"Condom," she said with that dimpled smile, and damn if he didn't almost weep with gratitude.

What the hell. It was dark. He was gone. And all this sultry woman heat had him damn near hypnotized by the prospect of her doing him, right here under the flashing neon *Quilmes* sign.

He skimmed his palms down her sides, pressed the heels of his hands against her breasts then slid them lower again, gripping her hips and rubbing her against his raging erection.

All the while, she had one hand on her purse, while rooting around inside with the other.

"Damn, darlin'. If you don't find that thing soon the party's gonna be over."

Just then he got wind of a scent . . . and got sober real fast.

He grabbed her wrist, pressed her hard against the wall, and pulled her hand out of her bag: a set of handcuffs dangled from her red-tipped nails.

"Talk about bling. Now, I'm all for kinky sex, but there's no way in hell you're going to slap a bracelet on me."

She wasn't smiling now.

He shoved her harder against the wall. "And nice perfume. Eau du le gun oil?" He felt the outline of a pistol inside that sparkly purse. "Shoulda gone for Shalimar, chica . . . the smell of that stuff makes me stupid."

"That's not all that makes you stupid," she muttered, and jammed a knee hard into his gonads.

He doubled over with a roar of pain, helpless to fight her when she slapped the cuffs around his wrists.

"We can do this easy," she whispered close to his ear as he gasped in agony, "or it can go real hard on you."

Well, of course, he wasn't going to go easy.

He drove a shoulder toward her stomach—which she easily dodged—and landed on his face in the alley's pocked, filthy pavement.

By the time he felt the prick of the needle in his arm, it was all over, except for the headache he knew he was going to have when he woke up. *If* he woke up.

Which, unfortunately, he did.